A season for wishing

Jim, Delia and Terry stood beneath the mistletoe and made wishes for the year to come. Warmed by claret cup and seasonal good feelings, they hugged one another and became the children they'd once been together.

Delia's beauty and fame as an actress were temporarily forgotten, and she was once more the wild, black-haired imp who'd led her cousins in a raid on Mr. Schneider's henhouse. Jim and Terry watched her as she lifted a rapt face to the heavens and wished for a better play than Rosaleen.

Jim wished mild misfortune on his Harvard history professor—and prayed inwardly for a kiss from Virginia Leonard at the ball on New Year's Day.

Terence wished for a hunting knife and an increase in his allowance.

"And what do you wish for, Kieran?" Delia called over her shoulder, feeling the spark that so often passed between the two of them.

Black-haired Kieran was standing ten feet away, and Delia's question caught him unawares. He lifted his glass in a mocking gesture.

"I wish that I had never been born."

The O'Donnells
AN IRISH-AMERICAN SAGA

the faithful and the few

ian kavanaugh

A DELL/JAMES A. BRYANS BOOK

Published by
Dell Publishing Co., Inc.,
1 Dag Hammarskjold Plaza
New York, New York 10017

Dell ® TM 681510, Dell Publishing Co., Inc.

ISBN: 0-440-03136-2

Printed in the United States of America

First printing—December 1982

To Kathleen Morris

We're children of a fighting race
That never yet has known disgrace
                    —Peadar Kearney

part one

1

It was a bleak day in January when they buried Liam O'Donnell—a wintry, joyless day that seemed to deny hope. The churchyard was on the westerly slope of a hill above Newburgh, and through the bare limbs of the trees, one could see the gray humps of the Catskills. As the family stood with bowed heads, a bitter wind blew down from the mountains. The women's veils were tossed mercilessly and the words of the priest were inaudible.

The O'Donnell plot was situated in a choice corner of the cemetery, and a marble headstone, carved as an angel gathering souls to his wings, would be erected to cover the gaping wound in the frozen earth. It was there that Liam O'Donnell was being laid to his final rest. Nearby were two small crosses marking the graves of his children, Dierdre and Thomas.

Dierdre had died at birth, but Thomas had lived until he was five, making his death so much harder. Another son, Robert, had his grave in the Atlantic Ocean, unconsecrated and unknown.

And what, thought Liam's widow, could a stranger tell by reading the words that would be engraved on her husband's headstone? That he had been born in Sligo, Ireland in 1828; that he had died in 1901; that he had been the beloved husband of Edith Holmes O'Donnell, the devoted father of Patrick, Robert, Thomas, Dierdre, Bridget, and Veronica. A stranger would see only the bare bones of a life which had been rich and full. There would be no way to guess at the turmoil and struggle, the triumphs and private griefs that had made Liam O'Donnell the man he was.

Edith straightened her shoulders and stared from beneath her crepe mourning veil, eyes dry. It was important to set an example for the young ones, her grandchildren. It was never too early for them to understand what it meant to be an O'Donnell. Not, mind you, that she wanted them to forget their heritage and turn into cold, priggish sorts like some of the Newburgh Protestant gentry—never that! But dignity was important. She didn't want it said that the O'Donnells had wailed and wept like Irish tinkers when her husband was buried. No one would ever see Edith weep. She would keep her sorrow to herself, giving into it only within the confines of her bedroom.

The rumbling voice of Father Finley washed over her, and she tried not to look down at the pit in the earth. Room had been allotted for her to lie beside Liam one day, and somehow she knew that day would be soon.

Patrick, Edith's only surviving son, stood next to her. He showed no emotion, but inwardly he felt a bewildering new pain—a solitary grief. Although he was only forty, robust and healthy, nothing now stood between Patrick and death. His father had been both mentor and friend to him, and he now felt as awkward and bereft as if he were still a boy.

He glanced sideways at his wife, Margaret. She was swathed in Fitzhugh furs, which she clung to as stubbornly as she did the Fitzhugh jewels she had inherited on their wedding day. The cold would not touch her slender figure, just as no grief would penetrate her thoughts. Margaret would not know how to comfort Patrick, and he wouldn't dare ask.

Patrick's sons both had tears in their eyes, but he knew that Jim's tears differed radically from those of Terence. Jim had been his grandfather's favorite and this was the first real loss of his young life. He was trying valiantly to contain his sorrow, but the tears came anyway.

Terence, who was only thirteen, hopped from foot to foot as if he were doing a slow jig. His tears were caused by the cold. He hated discomfort; he felt he had been born for pleasure and ease. Anything that smacked of duty made him sulky and his grandfather's funeral was merely duty.

Patrick squeezed his mother's arm with one hand. With the other, he restrained the unbecoming movements of his younger son.

His sister, Veronica O'Donnell Tyrone, stood with her husband and small daughter at the opposite side of the grave. Her daughter Bernadette, not yet six, leaned against her knees, away from the wind. Veronica was thinking of her father twenty years ago, when she was only twelve. All through the service, she remembered Liam in brief flashes, as if it were her own life passing before her. She remembered him beside her bed, the time she had the croup, holding her hand and telling her fragments of stories. She remembered him returning home with a face grey and drawn when the news had come about Robert, and she remembered him slapping his hands together in glee when he heard a Sligo reel.

Good-bye, Da, she thought. If you had faults, I don't want to know about them. You were the best of fathers.

Veronica's older sister, Bridget, stood directly across from her. Beneath her veil, Bridget was struggling to remain composed. She wanted to howl with the wind for the many losses her family had endured. It seemed proper. She didn't need to howl for her father—he had lived a full and relatively long life—but for those others. Robert, her brother, poor fiery fool, dead in his young manhood because he was daft enough to nurse ancient wrongs. Her brother, Tommy, who had drowned, and her own son Tommy, who had only lived an hour while his twin sister was blooming and rosy.

Bridget grasped her husband's arm and felt the pressure returned. Dear husband; ardent lover after all these years! Bridget and Michael's daughter, Delia, was the only grandchild absent at the funeral. How had Delia emerged as she was—cold and splendid as a fabulous gem, so exquisite it sometimes hurt to look at her? They had given her everything, but still she had run off when she was barely seventeen. Their beautiful daughter had wanted a career on the stage, and the miracle was that her desire had been fulfilled. Bridget agonized over Delia's lonely life in New York, but the alternative to Delia's loneliness was too dreadful to contemplate.

Her daughter had abandoned the name Flynn and used her mother's maiden name professionally. Delia O'Donnell, the prettiest girl on Broadway, and already famous. Her fame might be notoriety here in Newburgh, but what did *they* know? Bridget thought as she remembered the pride she took in her daughter's success. The people who whispered about her would probably give their eye-teeth to be appearing in a play in New York City instead of freezing their respectable bums in icy Newburgh. Delia had sent a huge wreath of hot-house roses to excuse her absence.

"Like it or not, Da, my daughter is your best chance at immortality," whispered Bridget. "I haven't done so badly, after all."

At the far end of the grave-site, in the place where the wind blew most bitterly, stood Kieran O'Donnell. In defiance of convention, he had refused to wear a hat. His face, stony and blessed with the same passionate beauty which had graced his cousin, Delia, was unreadable. He had come to say good-bye to his grandfather and nothing more. At seventeen, he was still capable of such a sentimental gesture. He was

the son of Robert O'Donnell, who had died at the age
of twenty-four. Kieran's mother had died bearing
him, and he had never known either of them. He had
been born in America. Alone, of all the O'Donnells,
he thought of Ireland as home, and yet he had never
set foot on Irish soil.

Good-bye, grandfather, thought Kieran. I am sorry
you died in exile.

A mourning wreath hung on the door of the O'Donnell house on Ridge Street. Like the churchyard, the
house stood on a hill, and on the fashionable side of
the tracks. It was a handsome dwelling, fit for a prosperous family. A smartly painted, three story white
frame, a cupola and rambling gallery-like porch, and
a stained-glass fan-light over the front door made the
house seem princely to its owner, who had been born
in a two-room cottage.

The carriages turned onto the street and moved
slowly up the steep incline. The horses' hooves were
muffled, out of respect for the dead. The maids at the
house saw the procession and rushed to make sure
everything was ready for the wake.

In the kitchen, Peg checked the hams and roast
chickens, and the salads and sweets. Upstairs, Rosie
glanced at the decanters of sherry and whiskey and
wondered if she had time to rush to the mirror and
check the angle of her white cap. A girl couldn't help
made some minor adjustments, pulling her cap back
a little to show her widow's peak. She was pleased
wanting to look her best at a wake.

She darted to the mirror above the sideboard and

with the shade of her hair. It was a dark, glowing red, like Master Terence's, not the pale, sandy color of Master Jim's. Jim was nice enough—he always had a kind word for Rosie and Peg, but he was bookish and plain. Terence would grow up to be a handsome devil, but she wondered how she could flirt with a thirteen year old boy? So instead, it was Kieran O'Donnell for whom Rosie primped. Rosie thought Kieran was the handsomest man she'd ever seen.

She ran to the door and opened it. A bitter blast of wind rushed in as the mistress stood, leaning on Mr. Patrick's arm, looking as if she'd been turned to stone.

"Come in out of the cold, madam," said Rosie, "you must be perishing."

"Thank you, Rose," answered Edith absently. She was carrying her head very high, but Rosie could see that her husband's funeral had taken its toll. Poor lady, she thought. Why couldn't she give in to it like anyone else and have a good cry?

Peg came up from the kitchen to help with the cloaks, and the two girls vied to take Kieran's. Rosie thought it was interesting how much you could tell about a person by the way they let you take their wraps. Mrs. Patrick O'Donnell had a way of stiffening her back as if an accidental touch of Rosie's hand would give her the plague, whereas Veronica and Bridget always smiled and said thank you. Terence let the maids do all the work, while he stood with a wicked grin, appraising them as if he were a grown man.

Nobody took Kieran's coat. Kieran took it off himself and slung it over the newel post of the long, walnut bannister. Watching him walk into the parlor, Rosie felt a little shiver at the base of her spine.

Mrs. Parker, the cook, had told Rosie about Kieran's unfortunate childhood during her first week in service. Rosie sympathized, and believed she would be able to comfort him if he would give her the chance.

"Sherry, Rose," said Veronica, "and plenty of it, please."

As Rosie passed the trays, she remembered all the things the cook had told her about the O'Donnell family. "If you ask me, Mrs. Patrick O'Donnell is riding for a fall. There's something queer there, can't put my finger on it . . ." *But I can,* thought Rosie. Margaret O'Donnell obviously would have preferred to drink whiskey, but would have bitten her tongue out before doing so in public. Rosie's own ma had been a drinker, so she knew the signs. The trembling hands, the not-quite-focused look in those cold, pale eyes. *Ah, yes, madam, look through me if you like, but I know your secret,* she wanted to say aloud.

Bridget Flynn liked a drink, too, but there was nothing secretive about it. She drank whiskey with the men, and never seemed to lose her head. Rosie wanted to ask her if she'd sent for the autographed picture of Delia as she'd promised to do, but decided to wait for a better time. It was one of the greatest disappointments of Rosie's life that Delia hadn't been able to come to Newburgh for her grandfather's funeral. What was the good of being in service at a celebrity's house if the celebrity never came up from New York City?

"Miss Delia, she's spoiled," the cook had said. "It's

partly on account of how beautiful she is, and partly because her little twin brother died when he was born, God rest his soul."

Rosie had seen photographs of Delia, and the thing that impressed her was how much like Kieran she looked. They both had that wild, black hair, dark as midnight, and their eyes were said to be the same shade of blue—like cornflowers.

Rosie glanced at Kieran's eyes as she handed him his whiskey. He lowered his dark lashes and nodded a curt thank you.

"Handsome is as handsome does," Rosie remembered the cook saying. "Mr. Kieran's father was a criminal, don't forget. He died before the child was born, and the shock of it killed his mother. Oh, she died in childbirth alright, but it's the shame and the shock that done it."

Rosie wasn't sure she thought Kieran's father a criminal. She had been born and bred in County Fermanagh, and she was more inclined to think of Kieran's father as a patriot.

"A drop more sherry, madam?" she asked, standing in front of Margaret O'Donnell.

Patrick turned a surprised look at her, then glanced at his wife. Margaret merely extended her glass, her pale eyes fixed across the room, on her sons.

"Never forget that Mrs. High-and-Mighty Margaret comes from old money," the cook had admonished. "She thinks she's gone down a step in the world. Can you imagine? With all her airs, she's ambitious for those boys of hers. She wants them to go into politics when they're old enough."

Rosie thought that was the stupidest thing she'd ever heard. A person only had to look at Jim to see he was far too shy for political life. He was too involved in his music. He'd rather climb up to the top of a hill and play his fiddle for the cows than get involved with politicians. As for Terence—Rosie knew he was born for trouble. Between the two of them, she was sure they'd break Margaret's cold heart.

Standing discreetly aside, making herself unobtrusive as a good servant should, Rosie observed the O'Donnell clan in their hour of sorrow. Only Margaret and Terence were unmoved by the death of the patriarch. They seemed totally absorbed in their own private worlds, and felt little for the others who were mourning, in their separate ways, a man they had loved. Even six-year-old Bernadette looked solemn.

By mid-afternoon, the house was full and the wake had begun to look like a fine celebration. Veronica O'Donnell Tyrone sat on the horsehair sofa with her young daughter, and greeted the people of Newburgh. Many of them she'd known in childhood—before she'd married and moved to New York—and the familiar faces flooded her with nostalgia.

Mr. Silas Leonard, the banker, came as did the ancient O'Shea sisters whose crabapples she used to steal when she was a child. An old man with a walrus moustache was none other than John Finnegan, the proprietor of the Coach and Four. He had always given her peppermints whenever she had gone downtown with her father.

"And who is this fine young lady?" Mr. Finnegan

asked as he bent down to look at Bernadette. Veronica introduced her daughter.

"How do you do, Mr. Finnegan?" said Bernadette, mindful of her manners. Veronica caressed her daughter's bright head and thought for the hundredth time that if she was fated to have only one child, she had been fortunate. The little girl was a carbon copy of her mother, only brighter, more newly-minted. Veronica's hair was a pale reddish blonde, her eyes a rather plain blue. Bernadette had the same coloring, but her hair seemed to crackle with energy and her eyes fairly snapped. She was interested in everything around her, alert and intelligent and sweet-tempered, and Veronica loved her more than anyone on earth.

"I believe I might have something here," said Mr. Finnegan, fumbling in his pockets with the rakish air Veronica remembered. He pulled out a sweet and handed it to the delighted child. It was exactly the same sort of peppermint he had always given her.

Veronica felt the tears build up behind her eyes and willed them to go away. Across the room her husband, Rob, was talking to a young man. No doubt they were talking banking, Rob's great passion. Marry a banker, she thought, and what else can you expect?

She shook herself irritably. It wasn't like her to feel sorry for herself. She had married well, so well, in fact, that all of Newburgh had been amazed. She had a beautiful house in New York, a loving and exceptional daughter. She had no right to want more, yet the longer she sat on the sofa, fighting tears, the more she wished Rob would—for once in his life— sense her need for comfort and come to her. I've lost my father, she thought. I am a grown woman of thirty-two, yet I need comforting.

It was warm in the room. The fire, the crush of people, the odors of the hot foods wafting from the dining room, all combined to make her feel weak and dizzy. She sent Bernadette over to Bridget and left the room.

Terence was at the foot of the stairs.

"Hello, Aunt Veronica," he said silkily, as if he had just noticed her. His smile was a bit loose, his eyes were bleary.

"Terry, you've been drinking!"

"No, never." He gave her his most cocksure grin and stumbled against the bannister.

"And you not even fourteen! What would your father say?"

"I only had a bit from Mr. Leonard's glass," said Terence. "He didn't notice."

This, she knew, was a lie.

"You won't tell?" he asked in a whisper.

Veronica shook her head. "No, Terry, I'll not tell. Best eat a sprig of parsley; it'll take the smell away."

She went on up the stairs, hurrying away from the babble of voices. Her old room was at the end of the long hall, facing west. It had been changed into a room for guests, but as she entered, she felt like she had finally found a sanctuary.

She looked at her old bed, the bed she had slept in until she married Rob, and the print of a hunting scene, *The Kerry Hunt,* that hung on the wall.

She sat on the edge of the bed and saw herself in the mirrored armoire. It hardly seemed possible that the neatly coiffed woman in mourning dress could be the same Veronica who'd first put her long plaits up in this very room.

"Where's Veronica?" Liam had asked, peering about comically and pretending he didn't recognize her. "Where's my little girl? All I can see at all is a fine looking lady."

Veronica remembered her father, and the sweet Sligo accent he had never lost. She let her tears flow unchecked.

Later she slipped into the bathroom and bathed her eyes with cold water. As she walked quietly back down the long, dim hallway, she paused at each door. At the door of her parents' room, she thought of her mother sleeping alone in the huge oak bed. Edith would not be alone in the house—Michael and Bridget lived with her, and Patrick and his family lived not five minutes away—but her life as a woman was over. Veronica's mother was now merely a widow, destined to sleep alone for the rest of her days.

Downstairs, Veronica heard the sounds of a fiddle tuning up. She knew it could only be Jim—sweet Jim who had shared her father's love for the traditional music. He would play several of his grandfather's favorites now, and she was glad she'd had her cry beforehand. Otherwise, at the first sounds of *The Road to Sligo,* she might have bawled like a baby.

It was Patrick who cried. Nobody noticed but Bridget, who was sitting close to him. She saw her brother's heavy brows contract, his lids squeeze shut, and watched as two large tears slid down his cheeks.

Somehow it was terrible to see a grown man crying—her own big brother, 'Patrick the Steady.'

Bridget looked to see if Margaret had noticed, but her sister-in-law's gaze was firmly fixed on the leaping flames of the grate fire. It embarrassed Margaret when her son played the fiddle; she thought it was peasantish.

Bridget got up and stood behind Patrick's chair. She put one hand gently on his shoulder. With her other hand she softly stroked his cheek. He turned to her, and for a moment they might have been children again. Damn Margaret for being such a cold fish! Bridget thought. Hadn't she any feelings? She then thanked God, as she did every day of her life, for giving her a warm, considerate husband. She looked lovingly across at Michael, who was holding Bernadette in his lap. The little girl lay against him, half-asleep, her head lolling on his chest. One of Michael's strong, square hands cupped his niece's cheek.

Bridget felt a familiar twinge of desire for her husband, and marveled that it should be so after eighteen years of marriage. Shame! she scolded herself. To have such thoughts at your father's wake! But secretly she knew that Liam wouldn't have disapproved. She squeezed her brother's shoulder, and went to sit beside her mother, reflecting that of all present in the room, her mother had lost the most.

"How beautifully he plays," murmured Edith O'Donnell to her daughter. "It's a true gift."

Together they watched Jim, who was so passionately absorbed in his music that he was unaware of the listening crowd. All vestiges of shyness melted away from the boy when he had his fiddle in his hand, and Bridget thought what a fine young man he would grow to be in a few years.

At sixteen, James O'Donnell was undistinguished looking. His sandy hair was lank, and he had inherited his Anglo-Norman mother's pale blue eyes. He had very fair skin that reddened quickly in the sun. He would never be the handsome man his brother Terence was fated to be, but Veronica thought he would be worth ten of Terry.

"Oh, Delia," she sighed. Thinking of Terry always made her remember her daughter, but she hadn't known she'd spoken aloud until her mother said: "It's a great pity Delia couldn't be with us."

Bridget nodded. The truth was that she didn't know her own daughter anymore. In spite of her proud musings in the churchyard, she often wished Delia had been less beautiful and headstrong. She yearned for a normal, affectionate daughter—a gentle child, like Jim.

"Well, mama," she said, "you know Delia."

That's what they always said, but who truly did, in fact, know Delia these days? Bridget's eyes flew to Kieran, who was sitting moodily in the corner, his legs stuck straight out before him. Even the garrulous O'Shea sisters avoided him—once bitten, twice shy. It wasn't that Kieran was rude, he was simply indifferent to most people. He had grown up in this house, been treated with the same affection as all the other grandchildren, but he had rejected it. Bridget attributed his moods and indifference to the fact that he was an orphan, but it didn't make sense to her.

There was something mysterious about Kieran, something even dangerous. He had never confided in anyone but Delia, and Bridget wondered if they confided in each other still.

Later, when the guests were standing about with great plates of food, Bridget made her way to Kieran's side. He regarded her politely, without interest.

"Kieran, have you seen Delia?" The blue eyes—Delia's eyes—looked into hers, waiting for her to clarify.

"What I mean, of course, is have you seen her recently? I haven't seen her for six weeks now."

He nodded, as if in agreement.

"Do you see Delia in New York?"

"Yes," said Kieran. "I see Delia sometimes. Do you object, Aunt Bridget?"

"Why ever would I object to Delia seeing her cousin?"

"I can't imagine, Aunt Bridget."

Rosie, the pretty little maid, was at their side, offering a tray of sweet liqueurs. Her eyes hung on Kieran with a desperate flirtatiousness. It irritated Bridget. She already felt flustered, bested by her insolent nephew, and yet she couldn't be angry at him, not really angry, because he looked too much like Delia.

"If you should see her before I do," said Bridget sarcastically, "please tell her that her mother sends kindest regards."

"I will," Kieran said, bowing slightly.

Really, the boy was like something from another era. According to her mother, Kieran spoke Gaelic fluently. He had learned it from Liäm. At least, thought

Bridget, he'd had a devoted grandfather. Not every orphan could boast of that.

While there was music, Kieran approved of his grandfather's wake. Liam's spirit seemed to hover in the room, enjoying Jim's fiddling, urging him on. The moment Jim put his fiddle away, however, the spirit vanished and the room was once again populated by fools and hypocrites. Kieran excluded his grandmother from this category, for she was neither, but everyone else who had come to mourn his grandfather disgusted him.

The old O'Shea sisters, half drunk now on sweet sherry and squeaking "I'm sorry for your trouble" at every opportunity—weren't they the very ones who gossiped about his "bad blood?" And Margaret, she was three sheets to the wind and thinking she was better than anyone because of her Anglo-Norman blood. And Frank Meyers who'd changed his name from O'Marra in the hopes people wouldn't know he was Irish. Even Jim, whom he liked, blushed every time he looked at Virginia Leonard, the banker's blonde daughter. Didn't Jim know the Leonards would as soon have Virginia court a stablehand as an Irish Catholic? Did he think, just because the Leonards came to pay their respects, that they'd ever regard the O'Donnells as social equals?

Kieran stood and made his way into the dining room. He poured himself a liberal tumbler of whiskey and drank it all in one gulp. If Mr. Leonard or Mrs. Whiteside had seen him they would nod, significantly, and exchange glances. He knew they would be thinking: "another drunken Irishman." Hadn't his Uncle Patrick been blocked from a seat in Congress by an anti-Catholic movement, and wasn't it true that they'd spread lies about his being a drunk, too? He wondered why Patrick wasn't angrier, bent on revenge. The years had passed, and his Uncle merely became more portly and prosperous. He ran the family business along with Michael Flynn, and was content to stay in Newburgh.

Rosie came sidling through the door, a tray in her hands. She was a pretty little thing, with her auburn hair and green eyes. Kieran was well aware of Rosie's glances in his direction, but he wasn't about to make *that* mistake. He could hear them now, babbling away in hushed voices, "they say he got the little maid in the family way, you know. Bad blood will out."

"Can I get you anything, Mr. Kieran? Will you have some port now?" Rosie asked, lowering her eyelashes at him. Her little pink tongue came out and flicked nervously at her full lower lip. Tempting.

"How old are you, Rose?"

"Nearly nineteen, sir."

"Well, I'm younger than you are, Rose. Under the circumstances, I think you might drop the 'mister.'"

Her eyes widened perceptibly. "But what would I call you then, sir? Not master, I hope?" She giggled at her daring witticism.

"Call me Kieran. I'm not your master. For god's sake, girl, have some pride in yourself. Do you think you were born to be a servant?"

Rosie bit her lip and blushed. "I'm sure I don't understand at all," she said at last. "What have I done wrong?"

"Nothing," sighed Kieran.

Rose fled down to the kitchen, and Kieran returned to the overheated parlor. Terence, sly devil, had disappeared altogether, and Jim was still casting longing looks at Virginia Leonard.

His grandfather, Liam, had come to America in steerage, lost his first wife and three of his children, carved out a niche for himself and his family, and had become a successful man—all without losing sight of where he had come from. Now that he was gone, Kieran felt that he was the last true Irishman left in the family. All the others were well on their way to becoming Americans.

2

They were packed in so tightly there wasn't room for her to stretch her legs out. It was so close, and dark, like being buried alive. Even if there were any food for her to eat, she couldn't possibly swallow it; the stench made her want to vomit. Soon the sea would be rough again, and the ship would pitch and roll. The others would cry out in fear, those with strength enough left to make a noise. How many had died? Was there an epidemic? Perhaps it was fever she felt now. Buried alive. Oh, help, for the love of Christ let me get out of here. . .

Someone was rescuing her, shaking her gently, then with more force. She was saying something about time. It was time.

Delia O'Donnell opened her eyes and beheld, with relief and gratitude, the round face of Sarah, her dresser. She was in her dressing room at the theatre. She had been napping on the velvet *chaise* and now Sarah had come to tell her it was time to paint and dress.

"Were you dreaming again, Miss O'Donnell?" Sarah's eyes were anxious but wary. She knew Delia was quite capable of getting angry if she sensed too much concern. She liked everyone to think she was invincible.

Delia sat up, pushing the long masses of her black hair back with a languid hand. "Dreaming, Sarah? Why do you ask?" She smiled. "Did I say something in my sleep?"

"No, dearie, but you were thrashing about."

Delia got up in one liquid movement and strolled toward the dressing table. "That will be all, Sarah," she said. "I won't need you for another half an hour."

Sarah withdrew, and Delia lowered her head to the dressing table. She could still feel the ghastly aura of the dream clinging to her; the fetid air, the pitching of the ship. Sometimes when she had the dream she felt ill for hours afterward. She couldn't afford to feel ill now; the curtain went up in an hour.

She poured herself a glass of mineral water, studying her face in the mirror. She watched her reflection, turning this way and that, searching for any blemish or imperfection. Finding none, she smiled. Looking at her face in the mirror always made her feel better. As a rich man counts his money, so Delia examined her face, and found it flawlessly beautiful. It wasn't vanity, or even pleasure in her own beauty that cheered her so. It was the certain knowledge that, so long as she had that face, she would never be poor.

She began to paint, making the glorious face garish so that it could be seen over the footlights. In real life, she needed no paint. Her skin was as white and smooth as rose petals, and along the high, rounded curve of her cheekbones there bloomed a delicate wash of apricot. Her heart-shaped face, beneath the mane of black hair, was breathtakingly lovely. The nose was small and straight, the lips full and curving, and the enormous eyes a shade of such profound blue that people, especially upon first meeting her, couldn't help but stare. Her eyelashes were as thick and naturally black as sable, her brows slender and delicately moulded.

It was this face which had been her passport away from Newburgh and into the theatre world. Delia had no illusions about her acting ability. She had a pleasant, melodious speaking voice and could sing a little, but she would never be a great actress. People came to see her because they had heard that she was a great beauty; she was in vogue this year.

Delia began to blacken the rims of her eyes with kohl, humming lightly. Next year she might be out of vogue, but she could always work and command a decent salary—provided, of course, that she kept her looks. She had just turned eighteen, and had every reason to believe her beauty would not fade for many years.

She knew some people believed she had come to New York to escape a life of poverty; it sounded more romantic that way. In actual fact she had lived well in Newburgh, had never known hunger or deprivation in her life. She would never understand why she feared what she had never known, but the fear was there, and it was very real. It made her dream, and it drove her onward, always in pursuit of more success, more face—more security.

She'd been nine when she first began to have the dream. She had been sitting in the kitchen, with Mrs. Parker, on the day it first happened. Mrs. Parker was rattling on, telling her what a fine man her grand-dad was to have prospered so well in America. "And him coming over in steerage," Mrs. Parker declared.

"What is steerage?" Delia had asked.

Mrs. Parker had told her, sparing no details, for she had come over in steerage herself many years ago, from Liverpool. "It was bad enough in my day," she said darkly, "but in your grand-dad's day they was coffin ships. So many people died, you see, and they just threw them over for the sharks."

That night Delia had the nightmare for the first time. In it, she saw herself being buried alive, and she woke up screaming. She knew that it was the talk of her grandfather's nightmare crossing to America that had given birth to her own nightmare. As she grew older, she compulsively read about the horrors of immigrating to America early in the century. Just as a person with a sore tooth is compelled to probe it with his tongue, so Delia fed her fears.

She read about the Potato Famine, and pored over horrid accounts of the starving peasantry of Ireland. She imagined the little children crying with the pain of starvation, their bellies swollen, their legs and arms like sticks. Once she read that whole hedgerows were thick with the dead and the dying, the latter too feeble to crawl out from beneath the corpses.

That was what she had come from. Her people were among the unluckiest of all the peoples of the earth. Her grand-dad had only survived by a miracle. His first wife had given birth to a little dead baby in steerage, and died. Once Delia tried to tell her mother of the fears that tormented her, but it sounded silly— even to her.

"Why Delia, girl, whatever can you be thinking of? Those days are long past. They can't ever come back, darling. You have everything a little girl could want, don't you lovey?"

How could she tell her mother that her life had changed forever on the day Mrs. Parker had told her about steerage? She had once vaguely imagined that her grandfather had been a great man back in Ireland; secretly, she had thought of herself as a sort of princess—the Princess of Newburgh. Now she knew that terrible things could happen in the world, and to people who were related to her by blood.

"Miss O'Donnell? Shall I dress your hair now, dear?"

"Yes, Sarah."

While Delia luxuriated in the pleasant feeling of those capable hands winding and coiling her hair, she recalled the promise she'd made to herself when she was fourteen: "I, Delia Mary O'Donnell, do solemnly swear that I will make my fortune for myself. I will never rely on my family, or on any man to do so. I will never be poor, or helpless, so long as I live. So swear I, this fifteenth day of May, eighteen-hundred and ninety-seven."

Now, four years later, she was about to step out onto the stage to tumultuous applause, and spend a pleasant two hours portraying a virtuous Irish peasant girl who marries a millionaire. The play had been written especially for her, after her success in *A Child of the Moors* earlier that year.

"Sarah, don't lace me as tightly tonight," Delia said, stepping from her dressing gown and standing up in chemise and stockings. "Even virtuous Irish peasant girls have to breathe, you know."

Delia had no way of knowing if the costume she wore as Rosaleen was authentic or not, but for *A Child of the Moors* she had created an accent which fell midway between Liam's Sligo sound and the burr of old Angus MacDougal, Newburgh's chief constable of police. The critics had loved it, but after her mother saw the play for the first time, she drew Delia aside backstage.

"That accent comes from nowhere on earth, darling, but oh, you did look beautiful." And then, face red with pride and anxiety, Bridget had burst into tears.

Sarah fastened the long, ragged skirt Delia wore in the first act of *Rosaleen,* and pinned the shawl to the chaste white bodice.

"Five minutes, Miss O'Donnell," called the stage manager.

Sarah handed her the basket of peat she was to carry over her arm, and then Delia went to wait in the wings for her entrance.

The curtain was up; she could hear the audience fidgeting and clearing its great, collective throat as it waited for the star. Delia wished her grandmother could see her in *Rosaleen,* but knew she would not come out of mourning for a year. Liam had died in January, and it was now May. Delia doubted very much if *Rosaleen* would run another seven months.

"Sure an it's a mornin' fit for Kings," the old character actor was saying on stage. Five more lines and she was on.

Suddenly, without warning, she had a sharp vision of Brendan Connolly's face. It seemed to hover in the wings, eyes scrutinizing her sorrowfully. Would she have wished Brendan to see her in *Rosaleen*? What was the use of wondering. He was lost to her. "Go away, Father Connolly," she muttered scornfully. "Go hear some housemaid's confession and leave me in peace."

"They do say this place is enchanted," said the character actor. The line was her cue.

Delia skipped onto the stage, her basket swinging gaily on her arm. "Good mornin, all," she trilled. "Can you tell me the road to Balincorry?"

The audience exploded in a cataclysm of ecstatic applause.

Spring in Newburgh was exceptionally beautiful. The furled leaves burst open against a sky that was the color of robin's eggs. Wild jonquils dotted the green fields like stars in a rippling sea, and the haunting odor of lilacs perfumed the air.

Edith O'Donnell could smell the flowers in her bedroom, where she lay alone in the vast oak bed. Sleep came to her easily, but often she awoke in the middle of the night, always remaining awake until dawn. Tonight she walked to her window and stood looking down at the moon-silvered lilacs in her garden. When she returned to the bed she took the pillow from what had been Liam's side and plumped it next to her. Then she turned and embraced it, drawing her knees up slightly. This is how they'd always slept, making spoons of each other's bodies. Long after love-making had become an occasional event, she had still needed his presence in her bed to sleep.

Down the corridor, Bridget and Michael slept fitfully. The moonlight illuminated a large, framed photograph of Delia that sat on their bureau. Their daughter seemed to watch over them as they tossed about beneath the covers.

"Lie still, woman," Michael grumbled as his wife's foot collided with his own. Bridget burrowed against him, half immersed in a dream. "The moon is too bright," she whispered.

Michael caressed her long, tumbled hair, soothing her back to sleep. A sudden memory of another spring night when they had made love in the moonlight took hold of him. She had been nineteen, and although they'd been married for almost two years at the time, she had never allowed him to see her unclothed. From the very start she'd been passionate. She was a woman made for love and had held back nothing—nothing but the privilege of looking at her naked body. Michael chuckled, remembering. He had persuaded her to slip her nightdress off in the moonlight and Bridget, drunk with the beauty of the night, had allowed him to see her for the first time.

How beautiful she was, and how that first sight of her had aroused him! She'd already had the twins—rest in peace Tommy—but her breasts were as round and firm as a virgin's. Her nipples were strawberry-colored, like her nether hair, and as she had lain back across the bed, all bathed in silvery light, she had surrendered the last shred of her modesty.

Michael slipped his hand down and stroked Bridget's thighs, warm beneath the nightdress. The memory had aroused him so that he felt as hard and urgent as a boy. She turned against him and he ran his hands over her breasts, coaxing her back from sleep. The perfume of the lilacs surrounded him—he couldn't wait. He entered her while she was still asleep, moving gently, furtively at first, gradually increasing the intensity of his thrusts.

Bridget's eyes opened; she moaned in confusion and pleasure. Then she buried her hands in her husband's dark hair and raised her hips to him joyfully. She would never be able to give him another child, but for as long as she lived she would give, and receive, this wonderful gift of love.

The only people who slept soundly in the house on Ridge Street that night were Peg and Rosie. Exhausted from their long day's work, they were oblivious to the moonlight. Tucked in their attic chambers, three thousand miles from home, they dreamed of the families and friends they had left behind.

* * *

Three streets away, in Patrick O'Donnell's house, Margaret lay next to her sleeping husband, eyes wide open in the darkness. He had touched her tonight while she was brushing her hair, and there had been longing in his touch. He didn't do it often, but when it happened she had to restrain herself from flinching visibly.

She didn't quite know when the revulsion had begun to claim her. Certainly, in the beginning of their marriage, she had allowed him to make love to her without feeling disgust. It had always seemed a kind, a benevolent thing to do. When Patrick arrived at the peak of his pleasure, she always patted his back as if he were a sobbing child. "There, there," she wanted to say.

Was it the dreadful pain of giving birth to James that had changed her? She didn't think so, for she'd gone on to have Terence. She liked to think of herself as a stoic, and so during those long, tortured hours of her two confinements she had scarcely cried out. How could she have confronted the servant girls ever again if they had heard her shrieking like a common peasant?

Her revulsion at the physical side of her marriage was only to be expected. Patrick, who had seemed such a gentleman to her when they were courting, was secretly coarse. It wasn't his fault. He was only one generation removed from the bogs. It always took at least three generations to iron out the peasant strain. Her boys would be gentlemen, more Fitzhugh than O'Donnell. They would succeed where Patrick had failed. Patrick. The first time she'd heard old Liam refer to him affectionately as "Paddy" she had felt her gorge rise. She had named her eldest son with a good, plain English name, but Patrick had insisted on an Irish name for the next one. Terence, thought Margaret, was showing more promise than Jim. He was bold and self-confident; he treated the servants with that little touch of good-natured contempt which distinguished a gentleman from a "Johnny-come-lately."

Now her mind was racing, seeking out the pitfalls which would prevent her sons from taking their true place in society. She thought another humiliation of the sort she'd endured when Patrick had failed to win a seat in Congress would kill her. Her nerves were humming with tension and she realized she was clenching her hands beneath the covers.

Cautiously, she edged up on one elbow and peered down at Patrick's sleeping face. He was snoring slightly, he would never know. Margaret slid from the bed and put on her dressing gown. She crept down the stairs like a thief and made her way to the dining room. The moonlight shone on the crystal decanters. A little whiskey would help her to sleep, she thought. She needed something for her nerves.

Above in his room, Terence was dreaming of Rosie, his grandmother's servant girl. Rosie was running up a flight of stairs, giggling and drawing up her skirts so he could see her flashing, slender legs.

The room next to his was empty, its owner having stolen away at midnight, unable to sleep. Jim lay in the long grass on the hill above Ridge Street, feeling he would die if something didn't happen to him soon. He was tortured by the odor of the lilacs; it spoke of something magical he couldn't touch.

His life seemed like a corridor of twisting alternatives. He felt lost. This would be his last spring in Newburgh if he went to Harvard College in the autumn. He had no desire to go to Harvard, but he couldn't bear to think of remaining in Newburgh unless—no, he wouldn't think of *her*.

Where, he wondered, was Kieran tonight? Kieran was only a year older, but Jim felt sure his cousin would not be alone on such a night. Kieran had gone back to New York again; perhaps he had a girl there. Jim writhed with envy at the idea. Nearly seventeen, he thought, and I haven't a clue in the world. Even Terry is wiser than I am.

Suddenly, he missed his grandfather acutely. There was nobody to play music with him now, nobody who understood how exciting it was to discover yet another variation on *Tom McCormac's Jig* or *O'Halloran's Reel*. When he and Liam had traveled together, collecting the old music, there had been a bond between them that nothing could shatter—not even his mother's disapproval. In Liam's will all the music they had collected was left to Jim, and with it a duty Jim understood clearly. It was up to him to see that it never died, that it was never forgotten or forsaken.

Margaret said the music he loved was common; it pained her when he played. His mother seemed almost Victorian to Jim, with her pernickety ways and sneering assumptions. Didn't she know this was the twentieth century? Queen Victoria had, in fact, died only a few weeks after his grandfather, and Margaret had insisted on wearing a mourning band for a week. How strange his family was! Kieran's father had been drowned trying to fix a bomb to the Queen's yacht—though no one ever mentioned it—and his own mother clung to the idea of being English as if her life depended on it.

What did it matter? Jim was proud to be Irish, if only because of the music, but he wasn't at all political. People were daft, they didn't see they were all approximately the same—struggling creatures trying to make the best of the few years they had on the earth.

Only one person in Newburgh seemed so exalted to him he could exempt her from the common lot of humanity. He couldn't help but think of her. No matter how hard he tried to banish her face, it appeared to him, radiant in the moonlight. She was an angel. The light in her soft, brown eyes seemed to melt his very bones. Her golden hair made the tips of his fingers burn with wanting to touch it. He thought he would be glad to die for her, if only she would let him.

Jim rolled over in the dewy grass and pressed his aching body into the fragrant earth.

"Oh, *Virginia*," he whispered.

Terry had been spying on the servant girls for several weeks, trying to determine which of them was most likely to make him a man on his fourteenth birthday. All he wanted was a real kiss, and maybe to be allowed to touch them in some intimate place. The bosom would be fine.

Rosie, his grandmother's girl, was the prettiest, but he had tailed her on her half-day off and discovered she only went to mass. For all her saucy ways, she was devout. Peg had a wall-eye and was quite old, perhaps twenty-five. All in all, he thought he stood the best chance with Eileen, his mother's maid, who was sometimes seen strolling at the edge of town with Dennis Dugan, the Leonards' stableman. Eileen was experienced. She had a broad face and was somewhat short in the leg, but there was a fine swelling in the front of her dress, and she was only nineteen. Eileen it would be.

He saw his chance a week before his birthday, on a sultry day in late August. His father was at the O'Donnell Company, as usual; his mother was taking tea at Mrs. Whiteside's. Mrs. Froelich, the cook, was taking a nap in the afternoon heat, and Eileen was alone in the morning room, dusting the frames of pictures on the walls.

Terry entered the room silently, leaning against the door-jamb. He observed Eileen's bottom as she stood on tip-toe to reach a large, framed print of a retrieving dog.

"Hello, Eileen," he said softly.

The girl jumped, then turned with her duster clasped to her chest. "You gave me a fright, Master Terence! I didn't know you was about." Her parted lips and heightened coloring made her even more desirable to him.

"It's my birthday, you know," said Terry.

"Why, not for a week more, surely?"

Terry favored her with his broadest smile, which he knew to be dazzling, irresistible. He was already at least six inches taller than Eileen; surely she could see he wasn't a little boy any longer?

"Was there something you wanted, Master Terry? I've my work to do, you know."

The shortening of his name infuriated him. It made him seem younger. He walked toward her, relishing her discomfort. "Yes, Eileen," he said. "I want you to give me a kiss for my birthday. Now's as good a time as any."

Her face flooded with color and she looked at him as if he'd gone mad. She was wringing her duster in her hands, her mouth had fallen wide open. Finally, she smiled nervously. "Ah, go off with you. Don't be teasing me, now. You should know better."

He was so close now he could see the little beads of perspiration above her upper lip. Her hair was damp in the heat; she smelled faintly of perspiration.

"You kiss Dennis Dugan, don't you? The great lout! I know you do, Eileen. I'm a better man than he is. You've got to admit that."

He knew exactly what she was thinking. She couldn't get too high and mighty with him, there was the danger of losing her position. Where would she go? Then too, he thought she probably wanted to kiss him. All she needed was a little urging. He reached out and grasped her arms, holding her fast as she stiffened and tried to move away. Yes, she was frightened. Quickly, he brought his hands up and clamped them tightly to her cheeks. Now! He bent and

pressed his lips to hers, but instead of melting, sur-
rendering, as he'd imagined, Eileen twisted her head
and gasped with indignation.

"Ah, don't, Eileen. Be sweet to me." He ground
his lips against hers painfully. There wasn't much
pleasure in it, as far as he could see. She continued
to resist him, pushing at his chest with frantic hands.
Terry stumbled back, furious.

"Stupid *slut*," he hissed at her. "Ignorant, peasant
slut!"

The bewildered look in her wide eyes, the harsh
sound of her breathing, enraged him. He placed both
hands on her breasts, and she began to cry. How red
her face was! Really, she wasn't pretty at all. He felt
the warm mounds of her breasts beneath the cloth of
her dress. They, at least, were nice. He squeezed, hard,
wondering if that was what Dennis Dugan did to her
in the fields.

She was blubbering now, calling him a devil, hating
him. Wretched girl. He dropped his hands and walked
out of the room in disgust. He'd been a fool to think
a bog-trotting slattern like Eileen would know how
to please a fellow.

It wasn't until his mother was due to return that
Terry's anger turned to uneasiness. What if Eileen
told on him? His mother would never believe her,
but just imagining the supreme look of disgust on
Margaret's face was enough to make him sweat.

His mother was the only person he feared, the only
one who could wither him with one look from her
pale, knowing eyes. When she returned, he went to
her with his most ingratiating smile. Solicitously,

he asked if he could fetch her fan, and inquired politely about Mrs. Whiteside. When she was well-primed, he said—as if the thought had just occurred to him— "By the way, Mother, I don't think Eileen is the sort of girl we should have working here."

"What makes you say such a thing, Terence? I consider her industrious, honest and loyal. Have you been listening to kitchen gossip?"

"Of course not, Mama. I just don't think you can trust her."

"I demand an explanation, Terence. This is a serious accusation."

Terry furrowed his brow, hoping he looked fair-minded and earnest. "I've been noticing the decanters," he said. "The whiskey decanters. The levels keep changing. I think Eileen tipples, Mother. I believe she steals our whiskey from us."

Margaret reacted astoundingly. Her normally pale face turned ashen, and she closed her eyes as if in pain. When she opened them, she gave Terry the very look he dreaded.

"The whiskey in this house is not your province, Terence. I would not expect a boy of your age to notice such things. I am quite sure you're wrong about Eileen, and I don't want to hear another word about it." She rose, her back stiff and uncompromising. "I am going to my room before dinner," she said. "When your father comes home, tell him I shall be down at eight."

"Yes, Mother."

Terry went out to the porch and sat, screened behind a wisteria vine. Heat shimmered over the mountains, and insects droned their late summer cadence. He imagined a scene, far in the future, in which his mother would come to him for help. He would be a United States Senator—just as she wished—living in a mansion. She would be destitute.

"Yes, Mother," he would say impatiently, "of course I'll help you. Don't snivel so. See my assistant—he'll book an appointment. No, I don't want to hear another word about it. Financial matters are not your province."

A week later, Terry turned fourteen and received so many splendid gifts he forgot his pique. At the large birthday dinner given for him, he was served by Eileen. She was courteous and neutral, but he knew he could never look her in the eye again.

When he returned to school in the autumn, he told his best friend, Fred Carstairs, that his mother's maid had let him steal a kiss and look at her legs in honor of his birthday.

"No, go on," said Fred reverently. "How was it?"

Terry shrugged. "It was alright," he said. "Mind you, I've seen better."

3

Lately, it seemed to Veronica, the world was growing more violent. In September, President McKinley had been assassinated in Buffalo. Veronica thought about this tragic event, trying to find some meaning in it. She had also begun to be curious about the war in South Africa. Sometimes she felt closer to the people she read about in the newspapers than she did to her own friends in New York.

On the day after McKinley's assassin—a man named Czolgosz—was electrocuted in Auburn, she lunched with Elizabeth Mallory at Child's. Elizabeth's husband was a colleague of Robert's. The Mallorys were important people, established, and Rob was proud of his wife's friendship with Elizabeth.

"'I thought Amelia was looking peaked Monday night," said Mrs. Mallory thoughtfully. "She needs to get out more. Sometimes I think . . . Veronica, have you heard a word I've been saying?"

"Yes, I heard you."

"I must say, you don't seem frightfully interested," Elizabeth said petulantly. She was a pretty woman, in her mid-thirties, like Veronica. Her blonde hair was elaborately dressed. By contrast, Veronica looked handsome but plain. She hadn't the patience for fussy coiffures, or the interest in jewels and new fashions which seemed to endlessly occupy Elizabeth. She wondered what her friend would do if she introduced a topic of real importance, just for once? The alternative was to discuss the reasons for Amelia's alleged peakedness. She speared a prawn, half-lifted it to her lips, but returned it to the plate.

"Elizabeth, do you know who Emily Hobhouse is?"

Her companion looked up in lady-like confusion. "Is she one of Mary Lowrey's cousins?"

Veronica sighed. It was just like Elizabeth to associate everything and everybody with her own small circle. And yet Elizabeth was an intelligent woman. On the rare occasions when she permitted herself to discuss matters more daring than fashion or local gossip, she could be articulate and incisive.

"Emily Hobhouse has just been arrested by Lord Kitchener in Cape Town. I read about it in the *Times* this morning."

"How very unpleaseant," said Elizabeth. "Is she a common criminal?"

"Far from it. She was sent by an influential group of women to inspect the camps in South Africa. That was last spring. When she returned in October, Lord

Kitchener claimed he hadn't given his permission. He had her arrested in Cape Town and deported back to England. She resisted quite violently." Veronica spoke with admiration.

"Camps? What sort of camps in South Africa?"

"Oh, Elizabeth, surely you know there's a war on there?"

"Yes, I suppose so. But really, Veronica, what does it have to do with us? A native uprising of some sort? And this Hobhouse woman—what sort of creature is she to involve herself? She can't be a lady, dear."

Veronica felt her lips tighten with impatience. Suddenly she felt quite capable of pouring her drink over Elizabeth's feathered bonnet, just to see what her friend would do.

"Are you aware," she said haughtily, "that thousands of Boer women and children have been left homeless? Their farms have been burned, desolated. They've been put in camps, Elizabeth. That is what Emily Hobhouse was sent to investigate."

"Well, it's a pity of course. The women and children are always the ones who suffer, and they're not to blame. But there is no excuse for an Englishwoman to go poking her nose into things which are none of her concern."

"Someone must," answered Veronica.

"I'm sure Lord Kitchener has able deputies for that purpose. It is not the proper sphere of a lady to concern herself with politics."

"And what should be of concern to us, Liz? Amelia's complexion?"

"Now you're being sarcastic, dear, and it doesn't

become you. I think you just got out of bed on the wrong side this morning. Now tell me—what are you planning to wear to Julia's theatre party?"

In the carriage, going back to her house on East 38th Street, Veronica considered why it was that women like Elizabeth Mallory shunned important topics as they would a plague. It was only quite recently that she herself had begun to read the political sections of the newspaper; what she read made her indignant and curious, but there was no one to whom she could talk. Robert, her husband, had much the same attitude as Elizabeth Mallory.

A few flakes of snow danced in the weak sun above 14th Street. It was that cheerless time of year when autumn had gone and winter hadn't quite arrived. Limbo. Veronica thrust her hands more deeply into her muff and shivered. A terrible thought had crept into her mind. She had suddenly realized that she had entered into that time in her own life between autumn and winter, and that it was far too early.

"Surely," she thought, "thirty-three isn't old. I have thoughts, and energy, and opinions, and nobody wants to hear them." Robert was content for her to run the house and manage Bernadette and be charming to his colleagues and their wives—he required nothing further of her. Very occasionally, if he had taken too much to drink, he slid into her bed like a thief. Furtively, apologetically, he took his pleasure, and then departed through the connecting door of his dressing-room, for his own bed.

If she had been able to have more children, her life would have been fuller. She was a good mother and would have happily borne a half-dozen more babies, but Bernadette had not come easily into the world, and the doctor had told her she could never have another. Guiltily, she acknowledged that she didn't care that Rob had no heir. Her sadness was for quite another reason. She planned to see that Bernadette had the best education available to a girl, and it seemed regrettable that her determination and Rob's fortune could not have been used to raise more than just one child.

The carriage was about to turn into her street, but she rapped on the roof and asked the driver to continue on uptown. She wanted to pass the theatre where Delia was performing. It pleased her to see her niece's name in bold black on the playbill:

DELIA O'DONNELL IN ROSALEEN—
A HEARTWARMING IRISH DRAMA

Veronica had seen Delia in *Rosaleen*. She agreed with Kieran, who thought the play a piece of ripe old trash, but it still pleased her to know that the radiant girl on stage was an O'Donnell, her sister's daughter.

The theatre district by day wasn't nearly half so glamorous as by night. Shivering urchins skidded about almost beneath the carriage's wheels, flakes of snow frosting their dull hair. Everywhere she saw the effects of malnutrition, especially in the forms of her countrypeople. The Irish were pale and narrow, their faces drawn and pasty. These were the children of the poor—children such as she and her brothers and sisters might have been if Liam hadn't been so enterprising.

A redhaired girl of about ten huddled in a doorway, a shawl clutched to her meagre body. Her narrow eyes were shifty, and too old. *That might have been me,* thought Veronica, *or Bridget.* If Liam hadn't been thrifty and shrewd, and if he hadn't worked like a dray horse, where would they be today? Liam's fortune was the product of farsightedness, and also some good luck. Whose wasn't? All the hard work in the world wouldn't have benefitted the O'Donnells if the land her father bought had been worthless. If the railroad construction companies had had no use for the gravel, O'Donnell & Sons Construction might not exist today, and she, Veronica, might have been the urchin in the doorway.

Robert was ashamed of her family's background. That their money had come through trade was something which galled him, but his own Anglo-Irish antecedents were spotless enough to make up for her lack of aristocratic blood.

Stop it! What could she expect? Should Rob say: This is my wife; her family are in the gravel business? Oh, shame, Veronica. He's a good man; he's given you Bernadette.

All the same, as the carriage rumbled past Delia's theatre, Veronica gave a silent cheer for her niece's willfulness. Say what you would, Delia was her own woman. It would be different for the next generation. Delia, Bernadette, Jim, Terry—in their own ways they would all be independent. Only Kieran worried her, and not for any reason she could fathom.

"Is Mr. Kieran at home?" she asked when the carriage had returned her to the house on 38th Street.

"No, madam," said Brinks, the ancient butler who had been with the Tyrone family since Rob was in short pants. "He's gone back to Newburgh."

She was home, back in her familiar drawing room. Safe, protected. She looked with pleasure at the Turkistan carpets (nothing braided here; nothing country-like or Irish), at the oil paintings of Rob's stern northern ancestors, at the fashionable Egyptian *frieze* above the mantle. Her maid, Betty, had laid a fire, and the curtains were drawn against the dull, grey afternoon.

The door burst open and Bernadette, three steps ahead of her governess, hurled herself into Veronica's arms.

"Mama! Only guess! I can count to ten in French. Listen!"

Veronica looked at the round face, the intense eyes. The child was counting for her, fiercely proud. Bernadette had progressed to *huit* when her mother could restrain herself no longer. She hugged Bernadette so hard the little girl squirmed and gasped. "You're *hurting* me, mama."

"I'm sorry, darling. Mama's very naughty today. Begin again."

The light from the leaping fire struck coppery flares in Bernadette's bright hair. As she looked at her daughter, Veronica had only one thought. This bright, questing, untameable little girl would do all the things in life that her mother could have only dreamed of. All that had been forbidden to Veronica, withheld from her, would be accessible to Bernadette.

She rang for tea, and dismissed Madame LaPorte, the governess. It was customary for children to take tea with their governesses or nannies, but she wanted her daughter all to herself this afternoon.

When they were settled comfortably, in front of the fire, Veronica told her little girl about what was happening in South Africa. She pared the tale down for Bernadette's ears, leaving out the violent details which might upset her, but she presented the facts as they were, adding the story of Emily Hobhouse for Bernadette's consideration. She was very neutral, desiring the child to draw her own conclusions.

Bernadette listened, eyes grave. She understood everything, and did not ask, as Elizabeth Mallory would, why a woman would interfere in the business of men. At the age of six, Bernadette was already a very apt pupil.

The room on the docks was large and shabby, filled with smoke and the mixed aromas of whiskey, wet tweed, and cheap beer. A makeshift bar filled the forefront of the room; in back, three tables were reserved for a perpetual game of cards, run by a man named Leary. To gain access to the waterfront gambling club, a man knocked on the bolted door, called out his name, and was submitted to the scrutiny of a giant employed by Leary to screen the guests. The giant, late of County Cork, had a gentle nature, but his height and features were so forbidding that no one would know it.

On a wet night in October, Kieran knocked on the

door and waited for the grill to slide back. He had left his Aunt Veronica's earlier in the day, and thought he might do well to play a few hands before returning to Newburgh. His money was running low, and rather than ask his Uncle Patrick for an advance on his allowance he had decided to try his luck. It wasn't the first time.

The grill slid back. The baleful eyes of the giant glared at him. "Who?" he asked.

"Gerry Ryan," answered Kieran.

The door opened and Kieran stepped in. "Good evening," he said to the giant. "It's a night to freeze your parts, Tim, it's that unpleasant."

"A bloody climate," agreed Tim. "Not fit for Christians."

It had turned cold quite suddenly, the earlier snow resolving itself into a hard, freezing sleet.

"Will you play, or drink, Ryan?"

"Both, I should think."

After a little sloe-eyed barmaid had bustled over to hand Kieran a whiskey, Tim showed him to one of the tables. An empty chair waited, and Kieran seated himself.

"Evening all," Kieran said with a broad smile. "Deal me in."

He had developed a good style at the tables, raffish and serious at the same time. He had only thirty dollars, apart from his train ticket, but nobody would know that. He glanced around to see who his opponents were. Three of the men he had played with before; one was a longshoreman named O'Brien, the other two were Tammany underlings. The fourth he had never seen before. He was a large man, with a hardened look in his dark eyes. He was a swarthy Irishman, his hair as black as Kieran's own, but he must have been at least fifteen years older. He glared at Kieran, and shifted uneasily in his chair.

They played a hand, and Kieran dropped out on the fourth card. Five dollars down.

The dark-skinned bloke shifted his cigar in his mouth. "Des Malloy," he said by way of introduction. His voice was pure Kerry.

"Gerry Ryan," said Kieran. He kept his impassive face, but inwardly he was impressed. He had heard of Desmond Malloy, and knew he was a man to be reckoned with. He was a former boxer, a middleweight, who had a voice in union matters. He was rising in Tammany fast.

"Where do you come from, Ryan?"

"From upstate New York by way of Sligo, Mr. Malloy."

"Fancy that," said Des Malloy, backing up the ace showing in his new hand with a five dollar bet. "Fine young feller like yourself. And what brings you to Leary's?"

"Oh, it's often I've been here, sir," said Kieran, sneaking a look at the buried king which matched the one showing in front of him. "Raise you five."

O'Brien, the longshoreman, dropped out. The other two matched the bet.

"I wonder," mused Malloy, accepting another spade which might well bode a flush, "are you old enough to play with the grown men?"

"Fully eighteen, sir," answered Kieran. The dealer

spun another king his way and the dark-skinned Kerryman regarded the table with interest.

"Ah, boyo," he said, "isn't cards just like life? You might have anything a'tall buried there, and you might have piss all. Raise you ten."

Kieran pushed ten dollars into the pile and watched while the other two folded their cards. Even if Malloy had two aces it wasn't a match for his three kings, and the chances against a flush were great. He had always been lucky at cards. The last one dealt him signified nothing, while Des Malloy received another spade. Malloy bet another ten, and Kieran placed his last ten dollar bill on the table.

"The moment of truth," said his opponent, teasing the buried card upward. "Ah, what a shame, Ryan, looks like I've been dealt a bloody flush. Now there's a lesson, boy! Three kings are noble to look at, but they can't triumph over the persistant voice of five spades. Sorry for your troubles."

Kieran felt his color rise despite his efforts to remain calm. He smiled and pushed the pile of notes in Malloy's direction. "I'll be saying good-night," he said.

"Not so early, Ryan? The evening is still young."

"I'm skinned," answered Kieran. He stood up, retaining his dignity, and walked away from the table. Now he would have to walk to the bloody train station, through sleet and driving rain. He had reached the door, ignoring the plaintive look of the barmaid, when Malloy's hand plucked at his coat sleeve.

"Newburgh, is it lad? Is that where you're headed?"

Kieran simply stared at him. He'd be damned if he'd give Malloy the satisfaction of his astonishment.

"Gerry Ryan—whatever you want to call yourself—don't be a stranger. I know exactly who you are, that's my business. Now, have you money to get where you're going?"

"I have," answered Kieran.

"Good, then. Here's my card, boyo. When you're back in New York, come see Des Malloy. You've some growing up to do, but you'll get there."

Kieran took the card and thrust it into his pocket ungraciously. He was trying to make his face a mask, but he had the feeling that the older man could sense his bewilderment.

"I knew your da," said Des Malloy.

Then Tim opened the door, and Kieran was alone in the raw, unfriendly night. He shook himself irritably, like a puppy, and began the long walk to the station.

Every year, during the week following Thanksgiving, Patrick O'Donnell escaped his wife, his construction company, and Newburgh, and traveled to far-off cities on business. O'Donnell & Sons was left in the capable hands of Michael Flynn, and Patrick took his leave with no regrets.

Technically, the men who gathered in Boston or Philadelphia or Chicago were there to trade views on the construction business and return to their companies with fresh perspectives. Patrick had, in fact, picked up some valuable tips at these conventions and had made some strong contacts, but it was the freedom from Margaret he prized most. He felt very guilty about it, but the guilt was less than the pleasure.

He stood in his compartment, locking his knees against the swaying of the train, and brushed his hair with Liam's silver-backed military brush. The face in the mirror was not, he thought, such a bad one. He had put on weight, as prosperous men did, and his cheeks were well-padded, but his complexion was still fresh and ruddy, his brown hair thick and only lightly touched with grey. He slapped bay rum on his cheeks, and rubbed his hands briskly together. He would have a good meal in the dining car, and wine. Perhaps he would have a chance to talk to the attractive woman who had nodded to him as they were boarding.

The train was rocketing through the green hills of New Jersey. The next day he would be in Chicago and, if all went well, he would be able to return to Newburgh at Christmas prepared to face another loveless year. It humiliated him to acknowledge the fact that the chief reason for his yearly trip to Chicago was to seek female companionship. How shocked he would have been, back in the early days of his marriage, if he could have seen ahead to these planned infidelities. He had idolized Margaret, and perhaps that was the problem. If he had seen her in less idealistic terms, she might have learned to love him.

On the way to the dining car, Patrick thought of Margaret's good-bye to him. A chaste kiss on the cheek, delivered unwillingly. A murmured farewell.

It made him burn to think of the times he'd forced himself on her because he couldn't help it. He was a man, wasn't he, not old or past it, not feeble or joyless? At first, when Margaret had begun to turn away from him, he'd thought he was to blame. He was too rough, too crude, for a woman of Margaret's delicate sensibilities. He had been infinitely gentle, then, bending over backward to try to seduce her, but it hadn't worked. Instead of being seduced, Margaret had taken it as a sign that she no longer had to participate in that side of marriage which was so distasteful to her. He'd be damned if he'd beg for scraps from her. She was as cold as they came, his Margaret—a cold fish!

The dining car gave him a sense of peace. The white napkins, the heavy old silver, the respectful attentions of the red-jacketed Negro handing him the menu—all these pleasantries were just the beginning. Chicago was full of pretty women who would dine with him, laugh at his jokes, stroke his hair and wriggle happily in his bed. Sometimes he paid for their company, but twice he had managed to attract women who were neither prostitutes nor low. One, in Pittsburgh, had been the wife of the local police chief.

He ordered a mixed grill and a bottle of expensive French wine, forgetting whether it was proper to have red or white.

Bugger that! Leave that sort of thing to the Margarets of the world.

The door to the dining car opened and the woman he had noticed earlier was ushered to a table across from his. She had fair hair; he thought she might be

Polish, or Scandinavian. She nodded to him, and the little plumes on her bonnet danced. She was wearing a mauve traveling suit; there were two rows of jet buttons gleaming on her neat little bosom. He nodded back.

All during his meal, he watched her covertly. She seemed respectable enough, a young widow, perhaps, and he doubted very much his ability to coax her to his compartment. What did it matter? If not her, someone else. The world was full of women. That was the joy of traveling—you never knew what adventure lay in wait. *Mea culpa,* thought Patrick. I am guilty of the sin of lust a hundred times over.

And yet, if Margaret had only loved him as a woman ought to love her man, he would never have strayed. Surely that made him less guilty? Night had fallen outside the windows and the train plunged on into Pennsylvania. The woman in the mauve traveling suit rose from her table and prepared to leave. She again nodded in Patrick's direction, and he—full of wine and anticipation and the foretaste of guilt—got up and followed her from the dining car.

He kept a discreet distance, swaying slightly with the wine and the movement of the train, and when he entered his own car it was just in time to see her mauve skirt disappear behind the door of her compartment. Never mind. Plenty of others.

He lay in bed for a long time, listening to the rhythmic clicking of the train's wheels, the haunting bells at the cross-roads. *Mea culpa, mea culpa* the train sang. Just before he fell asleep, he had a startling thought: Margaret should have married Robert Tyrone, his sister's husband. They were two of a kind.

"Will we do the little wreaths of holly, madam?" Rosie asked.

Edith O'Donnell nodded.

"And the mistletoe?"

"All of it, Rose. Exactly as it was last year. I want this house to be as festive at Christmas as it was when Mr. O'Donnell was alive."

Rosie bobbed her head and retreated. Edith knew the girl was puzzled, but glad. Puzzled because her mistress, not out of mourning yet, wanted the house to be gay; glad because, poor mite, she was still a child herself and liked all the trappings of a holiday.

Edith felt all her responsibilities keenly. She had a responsibility to her grandchildren, all of whom, except for little Bernadette, would be in Newburgh, and a responsibility to her serving girls, who were far from home without families of their own. She also believed she owed it to Liam, who had loved festivities, to carry on the tradition of a proper O'Donnell Christmas.

Therefore, the house on Ridge Street became transformed in late December. Holly wreaths graced the posts of the gas lamps and the large front door, and a fifteen-foot spruce, trimmed with garlands, baubles and candles, stood in the drawing room. Pine boughs lay on the mantle piece, dispensing their rich odor, and little garlands of mistletoe crowned the chandeliers and hanging fixtures. Mrs. Parker spent days baking fruitcakes and plum pudding, and on Christmas day, she would roast a fat goose. It would all be exactly as it had been.

Jim was coming home from Cambridge, and Kieran would be with them. Even Delia was making the journey from New York. *Rosaleen* had closed in late November, and she was rehearsing for another play, but she had promised to come for three days. Her mother was ecstatic. Only Veronica would be absent. It was her turn to go with her husband and child to Baltimore, where Robert's parents lived.

Edith worried about her younger daughter. Veronica, unlike Bridget, had been unlucky in marriage. Robert Wilson Tyrone had made her a rich woman, transported her to the city and a social life which could not be had in Newburgh, but he had failed to make her happy.

Edith knew her children very well, and although Veronica never complained, she was sure her daughter was dissatisfied. Patrick, too, was unhappy in his choice of a mate, but as a man he had other things to occupy his life. He had the company and the careers of his two young sons to consider, whereas Veronica had only little Bernadette to think about. It seemed hard to Edith that she could not have safeguarded the lives of her children more thoroughly, but that was being unrealistic. Sometimes she dreamed of Robert, her first born, and wakened to the knowledge that—for all her love—he had nurtured dark, revolutionary thoughts and died for them. It still pained her to think she had known him so little.

Robert's son, Kieran, was also a mystery to her. She feared for him, as she had failed to do for her own son, and prayed every night that he would not follow the hard path laid down for him by a father he had never known.

While the festive preparations continued around her, Edith looked out at the cold, deep snow blanketing Newburgh, and wished with all her heart that those she loved might have happy lives.

Jim, Delia and Terry stood beneath the mistletoe and made wishes for the New Year. Warmed by claret and good will, they hugged one another and became the children they had once been.

Delia's beauty and celebrated status were temporarily forgotten, and she was once more the wild-haired girl who had led her cousins in a raid on Mr. Schneider's hen-house in 1891. Jim and Terry watched her as she lifted a rapt face to the heavens and wished for a better play than *Rosaleen.*

Jim, abandoning the new dignity he had brought back from Harvard College, shouted out a fervent request that his American History professor be struck down, albeit not fatally, by the hand of the Almighty. Inwardly, he prayed for a kiss from Virginia Leonard at the ball on New Year's Day.

Terry wished for a hunting knife and an increase in his allowance.

"And what do you wish for, Kieran?" Delia called over her shoulder.

Kieran was standing ten feet away, watching his

cousins indulgently. Delia's question caught him unawares, and he lifted his glass to them with a mocking gesture.

"I wish I had never been born," he said. And then, as if to prove he had been joking, he grinned and drank to them. "*Slainte,*" he said, using the Gaelic toast. "Here's to 1902. May it bring luck and happiness to all of us."

"Hear, hear!" cried Jim.

"To 1902!" bellowed Terry.

"Luck and happiness to all of us," said Delia quickly.

4

The good fortune Delia had wished for her family in 1902 came to some of the O'Donnells but not all. In the stock market crash precipitated by Northern Pacific Railroad, Patrick lost five thousand dollars. This was not a sum great enough to ruin him, but it seemed a bad omen. One of Veronica's friends woke up a rich woman and went to bed a pauper. Her husband had been ruined when his holdings plunged, and, convinced that the stocks would never rise again, he shot himself.

Edith O'Donnell caught pneumonia in the spring and was desperately ill for three weeks, but Bridget's devoted nursing helped her through the crisis.

The best luck came to Jim, and to Delia herself. Jim had made friends with a young man distantly related to the Morgans. This fact so impressed Virginia Leonard that she allowed Jim to kiss her when he came home for Easter.

Delia's new play, more serious than *Rosaleen*, received such good notices that it was sure to run for the entire year. She still lived quite frugally in a respectable boarding house, but the handsome salary she commanded went straight into her bank account; at nineteen she was an independent woman.

"Do you mean to say you've never been in love?" Mrs. Throne asked as she arched one eyebrow playfully.

Mrs. Throne and Delia had become good friends. She was old enough to be Delia's mother—which, in fact, she played on stage—and Delia felt she could trust her. She paused now to consider the question.

"Of course, I don't mean to pry, dear," Mrs. Throne said.

Delia smiled. "I was only wondering what you meant by 'in love', Nettie."

"I should think that would be perfectly clear. When I was your age I'd been in love a half-dozen times. That was before I met Mr. Throne, of course. My little love affairs were quite innocent, you understand, but my, how *consuming* they seemed at the time!"

She leaned forward to pour more tea.

"Perhaps girls are different nowadays, Delia, but you can't look me in the eye and say you've never, ever felt a special emotion for some young man."

Delia stretched one leg out, admiring the rosettes on the tips of her kid pumps. Her pumps were blue, to match the stripes in her frock.

"I did," she answered abruptly. "When I was sixteen, I thought I loved someone. I was wrong, though. He turned out to be a great fool."

"Many of them do, my pet. What was he like? Tell Nettie."

"His name was Brendan. He wasn't terribly handsome, but he had the deepest, darkest eyes I've ever seen. I used to imagine I could drown in them."

Nettie sat forward, enthralled, and even as Delia heard her own trite words spoken, she knew how true they were. She *had* felt that way. Brendan's eyes made her feel that way, and his voice made her think of dark velvet. She'd been drunk with power, sure that Brendan would abandon his foolish convictions for her. She had thought he couldn't stay away from her, no matter how hard he tried.

"We used to walk together, at dusk, through the fields in the town where I was born. He never touched me, except to take my arm at the stiles, or if there was a rough place. He was afraid to touch me, you see."

"Why was that, dear?"

"Because he was meant to be a priest. He had the vocation."

"Oh, how tragic, how—" Mrs. Throne suddenly narrowed her eyes. "You wouldn't be having me on, would you dear? It's just like that novel I read—what was the name of it? It was all about a beautiful young girl who falls in love with a priest."

"Brendan wasn't a priest, Nettie. Not then. But he was destined to be one. The year I turned seventeen he went off to the seminary and I never saw him again."

"I see," said Mrs. Throne. "And you considered him a fool to prefer the priesthood to you?"

"I did. A man who can fall in love with a woman isn't cut out for that life."

"And are you sure he loved you, Delia?"

Delia smiled and touched her black hair. "Oh, very sure."

She would never forget the one time Brendan had kissed her, standing under the clump of alder trees at the edge of the river. He had caught her up against him almost roughly, and in the moment before his lips sought hers she had known a thrill of triumph so wild and sweet she'd laughed out loud. Brendan hadn't laughed. His voice, murmuring her name, had been full of despair. "Delia, Delia, Delia . . ." She could still hear it.

Mrs. Throne looked at her with less sympathy than Delia would have expected.

"Perhaps you loved him *because* he was studying to be a priest," she said rather curtly. "You were testing your power, my girl."

"Ah, well, it doesn't matter now."

Mrs. Throne softened at the plaintive tone. "And there's never been any other young man you might care for?"

Delia decided that she had parted with enough information about herself for one afternoon. She shook her head. She and Nettie discussed the 'stage-door-Johnnies' who hung about with flowers and sweets, hoping to entice Delia out with them, and Nettie congratulated her on her wisdom in turning them away.

"There's nothing to them, dear. They'll ruin an innocent young girl soon as look at her. And something else," Mrs. Throne said and winked, "most of them are married, anyway."

Later, in the carriage going uptown, Delia pondered Mrs. Throne's last question. There was, in fact, another young man for whom Delia had always had special feelings. Under other circumstances, she might even have loved him. As it was, she remained his friend. His only friend.

Kieran was her cousin, almost like a brother. His strange, dark moods, his solitary position in life, his pride and arrogance, all moved her. She felt a cloud hovered over Kieran and wished she knew how to rid him of it. Sometimes she wondered what it would be like to be in Kieran's arms, to look into those eyes that were so like her own. It made her shiver, because to make love to Kieran would be like making love to herself.

Now that he was a student at Harvard, Jim commanded more respect in Newburgh. It was well known that he had visited the home of his new friend, Maynard Hill, in Philadelphia, and some people even speculated that he might have invitations to Newport for the summer.

"I always said as how Mr. James would grow up to make the family proud," said Mrs. Parker to Peg and Rosie. "He's been accepted by all the best people now."

The truth, in fact, was rather different. Jim O'Donnell and Maynard Hill had become friends simply because they both loved music. Maynard was the very model of golden American youth. Tall, blond, rich, Protestant, quick-witted, graceful, and athletic, he was precisely the sort of boy who might have been expected to snub an Irish boy from Newburgh.

Certainly others of Maynard's social status had snubbed Jim. They weren't crude or cruel about it. Nobody said an unkind word to him or poked fun of him, but they made it quite clear that he could never hope to be taken into the charmed inner circle of the 'Insiders.' 'Insiders' were native Americans of English, Dutch, or German backgrounds, or the occasional unblemished foreigner, like the younger son of an English earl. Boys whose names began with an "O" or a "Mc" were immediately branded as outsiders; even those of Irish extraction whose families had changed their names to more Anglicized versions of the original were not quite up to 'Insider' status.

Only Maynard Hill, a true 'Insider,' could befriend a boy like Jim without inviting ridicule. Maynard could do what he liked. In many ways, Jim considered Maynard the perfect all-American male, but Maynard shared what was considered a major flaw with Jim: he did not wish to become a banker, any more than Jim wished to become a lawyer.

They had met at a concert. During the intermission, Maynard had pointed out certain mistakes in the performance which Jim hadn't even noticed. They continued their discussion in Maynard's rooms, drinking port, and Jim discovered that Maynard was also knowledgeable about classical music, and that he was a would-be composer.

The Hill family frowned on their son and heir's ambition, pronouncing it unmanly and Bohemian. So when Jim confided his mother's prejudices, shyly confessing that she thought traditional music "low," Maynard collapsed with laughter. They were both torn between their need to be dutiful sons and their desire to pursue what they loved best.

All during the term, they met to discuss music. Jim brought his fiddle to Maynard's rooms and played tunes which Maynard had never heard.

"But you know, old man, that is an *immensely* complicated, a *sophisticated,* piece of music!" Maynard murmured on hearing *Patsy Kelly's Jig.*

Elements of the traditional Irish music began to creep into his compositions, which he then played for Jim on the battered piano in a saloon off Sculley Square. By the end of the school year, they were such good friends that Maynard arranged to visit Jim in Newburgh on his way to Virginia, in July.

The house where Jim's parents lived, although grand by Newburgh standards, was very modest when compared to the Hill residence in Philadelphia. Neither Jim nor Maynard cared, but Margaret O'Donnell was thrown into a panic at the idea of entertaining a young man connected to the Pierpont Morgans.

At dinner she wore the Fitzhugh jewels and embarrassed both young men by making many references to her presentation at Court in 1882. When Patrick teetered back in his chair or wiped his mouth vigorously on his table napkin, she shuddered, visibly. Her accent became slightly English, as if to compensate for the hint of Irish which still hovered at the edges of her husband's vowels.

"Your mother's an unhappy woman," Maynard said to Jim one evening. They were sitting on the porch, screened by the wisteria vine, after dinner. Maynard was smoking a cigar, his long legs propped lazily against the railing.

"Why, yes, I suppose she is," Jim answered. "How could you tell?"

"My mother is, too. I've learned to read the signs."

It had occurred to Jim only recently that his mother might be a secret drinker. He felt humiliated that his friend had noticed Margaret's oddity, but grateful for the confidence.

"Your father seems a good sort. I like him."

Suddenly, Jim found himself pouring out a torrent of thoughts, as if he had been un-dammed. He told Maynard of his grandfather's flight from Ireland, Liam's long struggle to gain a toe-hold in the New World, and the tragedies that had befallen the O'Donnells. He explained that he felt torn between the need to honor Liam's last wishes and his parents' aspirations for him. "I'm not one thing, nor yet another," he concluded unhappily.

"You're lucky," said Maynard, puffing fiercely on his cigar. "At least there's some passion left in your family. It's all been bred out of mine." He brought his feet down from the railing in a violent movement. "I tell you, Jim, you're damned lucky! You're still close enough to what you came from to feel it! You may not like what you feel, but it's better than being a ghost. The Hills have invented themselves; they don't

know who they are anymore. Invented families produce ghosts."

"You look real enough to me," said Jim, shaken by
the passion and bitterness in his friend's voice.

Maynard laughed, but it wasn't a happy laugh.
They sat in silence, listening to the cicadas. The tip of
Maynard's cigar glowed like a small beacon in the
warm, dark night air.

The only confidence Jim had never shared with
Maynard was his love for Virginia Leonard; it was
something he couldn't bear to discuss with anyone.
But the following day, at a lawn party she had invited them to, he wished he had.

Virginia came toward them, seeming to float down
the long lawn in her white dress. Jim felt his throat
tighten at the sight of her. Her golden hair was looped
up beneath a rakish leghorn straw hat. A white ribbon was wound around the hat and streamed down
her back. Jim thought he'd never seen anything so
lovely as Virginia in her summer frock.

"Hello, James," she said, extending her little hand
to him. However, when she was introduced to Maynard she became twice as animated. She smiled so
radiantly that the corners of her eyes crinkled. "Good-
ness, Mr. Hill, imagine your coming to dull old Newburgh! I only hope we'll be able to entertain you—it
makes me feel quite anxious." She pouted, her hand
still in Maynard's.

"I would never want you to be anxious on my
account, Miss Leonard. I give you my word that I
shall be marvelously entertained."

Jim discovered that it pained him to watch his

friend and Virginia together. They looked somehow right, standing on the green lawn in their summer whites. They were graceful, elegant, beautiful—a golden couple. And how easily Maynard was able to banter with her! He struck the perfect note, half-way between courtesy and flirtatiousness. Jim was so awed by Virginia he could never think of anything clever to say. He winced, remembering the kiss she had given him last Easter. It had been the most perfect moment of his life, until she drew away and said: "Oh, Jim, now you'll think less of me, won't you?"

Instead of replying with a tender whisper, the way Maynard would have, he stammered, "I love you, Virginia. I've always loved you. I could never think anything but the best thoughts about you. You're an angel."

Virginia had giggled, uneasy at such a passionate declaration. "I'm not an angel," she said, "and you mustn't talk about loving me. We're friends, Jim, aren't we?"

How, wondered Jim, could he have gone back to Harvard thinking it possible Virginia would grow to love him? He had remembered only the kiss, and not the aftermath.

Virginia led them down to the little pavilion at the foot of the garden where her parents were receiving people. Jim saw his mother, deep in conversation with Mrs. Whiteside. His father was playing croquet, while Terry hovered near the long table under the oak tree, snatching up cakes and eating them greedily. They suddenly seemed so provincial.

His Aunt Bridget, a daisy fastened in her red hair, called to him, her voice sounding more Irish than usual. "Jim, lad, you look grand today. Quite the grown-up gentleman." Jim blushed and wished the earth would swallow him, but Maynard and Virginia hadn't heard.

"We have a surprise for our guests, Mr. Hill. When you see it, you won't think us so backward." She smiled at him, as she gestured to a large object under a tarpaulin. "Papa is going to unveil it, later, exactly like a statue."

Jim discovered his nervousness melting away as he drank more punch. He talked to old Ada O'Shea and Mr. Leonard. He made Beatrice Schneider, Virginia's closest friend, laugh twice. But all the while he was watching, like a spy, the emotions that filtered across his beloved's face. He noticed that she darted glances toward Maynard whenever she could, but then quickly looked away. When Maynard continued to talk to Mrs. Beach, an attractive widow, for nearly a quarter of an hour, her lips tightened, and when at last she came to his side, it was only to say: "Your friend is a perfect gentleman, Jim."

"Unlike myself," snapped Jim. His words were lost in the general clamor of the unveiling of the surprise. Mr. Leonard whisked the covering away to reveal a large green table divided by a low net. There were squeals of glee from the younger people.

"What would that be?" Miss O'Shea asked loudly.

"Oh, Ada," snorted her sister, "you're behind the times. It's a ping-pong table—they're all the rage."

The guests lined up to play on Newburgh's first

ping-pong table, laughing and calling out good-natured jibes. Patrick proved to be a good player, as did
Mrs. Leonard and Michael Flynn. Bridget was hopeless, laughing too hard at her fumbling to be able to
see straight. Virginia commandeered Maynard for a
partner, and they played a doubles match with Jim
and Beatrice Schneider, winning easily.

For the rest of the afternoon, Jim tormented himself by listing the ways in which Maynard was superior to him. He saw himself as he thought Virginia
must, and felt despair. The players continued their
sport at the ping-pong table until it grew too dark,
and when at last it was time to go, Virginia pressed
Jim's hand and gave him a special smile. Hope leaped
up once more, and he fell asleep that night convinced
that she preferred him.

Just before Maynard left Newburgh, Jim asked him
what he thought of Miss Leonard. It puzzled him that
Maynard had never mentioned her.

"Why, she's a most attractive girl," said Maynard.

"I think she's the loveliest girl I've ever seen," said
Jim, stung by his friend's tepid response. "The nicest,
too."

"Yes, very nice," said Maynard. But something in his
eyes belied the words. For some reason, Maynard
didn't approve of Virginia. Jim felt unhappy about
it, but relieved.

In the autumn of 1902, Veronica Tyrone com-
mitted the unforgivable. At a large dinner party, in
front of two dozen prominent New Yorkers, she con-
tradicted her husband, Robert.

The country was in the grip of a vast coal strike. Thousands of miners had walked off their jobs in May, and now, as the temperatures dropped and the price of the few remaining carloads of anthracite soared, people could talk of nothing else. President Roosevelt had tried, personally, to mediate the strike, and failed. Violence had broken out at Wilkes-Barre, where strikers wrecked two trains and blew up a bridge leading to the Slattery Colliery. In Shenandoah, a soldier shot a miner. The president was rumored to be considering the use of federal troops to restore order.

"They should all be shot," pronounced Mr. Van Sickle, the host. "Lawless, greedy ruffians—the lot of them."

"Things have gone too far when the country can be brought to its knees by a group of illiterate laborers," remarked his wife.

Elizabeth Mallory's husband said too much was being written about the rights of the laboring man. "What about the rights of ordinary, decent citizens?" he asked.

Veronica listened to the well-fed, well-heeled people at the table with growing distaste. Conversations like this were typical in Robert's circle. She had always wondered, uneasily, what they might say if she were not present. She imagined the word "Paddy" would emerge. *Illiterate Irish. Violent, thick-headed paddies.* Slighting remarks about Italians, Poles, and Jews were common, but out of deference to her—or to Robert, really—these members of the ruling class curtailed their contempt for the Irish.

"What I can't understand," said a plump woman wearing pink taffeta, "is why unions aren't outlawed. It was a great mistake to allow them in the first place."

Everyone laughed indulgently.

"It is time," added Mr. Van Sickle, "for Roosevelt to apply the big stick he is so fond of mentioning."

"What we are observing here," said Robert Tyrone, "is anarchy. Anarchy is invariably the result of putting large ideas in small minds. The wretched miners are being manipulated to suit the purposes of union criminals." He stopped and took a sip of wine, smiled drily. Veronica knew this meant he was about to make a joke. "If the miners *did* get an increase in salary, it would only make conditions more dangerous for them."

"How's that, Robert?" Mrs. Van Sickle asked, unwittingly playing the straight man.

"Every spare penny would go for drink, my dear. Can you think of anything more dangerous than a mine-shaft full of drunken men?"

"That is contemptible," said Veronica. She could feel the hot blood in her cheeks. Her fingers trembled on the stem of her wine glass. Everyone fell silent.

"I beg your pardon, Veronica?"

"I said your thoughts on the matter are contemptible, Robert. How can you, who have never known a moment's deprivation in your life, understand what it would be to work twelve hours a day, in unspeakable conditions, for less than six hundred dollars a year? Do you honestly believe these people are less human than yourself?"

For once in his life, Robert was too stunned to

speak. Mrs. Van Sickle tried to create a diversion, but the entire table waited to hear what he would say.

"There are children working in the mines," Veronica continued, "children who have to turn their entire wages over to the company store. And do you know why? Because their fathers were killed in the mines, owing money. Killed because of negligence on the part of the owners."

"I really think," said Robert finally, "that the dinner table of our excellent hosts should not be turned into an arena for your peculiar views, dear. Are you feeling well?"

Veronica thought that she had never felt better in her life. Soon she would be appalled, probably, but in the heat of the moment it was bliss to speak her mind. Recklessly, she smiled at her husband across the table. It was a smile meant to convey to him that she was declaring war, after years of submissiveness.

"I feel splendidly well, thank you. If you can joke about the misfortunes of desperate people and still feel well yourself, then it is *your* views which are peculiar, Robert." She turned to the man on her left and asked him what he thought of a new article in *Harper's*, and gradually conversation resumed.

Robert took her home immediately after dinner. He was stiff with rage and could hardly bear to look at her. When they were home he poured himself a large tumbler of whiskey and stood before her in the drawing room, like a head-master about to punish a pupil.

"I cannot understand you, Veronica. Your behavior tonight was unforgivable. You appeared to have taken leave of your senses. People will be talking about this, you know. They'll be saying that you are unstable."

"Will they? Well, I won't have to hear them, at any rate."

"I shall expect an apology."

"You'll be a long time waiting for it," said Veronica quietly. "I don't intend to apologize to you."

"And yet you propose to go on, as my wife, enjoying my esteem and affection as if nothing had happened?"

"Your esteem?" Veronica mused. "Is that what I've been enjoying all these years, Robert? Dear me, I hardly noticed it was there!"

"You're not yourself," said Robert. He finished his whiskey and placed the glass with a decisive thud on the mantel. "When you've returned to your senses, perhaps we can talk."

"Perhaps," she answered as she watched her husband walk from the room, his shoulders stiff with anger. She began to realize the enormity of what she had just done, and instead of exhilaration she felt a sickly feeling of fright. She had Bernadette to think of, and Robert was, after all, Bernadette's father.

"Let nothing come between me and my daughter," she whispered in the silent room. "Not ever."

"Kieran."

He had been dozing in her arms, enjoying the light half–sleep that came to him after making love. Inga's voice was gentle at first, then insistent. She was shaking him, her hands on his bare chest. "Kieran, wake up. Talk to me, darling."

He groaned and rolled over, protesting. His face

nestled against Inga's large, round breasts. He opened his eyes on vistas of creamy flesh. "Ah, Inga," he whispered, "give us a rest." But she had buried her fingers in his hair and was forcing him to look up at her. Her oval, smooth face was serious; it wasn't more love she was requiring from him now. Her large grey eyes were solemn. If it hadn't been for the wild disarray of her honey-colored hair and the closeness of her warm, bare body, she would have reminded him of an earnest school mistress. He caught a strand of her hair and pulled her down to him, kissing her lazily, but Inga squirmed away, determined.

"Kieran, we must talk now. I've been thinking about you while you were asleep," she said as she disentangled herself and rose from the bed.

Kieran admired the lines of her body as she walked away from him. Inga was twenty-seven, eight years older than himself. She was tall and voluptuous, a sturdy peasant girl with round thighs and lovely breasts, and hair you could swing from. She had immigrated from Sweden at the age of sixteen, married a shopkeeper in New York, and lost him when he caught gold fever in '94. One day he had gone west, hoping to make a fortune in Cripple Creek. He had written to her at first, assuring her he would send for her as soon as he had staked his claim, but his letters grew scarcer and finally ceased altogether. Inga had last heard from him in '95, when he was on his way to the Klondike, but never since. She didn't know whether he was alive or dead, but she was a phlegmatic girl and didn't seem to care. He had left her with two young children and his tobacconist's shop; the proceeds from the latter paid for the former, and Inga seemed perfectly happy.

"You've a lovely arse, sweetheart," murmured Kieran from the bed.

Inga looked at him over her shoulder, smiling, and then slipped into her ruffled dressing gown. She left the room and clattered about in the kitchen for a time, returning with two cups of tea and one of the sweet almond cakes she knew Kieran liked. She set the tray on a low table near the bed and then opened the curtains. Dull, wintry light penetrated the room. Clearly, this was to be their first serious conversation. Kieran sighed, drew the covers up over his naked body, and folded his arms.

"You're nearly twenty, darling," said Inga. "It's time you made something of yourself."

Kieran grinned. Bloody women—always wanting to meddle and spoil a good thing. "Leave it alone," he said mildly.

"I am serious. It's plain to me that you're very intelligent and—"

"Is it my intelligence prompted you to take me home with you that first time?"

"No," said literal-minded Inga, "it was because I wanted you to make love to me. Please not to interrupt, Kieran. You tell me nothing about yourself, but I can tell you're a gentleman. Gentlemen don't drift about from pillar to post unless there's a reason. What could be the reason that you wander? I said to myself: 'Inga, he is poor. He has no money. He is from a good family, but they lost their money.' Am I right?"

Kieran propped himself up on one elbow and looked

at her incredulously. She flushed a little under his gaze but continued determinedly. "This is a great country, Kieran, full of opportunities, but a young man must educate himself. You should be at a university, so you can become a lawyer, or a doctor."

She was so earnest that he couldn't help laughing. Inga looked at him with reproach. "I have some money my man left for me. I've never touched it. The shop does fine for me and the children; we don't lack for anything. The money is yours, darling. You can pay me back when you become a success."

"What are you saying, Inga?" He felt a great sadness and didn't know why.

"I want to send you to school," said Inga simply.

Kieran got up from the bed and walked across the room. He knelt by Inga and held her face in his hands. "You would do that for me?" he whispered. She nodded. "But *why*?" Her docility made him angry. He shook her. "*Why*, Inga?"

"Because I love you. I want to help you."

Suddenly, Kieran wanted to cry. He had not cried since he was very small, but now he wanted to put his head in Inga's lap and weep. That this simple, pretty woman, who meant nothing more to him than the pleasure they shared in her bed, should be willing to give him her savings, seemed inexpressibly pathetic. He carried her to the bed and removed her dressing gown with gentle hands. While he stroked her body he told her he had no need of her money.

"I don't want to go to university," he whispered, lifting her heavy hair so he could kiss her throat. "I know everything I need to know, sweetheart."

She protested, but he covered her lips with his own. He wanted to please her as never before, because it was the only means he had of thanking her.

Inga was always quickly aroused, but today he caressed every inch of her willing body, feeling her flesh ignite beneath his touch. Her protests turned to moans of pleasure. Carefully, mechanically, he brought her to a pitch of desire. For the first time, he did not allow pleasure for himself, because this was to be his parting gift. He looked down at Inga, writhing on the rumpled bed, holding out her arms to him and crying out in Swedish and English, both.

His hands stroked her breasts. He felt the spiky, coral-colored nipples hard against the palms of his hands and thought that he would miss them. When he plunged into her she threw her long legs around him, gripping him as if she would break him in two, and bit his shoulder hard enough to draw blood. She was singing his name, as if it were an aria.

Later, when she lay sleeping beside him, spent and still shuddering, he left the bed and dressed in the semi-dark. It was best to leave like this. There would be no tears, or recriminations. When he was ready to leave, he took one last look at the woman who had been his mistress for the past six weeks. Inga lay with one arm thrust out, as if searching for him. Her fair hair was tumbled over the pillow, and in sleep her lips seemed to smile. *Good-bye, Inga,* he whispered.

Inga had made the mistake of telling him she loved him. Kieran preferred older women because they were less likely to be sentimental, but Inga—who had seemed to be pure need and sensuality—had betrayed him by confessing love. He could not afford the luxury of letting women love him; it wasn't a part of his plan.

He let himself out of her flat quietly, loping down the brownstone steps and heading west. Sweet, daft woman—she had wanted to send him to *school*. That had doubtless been Liam's intention, too.

The money Liam had left for his grandchildren was scrupulously parcelled out—each had an equal share. Only Terence and Bernadette were too young to touch their inheritance. Delia didn't need hers, and Jim had sensibly banked his. Of all the O'Donnell grandchildren, Kieran was the only one who had need of the money.

He hailed a carriage and instructed the driver to take him to an address near the Hudson River. Inga had wanted him to become a doctor, or a lawyer. Anna, an Italian girl he sometimes bedded, had marriage on her mind. Catherine was showing signs of jealousy. Mother of God, wasn't there a woman in the world who wanted nothing from him but the pleasure of his company?

A doctor or a lawyer! Kieran knew exactly what he was going to become, but it wasn't the sort of thing one confessed to avid ladies in bed. He was training himself; it wouldn't be long now. In his unlucky life, one stroke of luck had glanced the right way. The time was almost ripe, and when it ripened, Kieran would be ready.

5

In the spring of 1903, Bridget and Michael Flynn went to New York City to see their daughter in a new play. They stayed with Veronica and Robert in the house on East 38th Street.

"What do you think, Michael?" Bridget asked as she brushed out her hair in the sumptuous guest bedroom, preparing for bed.

"What do I think about what?" Michael, attired in a dressing gown, lay on the bed and watched his wife fondly.

"About Veronica, of course! Haven't you noticed anything?"

Michael laughed. "I've noticed Bernie looks more like her every day. That one's as smart as a whip."

Bridget laid her hairbrush down and went to sit beside her husband. "Here's what I think," she said. "I think that Robert and Veronica wouldn't be speaking to each other at all if *we* weren't here. They avoid looking at each other, and they never touch."

"Well, girl, not all old married couples are as lusty as we are, eh?" Michael teased and cupped his wife's face in one hand. "You can't judge Veronica by yourself, darlin', you've always been that different. Veronica was never a jolly sort."

"That's not true, Mike. When we were little she was so eager—just like Bernadette is now. She was as happy, learning about things, as I was doing them. Robert has made her miserable, and I hate him for it! He's a mean, dry devil of a man. He's got no juice."

"There's truth in that, but she chose him, didn't she? There must have been a reason, and, knowing her, it wasn't his money. Other people are mysteries, girl. It's not your business to try to understand them."

At breakfast the next day, Bridget watched her sister carefully. There was a remote look in Veronica's eyes, as if her real life were going on somewhere else. As soon as she could, she cornered her in the morning room.

Veronica was writing a letter. Next to her, on the fruitwood desk, lay a pamphlet. The bold print read: *The Shocking Truth About Working Conditions for Women in America's Factories!*

Veronica laid down her pen. "It's so good to have you here, Bridget. And tonight we'll see Delia! I wish we could all have remained closer." She smiled apologetically. "Sometimes I wish I had never left Newburgh."

"Vera, what is it? I can see you're troubled. Tell me, Vera. After all, what are sisters for?"

The use of the old childhood diminutive seemed to touch Veronica. She put her hands to her temples and shook her head. "There are so many things in the world, Bridget, things I never thought about before. The injustices! Do you know about Jane Adams, in Chicago? Do you know about Hull House?"

"No, dearie."

"For over a decade now she's been trying to win a better life for the poor. Volunteers come from all over America to work for Hull House. Medical help, work reforms, protection for widows—that's a life worth living, surely?"

"And you wish you could help?"

"I wish it passionately. If it weren't for Bernadette, I think I would devote my life to founding a settlement here."

"That can't please Robert," said Bridget neutrally.

At the mention of her husband's name, Veronica took up her pen again. "I am done with trying to please Robert," she said flatly. "Our sympathies are wholly different. I will try to educate Bernadette as best I can, and what time is left over will be spent in pleasing myself."

Bridget bent over the desk and hugged her sister. "Oh, Vera," she said sorrowfully, "I wish you could be happy."

27 May, 1903
Tonight Mama went to the theatre to see my cousin Delia in her new play. Uncle Michael

*and Aunt Bridget went too, but Papa had busi-
ness. I wanted to go, but Papa said I was too
young. In two more years, when I am 10, Mama
says she will take me. They all came back here
very late, to have a Good Talk and a Mid Night
supper, and cousin Delia came creeping up to the
nursery to give me a kiss. How beautiful she is
and smells so sweet, like roses. Delia and my
cousin Kieran are the most beautiful people in the
world, but I love Mama best. Some day Mama
and I will go off and have adventures, she
promised me. Today I learned about Napoleon.
My French is going well, and soon I will have
Latin. Papa is not proud of me, I wonder why? I
was wicked and listened when I should have been
upstairs and I heard him say girls were not meant
to learn so much. Sometimes I remember grandfather, and I wish he could come back and talk to
Mama. He always made her laugh and be happy.
It is One O'Clock, the latest I have ever been
awake. I can hear Aunt Bridget laughing down
below. That is because Delia is here. God bless
my family. Goodnight now.*

Just before the end of his second year at Harvard,
Maynard Hill *vanished.* There was no other word for
it—he simply disappeared. It was several days before
the police appeared with their discreet questions, and
as Jim had been his closest friend, they questioned him
the longest.

"Was there a woman?" they asked.

Jim knew Maynard was sweet on a girl from Philadelphia called Daisy, but she was not the sort of woman the police were referring to, so he answered no.

Did Maynard have gambling debts? Had he become involved with unsavory people? Was he worried about his studies? To all these questions, Jim replied in the negative. Maynard's father made the journey to Cambridge to ask Jim the same questions. During their interview, he refused to look Jim in the eyes. Although Jim had been a guest in his house, he seemed not to remember him. Mr. Hill conducted his interrogation as if he were a barrister and Jim a felon.

"I can't stick it much longer, old man," Maynard had said not two weeks earlier. Although they were uttered with his customary cavalier air, Jim knew he was serious. He also knew—although the police and the Hill family would never understand—that Maynard was thoroughly tired of being a Hill, of preparing for a life which did not attract him. Sometimes, during the questioning, Jim found it hard to suppress a smile. The truth was that Maynard had escaped. He had gone west, or south, or even across the ocean, to manufacture a new life for himself. He was free, and Jim was glad for him. Nothing could have forced him to tell the authorities the smallest detail about Maynard which would allow them to catch him, and bring him back.

When Jim returned to Newburgh in the summer he found his family much the same. Patrick was enthusiastic about the possibility of putting flying machines into the air. A lunatic pair of brothers named Wright in Kitty Hawk, North Carolina, were experimenting in this direction, and Patrick could hardly wait for them to succeed. It was his ambition to be one of the first men to invest in the flying machine market.

Terry, now nearly seventeen, was as sly and devious as ever. He pestered Jim with accounts of his seduction of Aggie, a bar maid at the Coach and Four. Jim didn't believe him.

His mother, Margaret, mourned the loss of Maynard Hill as if he had been her own son. Tears streamed down her face when she recalled the occasion when Maynard had visited, and Jim felt both pity and embarrassment. His mother was more than a little drunk.

"But why?" Virginia Leonard cried. "Why would Mr. Hill go away and cause his parents so much pain? He was such a nice man, James. He wouldn't just disappear."

They were sitting at the end of the long Leonard garden, beneath the oak tree. Fireflies winked from the hedges. It was the first time he had seen Virginia since his spring break, and he had hoped she would be desperately glad to see him. All during the school year, he had written to her once a week. Her replies came less frequently, but in her last she had penned in her round hand, "Things are so dull here, James, and I shall be so glad to see you and hear news of the real world." It seemed all she wanted to know about was Maynard, and it pained him.

"He's alright," answered Jim, "wherever he is. Depend on it."

"Oh, how can you be so callous? I thought you were his friend." Her eyes flashed at him, even in the twilight gloom. She was wearing a white waist and a pale green lawn skirt. Her golden hair was flowing free, and Jim wanted to catch a strand and press it to his lips.

While Virginia told him about the dullness of her life at Miss Pritchard's School for Young Ladies, Jim felt his heart bursting with love and desire. She had kissed him several times last Easter, once at a social and once in this same garden. It was true she always pressed him for details about Maynard and the other socially acceptable people he must know in Cambridge, but he didn't associate the two acts.

"Virginia," he said, breaking into her anecdotes with desperation, "I've missed you so. I think of you all the time, every day. Haven't you missed me, just a little?"

"Of course I have," she said in a hushed voice. "You mean the world to me, Jim, don't you know that?"

Somehow he stumbled from his chair and knelt before her. He took her hand and pressed it to his lips. "Oh, dearest, dearest Virginia, don't forbid me to speak of my love. Let me tell you . . ."

He felt her hands on his hair then, and nearly swooned. She caressed him, and when he looked up adoringly she bent and kissed his lips. Even in the midst of his delight, Jim couldn't help noticing the expert movements of that kiss. Virginia opened her rosy lips with a confidence, an almost wanton confidence, she hadn't displayed last spring. He even felt her little tongue flick against his for an instant, and then it was withdrawn.

"Oh, God, I love you," he sighed. "I love you, Virginia."

"Jimmy?" Her voice was small, submissive. He clutched the folds of her green skirt convulsively and waited for the blessed words.

"I've been thinking. Why don't you change your name? It would be so simple—you could dispense with the 'O' altogether. James Donnell! Doesn't it sound lovely?"

"But why would I do that?" His body was humming with the desire she had provoked; his head swimming. He felt thick, stupid. Why was she talking about his name?

Virginia sighed and pushed him away. It was a small movement, a mere shrug of her shoulders, but to him it felt as if he had been cast out of Paradise. "Oh, you're hopeless sometimes," she said.

At that moment, as if on cue, the voice of her mother echoed through the garden. It was time for her to go in; her parents were having a dinner party. "Will I see you tomorrow?" Jim whispered.

Virginia shook her head. Tomorrow was Sunday. In the morning, Virginia would go to the Anglican Church, while Jim attended Mass with his family at St. Joseph's. Afterwards, there would be long Sunday dinners.

"In the evening?" Jim pleaded.

"I'm afraid I shall be engaged," said Virginia. Then she rose and walked up the lawn toward the lighted house without a backward look.

When one of his foremen announced that a Miss Murphy wanted to see him, Patrick was bewildered.

Who was she, and why was she seeking an audience with him at O'Donnell & Sons Construction Company?

"Well, show her in," said Patrick. His office was a simple affair—a square room with a desk and two chairs and a framed photograph of Newburgh as it had been in the nineteenth century, when his father had founded the company. He rose to admit Miss Murphy, whoever she might be.

A square-faced young woman with wiry brown hair entered. Patrick reckoned she couldn't be over twenty. His puzzlement mounted, until she spoke, and then he recognized her. She was Agnes, from the Coach and Four. Finnegan's new barmaid.

"Good morning to you, sir," said Agnes.

Patrick drew out the spare chair for her and asked her to sit. He took his place behind the desk and waited.

"I've a delicate matter to broach, sir," she said. She pronounced 'sir' as 'sor,' the way his father had. Patrick knew she was from the west of Ireland. He felt his pulses race. If Agnes Murphy, barmaid, spoke of delicate matters in his private office, it boded ill. She was not one to waste words.

"The fact is, I'm going to have a baby, sir. It's me own damn fault—I should a'known better—but there it is. I thought you would help me, bein' a fair-minded man and all."

"But what have I to do with your baby, Miss Murphy?"

"Well, it's your son as is the father. I'm not complainin'—haven't I already said? But I'm a poor girl,

94

with no relations here, and I can't stay in Newburgh." She straightened her bonnet and smiled at him frankly. "If you could help me with the money, sir, I could go away, couldn't I? I'll be fine with a little stake of me own. I'll raise your grandchild proper, I promise you."

Patrick stared at her in disbelief. He couldn't see his Jim bedding Aggie Murphy; it wasn't like him. Jim was far too shy to seduce the local barmaid; and if he knew anything in life, it was that Jim was still untried. He had mooned about after the Leonard girl in a way that only a virgin soul could do.

"I'm sorry for your troubles," he said, "but I'm afraid I don't believe you. Someone else is the father of your child, Miss Murphy, and you're blaming my son Jim."

"*Jim?*" she said. "Your son *Jim?*" She began to laugh then, throwing her head back and emitting little shuddering shrieks. "Oh, Jesus," she said at last, her laughter subsiding, "I've never met him once, sir. It's not Jim, Mr. O'Donnell, I swear it's not."

"What are you saying?" Patrick felt he had passed from a world of sanity into a world of bedlam in seconds.

"Well, sir, it's your other son. It's Terry."

"But he's barely seventeen!" he shouted.

Agnes shrugged. "It's him all the same," she said. "It's Terry."

Patrick looked into the blue eyes and saw only the truth. Agnes Murphy would not have the resources to lie so convincingly; from the moment she had pronounced the name of his younger son, he'd known she spoke the truth.

He wrote out a check for a large sum, and then asked her if she would sign a document releasing Terence O'Donnell from all responsibility in the matter. When they had completed their transactions, Agnes Murphy rose from her chair and thrust out a reddened hand with good-natured complacency. "God bless," she said.

"When is your child due?" Beneath her cloak, he thought he could detect a thickening.

"In four months, Mr. O'Donnell. I'm not showing much yet."

"Why do you not go home?"

"What—to Ireland? There's nothing for me there. I'll stay here. I'll go to New York, or Boston."

"And where are you from, Aggie?"

"Mayo."

He watched the woman who carried his first grandchild leave, and felt a sadness so great he wanted to blot it out completely.

When he went home, he dragged Terry from his room and beat him with his belt. Although Terry howled, he did not compound his sin by pretending to be innocent. He knew exactly why his father was beating him, but he did not understand the passion that powered Patrick's arm.

The cousins were not together to welcome in the year 1904. Margaret had taken her younger son to spend Christmas with the Fitzhughs, and Delia remained in New York. Kieran's whereabouts weren't known. Veronica came to Newburgh with Bernadette, and consequently, Edith had only her youngest grand-child and James to pamper over the holidays.

"Are you happy away at Cambridge, Jim?" she asked on the last day of the year.

"Yes, grandmother. I didn't think I would be, but it's not half bad."

Edith studied Jim carefully. He had filled out some since his reedy, adolescent days, and had acquired more confidence, but she could detect misery in his blue eyes. She thought it was caused by the Leonard girl, who was leading him on a merry chase. Virginia Leonard liked Jim's attentions when she hadn't any-thing better to do, but her sights were set on a much grander match, and Edith didn't have the heart to tell him.

"Give us a kiss, Jimmy," Edith said. Jim bent and kissed his grandmother's powdered cheek. "Are you taking the Leonard girl to the ball tonight?" He nodded. "Well, that's fine, but there are plenty of fish in the sea, boy, and don't go forgetting it." Jim blushed.

When he left the room, Edith reflected on unhappy matches. She didn't want Jim to repeat his father's mistake, or Veronica's for that matter. Veronica had as much as admitted to her that she and Robert were on bad terms. They lived in the same house, but they led separate lives. "Don't fret, Ma," Veronica had said, "I won't disgrace the family with a divorce. Even if I wanted one, Robert would rather die than give it to me. He'd rather cut off his nose to spite his face."

As for Patrick, he had become active in the local Democratic club again. Edith knew her son's political activity was all on Jim's behalf. Margaret had her heart set on Jim being a politician.

When Jim departed to escort Virginia Leonard to the Newburgh Country Club, the women of his family assured him that he looked splendid in his evening clothes. Veronica and Bridget beamed at him, and Edith nodded with satisfaction. Bernadette climbed up on his wing-tip shoes and waltzed with him in the entry hall. "Oh, when will I ever be old enough to go to a ball?" she wailed.

Her mother smiled and touched the child's cheek. "All too soon," she said quietly.

The new year dawned bitter cold but full of promise. It was the year of the great Louisiana Purchase Exposition in St. Louis and 'progress' was the word on everyone's lips. Patrick contemplated buying a Packard "Pacific," even though it was Margaret's opinion that automobiles were unsafe and vulgar. President Roosevelt would defeat his opponent by a landslide, and Wilbur Wright would pilot his flying machine on a five minute flight—the longest ever—in honor of Teddy's victory.

Despite the optimistic feeling so prevalent in America, two of the O'Donnells still saw injustice and dreadful hypocrisy everywhere they looked. Veronica continued to educate herself on the misfortunes of others. Without telling her husband, she began to devote two afternoons a week to working at a settlement house on the Lower East Side. There she met penniless widows, pregnant, unmarried girls, and children suffering from malnutrition. She continued to appear with her husband socially, and rarely spoke her mind in public. It was a part of their pact. She would act the part of the good wife, and in return he would ask nothing of her. Veronica thought he had a mistress, and was relieved. She dropped the friends she had lunched with to please him; now, the only people who interested her were the women she met at the settlement, and her daughter, Bernadette, who was her greatest friend of all.

Kieran, too, was obsessed with injustice, but it was the plight of Ireland and not of his fellow Americans which moved him. He had joined a secret society known as the Irish Republican Brotherhood. He became Gerry Ryan to the men at Leary's card-game, and Patrick O'Rourke to the Society. The IRB was active on both sides of the Atlantic, but Kieran was impatient and the Brotherhood cautious. Whenever he went to hear Irishmen like Douglas Hyde of the Gaelic League speak, he was torn in two directions. He admired Hyde's eloquence and political wisdom and agreed with his principles, but something seemed missing. When the Brothers stressed the importance of biding their time for the right moment, Kieran burned. He was primed for action, and all he got was talk.

One night in early fall, Delia had three curtain calls and retired to her dressing room. It was the first week of a new play, and the tributes were always greatest when a play was in its infancy.

A huge basket of roses stood on the low table near her chaise lounge. There was also a bouquet of lillies, one of camellias, and a fanciful concoction of hot-house orchids. All were fresh offerings. She kept flowers for one evening only, after which she gave them to Sarah, her dresser, or brought them back to the boarding house where she lodged. Mrs. Hogan's boarding house was always full of Delia's flowers; the landlady's good luck at having acquired Delia O'Donnell as a permanent lodger was something for which she thanked God daily.

Delia sat at her dressing table and examined the cards. The roses were from Whitney Fellows III, a young society type who fervently hoped to seduce Delia and take the tale back to Princeton. His card asked if she would dine with him at Sherrys.

The lillies bore a card which said: "With profound respect and admiration for your talent and beauty, I remain, your most ardent admirer—Theodore Bart." A newcomer; a roguish millionaire with a reputation for philandering. He had once tried to gift her with a diamond bracelet, which Delia had duly returned.

The sender of the orchids was another newcomer. In a bold hand he had scribbled: "My respects to a glowing actress and a great Celtic beauty. If ever I can be of service to you, I shall be glad. Desmond P. Malloy." Delia had heard of Malloy; she guessed he was connected to Tammany in some unsavory way, but she couldn't put the name to a face.

"Excuse me, Miss. You have visitors," said Tommy, the elderly house manager, as he thrust a handful of cards through the door.

On each card was printed the name of an admirer, including the Princeton socialite and the unknown Mr. Bart. Only one was not a proper card. On a plain piece of paper was written the name of her cousin, Kieran.

"Send them all away, Tommy," said Delia. "All except Mr. O'Donnell. I'll see him in five minutes."

She sat at her dressing table and regarded her image critically. She was still wearing the pale green satin frock which was her costume in Act III. She reached for a bottle of mineral oil and applied it to some cotton to wash away the heavy stage paint. Then she bathed her face in water, shock her hair from the elaborate coiffure she wore as Lady Janet Bruce, and brushed it carefully. She was staring gravely into the mirror when Kieran entered her dressing room.

She watched him walk toward her in the glass. He was wearing a dark coat that look romantically raff- ish and not quite respectable. The collar was turned up. He was, as usual, hatless, and his black hair was tousled. She smiled at his image, at the face which might have been her own.

"Good evening, cousin," she said. "To what do I owe this honor? It's been half a year since you've favored me with your presence."

Kieran bent to kiss her cheek. His face was cold, as if he had been out of doors.

"You didn't see my play at all," said Delia. "I thought perhaps you'd relented." Ever since *Rosaleen,* which Kieran had pronounced a load of rubbish, he had refused to see her perform. "It's better than *Rosaleen,* Kieran, I promise you."

Kieran grinned and helped himself to a glass of champagne.

"You might pour one for me," said Delia reproachfully. She turned to face him at last, and was moved, as always, by the light in those blue eyes. He handed her a glass of champagne, then went to sit across from her, legs thrust out in the defiant pose she remembered so well. "*Slainte*, Dee."

"Where have you been? You never even wrote to me."

"Here and there. I'm sorry about not writing."

"I always know you're taking care of yourself, but poor grandmother would be glad of news. How long has it been since you've been to Newburgh?"

He shrugged, and gulped his champagne.

"Kieran, old darling, that's not whiskey, you know. It's very fine champagne, and it's meant to be sipped."

"Ah, what a lady you've become, Dee. Champagne and flowers everywhere—it looks like a bloody wake in here. Please don't patronize me; it doesn't become you."

Delia rose and stood behind him. "I've missed you," she said softly. "We're two of a kind." She put her fingers in his hair and tugged, teasing. "Haven't you missed me a little?" she cajoled.

Kieran was silent. He stiffened at her touch and pulled away.

"Have you a girl?" asked Delia.

"Not one. Dozens. They queue up. And you? Which of your lucky admirers do you favor?"

Delia made a face. "I've no time for that," she said,

dismissing the entire world of love and romance with a wave of her hand. Then she remembered the strange card. "Who is Desmond P. Malloy? He sounds just the sort of shady fellow you'd know."

"What makes you ask?"

Delia showed him the card. Kieran read it, then contemptuously sailed it across the room. "I'll set him straight," he said. "He's not to bother you."

Delia laughed aloud, delighted. "Oh, cuz," she said, "I do love you. You're so dreadfully fierce and secretive. Even I don't know your secrets, do I?"

Kieran took her hands in his and drew her close, until her knees touched his. "I'm going away, Dee," he said. "I came to say good-bye."

"Where are you going? When will you come back?" She felt an alarm out of proportion to the news; for a moment she feared she would never see him again.

"I'm going all over," said Kieran. "I'll be back sometime."

"Oh, splendid. Extremely clear. All over. *Sometime*."

He got to his feet, his color heightened and eyes glittering with—what? At first Delia thought he was angry, but he took her face in his hands and spoke gently. "I'll be back, Dee. I'll even write to you, if you like. You're a self-centered little creature, but I've always cared for you."

"Kieran, you're not in trouble?"

"No."

"You're thinking of doing something foolish. I know you are. I know you, Kieran."

His eyes bored into hers with their unreadable expression. She clung to him, aware of an overwhelming desire to throw herself into his arms. Her cousin's arms.

"Do you know the tale of Narcissus, Dee?"

"It's an opera, isn't it?"

He laughed softly, and pulled her to him. They had kissed, as children. Dutiful, sweet, cousinly kisses. Then Delia felt his lips on hers in a way that was anything but cousinly. She closed her eyes and let herself be borne off on a tide of feeling she had known only once before, with Brendan Connolly. Kieran's lips were so sweet; she wanted to drink him in. She felt the soft black hair beneath her fingers and realized she was clutching him to her, returning his kisses with a fiery passion she'd never known. She pressed her body to his and let her fingers wander over his face. She felt his sharp cheekbones, his silky brows and long lashes that were so like her own. When he pulled away, she traced the line of his full lower lip with adoring fingers.

"Kieran," she whispered. "Oh, love."

"Sweet Delia, wish me luck," he said with uneven breath.

"Luck!" she wished him sincerely as she touched his curling mouth with her fingers. "When shall I see you again?"

"A year from today; I swear it! Will you remember?"

She nodded. "Where will we meet?" she asked.

Kieran buried his face against her shoulder for a moment. He suddenly seemed vulnerable and very young, but when he lifted his head he once again showed her the controlled face she had come to expect.

"I'll find you," he said with determination.

Then he left, and she was alone in the dressing room. She stared into her mirror, hoping to call him back by looking into her own eyes, but he had gone.

For the first time since she had left Newburgh, Delia went to church. She did not partake of the Mass, but she prayed. Anonymous in a black shawl she might have worn in one of her roles, she knelt in a back pew and whispered silent words for Kieran. She pleaded with all her heart that no harm would come to him, and that he might return safely.

Delia knew what dark tides pulled Kieran away. She had always known, though they never spoke of it. It had never occurred to her to seek her parents' help and even if Liam had been alive, she never would have broached the subject to him.

Delia, like Kieran, believed in luck and destiny. Nothing could change Kieran's fate, not even her prayers.

6

13 *March, 1905*
Mama told me such a sad story it made me cry.
There is an Italian lady at the place Downtown
who is very sick from tuberculosis. She cannot
work any longer and must die soon. Her husband
is dead, and there are three little children, one is
just a baby. The two elder daughters, one is just
my age, nearly ten, work in a bonnet factory.
Their names are Maria and Nina. Nina has bad
eyes and is going blind. The work in the bonnet
place is very close, sewing feathers and plumes,
and Nina cannot see well enough any more to do
the work. Soon she will be discharged, and the
family will not be able to live on Maria's wage.
Mama says she would like to adopt them and the
baby, but of course that would not be possible. I

*feel very much for the Italian lady and her chil-
dren and I wish I could help them. I think the
world is a cruel place if such things could happen. I will pray for them, but I wonder. Does
praying do any good?*

For the rich and the fashionable, 1905 was greeted with sumptuous revelries. Four hundred and fifty
of the city's elite came to Mrs. Astor's ball, and ate a
nine-course meal at midnight. Mrs. George Gould appeared at James Hyde's Louis XV ball wearing green
velvet lined with ermine and embroidered with gold
and emeralds. The entire orchestra of the Metropolitan
Opera had been imported to play, but Mrs. Clarence
Mackay was not able to dance because the train of
her costume was so heavy it had to be carried by two
little Negro boys dressed in pink brocade. In some
quarters it was estimated that Hyde's ball had cost
two hundred thousand dollars and that much of it had
come from the pockets of the policy-holders, the Equi-
table.

Edith O'Donnell did not attend, but she subscribed
to the *World,* and her maids took great pleasure in
reading accounts of the decadent rich.

"Well, I never! It says here that Mr. Vanderbilt's ga-
rage on Long Island has space for one hundred motorcars," Mrs. Parker gasped. "Listen to this, girls. Mrs.
John Jacob Astor has got herself a two-ton bathtub
made from one slab of marble, and Mr. Guggenheimer
borrowed real nightingales from the zoo for his party
at the Waldorf."

"It's wicked," said Peg.

"I think it sounds lovely," said Rosie.

"Now, Mr. William Fahnestock," continued Mrs. Parker relentlessly, "has gone and decorated his trees in Newport with fruit made out of fourteen carat gold!"

"Do you suppose Miss Delia goes to balls and parties like the ones in the *World*?" asked Rosie.

"No, girl, never in this lifetime," said Mrs. Parker. "Miss Delia is an actress, Rose. I expect she has some fine times in New York, but them people wouldn't include her in. They're old money, you see—no O'Donnells can mix with Vanderbilts and Morgans."

As it happened, Mrs. Parker was wrong. Her words were true enough, generally, but Delia was an exception to the rule. Just as other actresses of remarkable beauty before her had crossed over into the world of High Society, Delia was preparing to do so in the spring of 1905.

Delia cared nothing for being included in the golden circle, but she quite liked a young man by the name of Philip Henry Warren. It wasn't her fault that Philip Henry Warren's family was a member of the Four Hundred, any more than she could help his being hopelessly in love with her.

Philip had seen Delia play Lady Janet Bruce six times before he summoned the courage to send her flowers and a note, and Delia was never quite sure what impelled her to respond to this note when she'd rejected so many others. She told herself she was bored with Lady Janet Bruce and a life devoted to work, but the truth was rather different. Kieran had

stirred something in her which had been lying dor-
mant for a long time. With his departing kiss he had
made her long for the very love she pretended to
scorn. It was this vague longing which prompted her
to accompany Philip Warren to Delmonico's for supper.

He was a tall, straight man with fair hair and dark
eyes that seemed at once shy and knowing. He had
been educated at Princeton and now, at the age of
twenty-six, he helped run his father's banking firm. He
had the courteous yet commanding air of the very
rich, and Delia found him a welcome change from the
good-hearted but raffish theatre people with whom she
spent most of her time.

"Miss O'Donnell, you can't imagine what pleasure
it gives me to meet you at last. I'm not in the habit
of writing to actresses, you know, but from the moment I saw you on stage I felt I had to make your
acquaintance."

Delia smiled. "I'm not in the habit of answering
letters, either, Mr. Warren. Not when they come from
strangers."

"I hope I shan't be a stranger to you," he whispered
as his eyes searched her face helplessly.

She'd seen this same longing in the faces of hundreds of men and always found it somewhat foolish, but somehow Philip Warren's admiration warmed
her. She looked at her own face in the gilt framed
mirrors at the far side of the restaurant, and knew she
had never looked lovelier. Well aware that women
dressed sumptuously to dine at Delmonico's, she had

chosen a simple dress of dark satin, trimmed in white. Therefore, all the other ladies in the room looked coarsely overdressed by comparison.

"I so seldom dine out," she said to her companion. "This is a great occasion for me, Mr. Warren."

"Good Lord, Miss O'Donnell, I'll take you here every night if you like. I should be honored."

The third time Delia dined with Philip Warren, she allowed him to press her gloved hand ever so discreetly. He had begun to mention his family, intimating that he would like to present Delia to his parents. Delia lowered her lashes modestly. "Do you think that wise?" she asked.

"Whyever not?"

"I am an actress, Mr. Warren. Your parents are not likely to welcome me. Then, too—I am Irish."

"Do you think I care what you are? I see only a radiant, innocent artist, Miss O'Donnell, a fine young lady any man would be proud to know. My parents aren't bigots. They would be honored to make your acquaintance."

Delia smiled. She knew differently, but his ardor touched her.

The following week she was included in a Warren family dinner party. Everyone there treated her with great courtesy. Philip's father confessed himself an admirer of her work and was especially kind to her. Only Mrs. Warren had trouble concealing her hostility. Philip's mother was a perfect social animal and wore an amiable mask, but in her handsome eyes Delia could read distrust and contempt.

"She thinks I'm a scheming little mick," thought

Delia. *"She's terrified for her son."* She smiled down the long table at Philip and watched his eyes melt with desire and love. Mrs. Warren saw this, and for one moment her mask fell away and revealed what had been there all along—hate.

When Philip took her back to her boarding house she allowed him to kiss her hand in the carriage. "Dearest Delia," he murmured. "Could you learn to care for me?"

"I do care for you. You've been so kind to me."

"If I am kind to you," sighed Philip Warren, "it is because you mean more to me than anything in the world."

She calculated that it would take him another week to kiss her properly. She was impatient, but it would never do to let him know.

During the late spring, Jim shut himself up in his rooms and played his fiddle for hours. As he played *Bright Love of my Heart* and *Roisin Dubg,* he let the sounds wash over him like the comforting waves of a warm and friendly sea. Only when he laid the fiddle down and turned to his studies did his pain return. He had had a letter from Virginia, telling him of her "close friendship" with one Jeremy Randall, a surgeon from Albany who had set up practice in Newburgh.

"Jeremy is from a very fine family," wrote Virginia. "His mother is English, his father American. I have told him about you, James, about how we have been friends since childhood. He is most anxious to meet you when you return from Cambridge. He said it would be almost like meeting my brother."

The words of this letter had burned themselves into his thoughts; he believed he could have recited them in his sleep. Sometimes, as he sat at his desk, the window open on the sweet spring night, he wanted to cry. Once, to his chagrin, he found tears dropping on his open book. He put his hands up to his eyes and discovered he had been weeping without knowing it. Another time he found his fists clenching with the involuntary desire to choke the life out of Jeremy Randall. It seemed the only remedy to any of this was to take up his fiddle and play.

In this state of grief and heartbreak, Jim took to wandering the back streets of Boston. On one of his sad rambles, he spied a familiar figure coming out of a saloon. It was his cousin, Kieran. Kieran walked toward him, preoccupied and frowning, but when he saw Jim he bellowed out his name and caught him up in a friendly bear-hug.

"I was thinkin' of callin' on you, James old flower, but what with yer studies an' all . . ." Kieran said and shrugged. "Now we've met, come have a jar with me."

Jim tried not to stare at his cousin. Kieran sounded as Irish as if he'd just got off the boat, and it wasn't put on for a joke. "What are you doing in Boston?" he asked.

Kieran grinned and said he'd become a traveling man and added that it didn't matter what he was doing so long as he could drink with his cousin. As he spoke, some of the brogue dropped away, as if he had suddenly become aware of it.

They entered a saloon together, arm in arm. It was a low place, full of sagging drunks and red-faced women. Sailors and stevedores drank standing up at the bar, but there were a few rickety tables in back. Kieran steered Jim to a table and asked what he'd drink.

"My round," he said. "Whiskey?"

Kieran drank ale with one hand, whiskey with the other. His eyes roved the room at intervals, but always they returned to Jim with a look of affection.

"Tell me, Jim-o, is your life in order?"

"It's alright. This is my fourth year, you know. I never thought I'd stick with it," he answered and took a long sip of his whiskey.

"Got yourself a girl?"

Jim shook his head. While Kieran lectured him on the necessity of regular love-making they ordered another round. After Jim's third whiskey, he found himself telling Kieran about the betrayal of Virginia Leonard.

"I was never good enough for her," he slurred. "She deserves better. This fellow had better make her happy, that's all. If he doesn't, I'll kill him."

Kieran listened, a cynical smile on his lips. When Jim repeated for the third time that he wasn't good enough for Virginia, Kieran shook his head impatiently.

"You're good enough for anyone, old flower. You're well rid of her. She was nothing but a small-town snob. A silly, climbing little bitch."

Jim sprang to his feet, nearly overturning the table. "You'll take that back," he shouted. "It's not true, Kieran. Take it back!"

"But it's the truth."

Jim drove his fist into Kieran's face, astounded at the force of his rage. His cousin staggered back a pace, looking surprised. Jim knew Kieran could beat him senseless if he wished, but Kieran held his hands up in a sorrowful gesture of truce.

"Sorry for your troubles, James," he said softly. Then he touched Jim's arm lightly and walked to the door. His tall figure vanished into the night.

The next day, waking with bruised knuckles and a throbbing head, Jim wondered if he'd dreamed the entire incident. Only the pain in his right hand had survived as proof of the encounter.

Patrick returned from dinner at the Democratic club to find his wife dead drunk. There was no other word for it. Margaret had come toward him weaving and mumbling like some ghastly apparition.

"You're very late, Patrick," she announced. "It has gone eleven."

He stared at her, dumbfounded. Her hair was disheveled, and her dressing-gown was half open. He could see one of her breasts partially bared. It was the only time he'd seen his wife's breasts in five years.

"Have you an explanation for your tardiness?" she demanded in the haughty, self-righteous voice of inebriation.

Still he couldn't speak. The fact that Margaret Fitzhugh—who thought herself too fine for the likes of him—should be as drunk as any low slattern, came as a revelation to him. The years of recriminations, of spoken and silent contempt, of being made to feel a peasant, came down to this one moment.

"I suppose," said Margaret, "you have all been sitting about contriving a career for the unspeakable Mr. Lynch. How proud America can be to have Mr. Lynch in congress! *I* would not allow him in my house."

"I'm sure you wouldn't, Margaret," he said as he walked toward her, smelling the whiskey in the air between them. Did she think he didn't know? It was possible she thought herself above suspicion; it would be like Margaret to believe that nobody could tell she'd been tippling. "Have you forgotten why I spend long hours at the Club? At whose urging did I get involved in politics, Margaret?"

"I never thought you'd mix with such low men. Mr. Lynch is disgusting."

"Why? I suppose because he's never lost his accent and keeps a picture of the sacred heart in his parlor. That's it, isn't it? He's a decent man, which is more than I can say for many in politics. What did you think it would be like, back when you pushed me into it? You thought you'd go to Washington and play fine lady with a lot of Fitzhugh types and folks with put-on British accents. Bloody illusions, woman."

"Your language, Patrick."

"What about my bloody language? Christ, Margaret, you're forty-one years old. Have you never heard anyone say bloody before? Are you so bloody thick you can't see what you're like at this moment?"

With each "bloody" Margaret shuddered as if he had struck her. "How dare you!" she cried. "It's you who are appalling at this moment. To come home and speak to your wife in such a fashion. Shame, Patrick."

"To come home and speak to my wife, who has drunk enough whiskey to fell an elephant," he said softly.

He heard the sharp intake of her breath, and saw her eyes widen with horror. She covered her mouth with her trembling hands and began to weep. It had been ten years since he had seen Margaret weep, and the sight of her tears filled him with sudden pity.

"Ah, Margaret," he whispered. "Never mind, girl. Don't cry so, Margaret, please. I'm sorry I spoke rudely to you."

Gently, he went to her and put his arms around her quaking body. She resisted at first, but as he whispered to her, comforting and cajoling, she allowed her head to rest against his chest. He stroked her wild hair until she had quieted, and then he picked her up and carried her to bed.

As he laid her on the bed her gown fell open. Her breasts were small, delicate things. Fitzhugh breasts, he thought. He fastened her nightdress and removed the dressing gown. He sat beside her, stroking her hair until her eyes closed. She held his hand very tightly, as a child would do, until she fell asleep and the fingers relaxed. Ah, my poor Margaret, he thought. Poor, unhappy woman.

Long after she slept he remained beside her. The fact that she drank, astounding at first, seemed finally something he had always known but never admitted. What amazed him far more was the knowledge that the love he had once felt for her was not completely dead.

26 September, 1905 (Only one more month until I am ten!) Today I asked Mama why we are Irish and Papa is not, even though his grandparents came from Ireland. She told me it is because he is a Protestant and part English and Scotch. That means I am too, but I feel more like Mama. I am an American and I am Irish. Mama also told me I must be proud of what I am, because our country suffered so much. She explained about the laws that said Irish people could not go to school or own their own land or speak their language. That was in the Old Days, but she says things are still hard for the Irish Back There. I can remember from when I was still very little, five years old, when grandfather was talking to Uncle Patrick. They thought I was asleep and grandfather read something in the newspaper and said 'What can you expect of those B —————y British!' Now I understand.

"Bloody British," said the man sitting across from Kieran, "they don't know the meaning of the word justice. If they had their way, Ireland would still be under the Penal Laws."

"They blather of progress in the Parliament, as if they was doing us a favor," said another man. "If they'd never bloody crossed the Irish Sea in the first place, we wouldn't be speakin' of *progress*. Devil take 'em, one and all."

There were a dozen men sitting around a deal table in the shabby room. The room looked very like Leary's waterfront dive in New York, but it was not a gambling club, and it was situated in a slum on the south side of Chicago, near the stockyards. As the men grumbled and cursed their ancient enemy, they looked to Kieran for confirmation. He was the youngest by many years, but he was also the reason for this meeting. *Clann na Gael,* the American counterpart to the IRB, had fallen into disrepute in Chicago. A corrupt scoundrel had played fast and loose with the *Clann's* money, and they had taken to murdering each other.

It was Kieran's duty to recruit new members for the IRB in Chicago—responsible men with a true feeling for the Cause. In addition to organizing and recruiting all across America, he was raising money.

"So," said a large bearded stockyard-worker named Finn, "you was born here, lad?"

"I was, and my father before me. You'll have heard of Bobby O'Donnell, who died in '82?"

There was a rumble of assent and Finn lifted his glass and drank to the martyr, Kieran's father. In letting the men know his true name, Kieran was violating one of the Organization's cardinal rules, but the High Command had agreed that his father's identity would help him in recruiting. Men twice his age might distrust a young, American-born hothead, but Kieran's credentials, thanks to the manner of his father's death, were impeccable. Kieran acknowledged the tribute to his father, and then went back to being Patrick O'Rourke.

An elderly fellow began to sing a patriot's song, but the others hushed him. Kieran waited patiently. He was familiar with the routine by now. In rooms like this in Boston, Philadelphia, Pittsburgh, Cleveland, San Francisco, he had become adept at determining which men were good fighting material and which were simply all talk.

Generally, these men liked to air their grievances before fellow Irishmen. Most of them were sons of families who had fled the Great Famine, and their grievances were many and bitter. Some had fought in the Civil War and been recruited by the Fenians; a few were recent immigrants who had brought fresh tales of horror and injustice from their motherland.

A man called Flaherty, whose parents had died on a coffin ship, recalled how he and his two brothers fought to keep from starving in the New World. Finn reminded the assembly that the British had looked on the Famine as a blessing, intended by God to decrease the population of a people they considered useless. At a time when two shillings would have kept a family alive for a week, thousands of pounds had been spent to pay homage to Queen Victoria while she visited their poor land.

Now, at the meeting, only two men remained silent. The first smiled wryly at Kieran, as if to acknowledge the futility of these common grievances. The other was expressionless, yet his arm was crippled and he held it to his side as if it pained him. These two, Kieran thought, were his true audience.

"There's been plenty of talk," he said, holding up a hand to silence the room. "Talk in the Parliament, talk in the newspapers. Negotiations. The British are fond of negotiations. They want us to be blinded by all the blather, so we won't notice how bloody slow they are in handin' out their reforms.

"As Mr. Toohey pointed out, the reforms wouldn't have been necessary if Britain hadn't crossed the Irish Sea. Boyos—the Bitch not only crossed it, she made it her own! The British Army has ravished Ireland from stem to stern for over seven hundred years! If plain talk could have solved the problem, wouldn't you think we'd be free by now?"

There were cheers and cries of "Up the Republic!"

"You can't talk to the British," said Finn. "They don't understand talk. Sure, they're barbarians."

"There is a way to make them listen," answered Kieran. "Even the British will listen to an Irishman who's got a gun to back him up. Ten thousand men with guns, lads, would make them listen fine."

For the first time the man with the withered arm spoke. "There's to be a Rising?" he asked quietly. "When?"

"When the time is right."

"Ah, more biding time, is it? You're young, Mr. O'Donnell . . ."

"O'Rourke," said Kieran. "Remember that."

"I've not much time left, O'Rourke."

Kieran spread his hands. "Friend, I wish to Christ I could say the Rising would begin tomorrow, but it won't. We have to be prepared. I'll tell you this much —we haven't enough to defeat the boys at Sligo Barracks, let alone the entire British Army." He paused and looked at each man in turn. "The Organization has been demoralized here. What you want is a strong group with new blood and firm purpose. Nobody ever won a war on talk and ideals alone. Money's needed."

The men cast shrewd looks at one another. Finn was the first to dig in his pocket and withdraw some grimy bills. He tossed them on the table.

"Keep your money, Mr. Finn. You're a working man and have need of it. Collect the money from those who can afford it." As he was talking, Kieran glanced at the wry man, who was still smiling. "You understand me?" he asked.

The man nodded. "I understand you fine, O'Rourke. I know a man in the ward who's a genius at gettin' money. For Irish orphans, a'course."

"You'll take new names for your work with the Organization. These names will be known only to fellow members. Someone will be by in a few months to see how you're gettin' on and pass the money back to headquarters." He lifted his glass. "I thank you one and all," he said. "*Slainte*."

As the meeting broke up, the men drifted down to the saloon belowstairs, but Kieran waited to speak to two men alone.

"I wish you success," said the man with the crippled arm. "I wish us all success." He spoke in a soft, cultured voice, unlike the others. Kieran wondered what had brought him to the meeting.

"What's in the Cause for you?" he asked.

The man smiled. "Do you see this arm?" he asked. Kieran nodded.

"I'm a schoolteacher now, and I've done well—but when I was a boy of ten I lived with my family in a village in Roscommon. There were fourteen of us, each hungrier than the next. One day I made myself a fish-hook of wire, attached it to a bit of old string, and went to the river. I thought I'd catch a fish, you see, even though it was prohibited to fish in those waters. For five hundred years my family had lived alongside that river, which the British now claimed as their own, and it seemed only right that the river should give me a fish. We were quite literally starving. I could see a salmon flashing about, and I became excited. I was too ignorant to know you can't catch a salmon with a bit of curved wire.

"A British soldier passed by while I was engaged in the vile sin of poaching. He called to me, and I was so surprised I dropped my make-shift fishing gear and whirled around. He shot me in the arm. To teach me a lesson, he said. The bullet shattered the bone above my elbow, and the arm was badly set.

"More than fifty years have passed since that day, but I can still feel the pain. I have no love for the British, Mr. O'Rourke."

It was nearly midnight before Kieran realized that a year had passed and that this was the day he had sworn to rendezvous with Delia in New York. He lay quietly on his narrow bed and pictured her as he had last seen her. It had been rash and dangerous to kiss her as he had. He had always wanted Delia, but she was shallow and untrustworthy. Nevertheless, he had meant it when he'd sworn to meet her, and it was the first time he had broken his word, ever. He suddenly felt obscurely guilty, and afraid. It was a bad omen. "Forgive me, Dee," he whispered.

The feeling soon passed. In its place came the image of a boy of ten trying to catch a fish because his family was starving. The man's name was Grady.

"I'll see you get your revenge, Grady," Kieran whispered aloud. "If it takes me all my life, I'll do it. For you, and my da, and all the others. I swear it."

part two

7

In the dawn hours of April 18, 1906, the glittering city of San Francisco was ripped apart by a mammoth earthquake. The earth rumbled and cracked open; buildings collapsed—hotels and theatres fell in upon themselves in vast piles of plaster and glass, and the cries from people trapped beneath the rubble were piteous. Fires ravaged the city, and the engine companies were powerless to do anything about them—the water mains were broken. For two days fire raged, claiming the old Palace Hotel and the Grand Opera House on Mission Street. Enrico Caruso had sung the role of Don Jose, in *Carmen*, on the eve of the calamity and had himself run through the halls of his hotel, shouting hysterically and brandishing an autographed photo of Teddy Roosevelt.

The devastation of one of America's most beautiful cities somehow touched everyone. Most were sympathetic. John D. Rockefeller gave one hundred thousand dollars toward the rebuilding of the city, and E. H. Harriman's railroads donated twice that sum. Sarah Bernhardt gave a special benefit in Chicago and raised fifteen thousand dollars in a single day.

Offers of help poured in from even foreign nations, but President Roosevelt declined their kindness stating that, under adversity, the American people would take care of their own.

A small but vocal minority claimed God had sent the earthquake as his judgment on a city more depraved, even, than Paris. The fact that twenty-five thousand buildings were reduced to ashes, four hundred and ninety city blocks ruined, hundreds of thousands of people homeless and over four hundred dead seemed proof of His displeasure. Why, however, did God burn down the churches and spare the Hotaling Whiskey warehouse, wondered the city's cynics.

Patrick O'Donnell sent a check for one hundred dollars to the embattled city. Veronica, drawing on the sum her father had left her, sent money to help the homeless and injured.

Virginia Leonard and Jeremy Randall were in a train mid-way across the continent, bound for the west coast, when the earthquake hit. Their honeymoon was a shambles.

For Delia O'Donnell, however, the tragedy had more personal repercussions. Her old friend, Nettie Throne, died when the roof of her hotel collapsed. Mrs. Throne had been playing in a road tour of a Dion

Boucicault melodrama; only two days before the earthquake, Delia had received a letter from her extolling the beauties of San Francisco.

Delia was sadly re-reading this letter when her maid announced that Mr. Warren had come to call. Listlessly, she told the maid to show him in.

Delia had moved into a new apartment in a house off Gramercy Park. She had known she couldn't stay in Mrs. Hogan's boarding house forever, but sometimes she missed it. At least she had felt free there, but in her new domain, constantly in the company of Philip Warren, she often felt as if she were in a prison.

"Good afternoon, darling. How beautiful you look in the light from the window," Philip said as he advanced toward her, his eyes soft with love and admiration. Delia looked at him dispassionately. Last spring she had seen his tall figure and fair hair as dashing; now they seemed altogether too familiar to her.

She gave him her hand, but he took her in his arms. "Delia, Delia," he murmured, his lips searching for hers hungrily.

She turned her head away. "I have a headache," she said softly. "Would you like anything, Philip? Shall I ring for Ellen?"

He retreated to a small sofa opposite her, looking wounded. "It's a fine day," he said. "I thought you'd like to go for a drive."

"Presently." She knew she was being difficult, but something about Philip prompted her to behave badly. Perhaps it was his unqualified adoration. She wondered what he would do if she emptied the vase of jonquils at her elbow on his head.

"Philip, I received two requests to appear in plays today. They came in the morning post."

Philip sat up straighter; his eyes narrowed slightly. Delia had not appeared on the stage for nearly six months now. She knew Philip was secretly pleased she had not been on stage, but he pretended otherwise.

"And was there anything worthy of your consideration?" he asked in a light, bantering tone. Philip continually argued that Delia owed it to herself to wait for exactly the right play before taking a part. He pointed out that her talent was far too great to waste on fripperies like *Lady Janet* or *Rosaleen*. But Delia knew if she waited too long the world would forget her. The world was notoriously fickle in that respect.

"Not really," she said. "But if anything half-way good should come my way, I feel inclined to take it."

Philip got up and walked to the window. His hands were clasped behind his back in a way she found priggish and annoying. "Haven't we agreed that you mustn't squander your gifts?" he asked.

"Perhaps squandering them would be better than not using them at all. This past half year I've hardly lived!"

"Delia!" It was a cry of anguish. "How can you say that of a time which has meant so much to me? It's been the happiest time of my life."

"I didn't mean *that*, Philip." She saw him flinch. The "that" she referred to so casually was their love affair. She was, as everyone in New York (and she hoped no one in Newburgh) knew, Philip Henry Warren's mistress. Not in the vulgar, ordinary sense of the word—after all, she had her own money and had paid for the rooms here herself—but because she had sexual relations with him without being willing to marry him.

He had begged her to reconsider, asked her to become his wife dozens of times, but Delia was adamantly against it. "I am fond of you," she had said. "There is no other man I wish to marry. I don't want to marry at all, I'm afraid."

When she had made it clear that she wouldn't object to his lovemaking, he had been shocked. "You would allow me to take that which is your most precious gift to confer, and yet you won't become my wife?" He had sounded so pompous. She laughed, remembering.

"Delia," he said, turning from the window and burying his face in his hands. "How can you be so heartless? Don't you know you wound me to the quick?"

Delia could predict each of the recriminations he would now toss her way. He would say that he loved her so dearly that she had a responsibility not to wound him. He would remind her that she had promised to reconsider marrying him, and accuse her of harboring false views of his mother's dislike of her. At the end of it all he would be pleading.

I wonder, she thought, if I have ceased to be respectable? By wearing the jewels he gave to her, and by going to Newport with him when they were not formally engaged, she had renounced all claim to respectability. If he had been willing to initiate her into the mysteries of love and then retreat, as she had wished, things would have been different.

". . . I love you so," he was saying. "If only you

would marry me, Delia, things would be different. I could make you so happy. It's all I wish, to make you happy."

"Fancy that," answered Delia. "What a dull life you wish upon yourself! What would make me happy, Philip, is to return to the stage as soon as possible. I was not cut out to be idle. You have been very kind to me, but I cannot bear to live only for you." She rose and went to him. She was wearing a brocaded Chinese dressing gown that touched her limbs like a caress. She moved slowly and sensuously. In bed he was quite a different man, passionate and fierce. She respected him there, for he brought her a pleasure she had never known. If he were just as masterful outside the bedroom, things may have been different.

"Phil?" she whispered as she watched the sleeves of the gown fall away from her bare, white arms. "Why must you always be so serious? Why all this talk of marriage and lifetimes? You don't have to possess me, you know. You couldn't if you tried, for I'll be no man's possession, either by law or by compromise. Why can we not be friends who share pleasure in bed together?" She twined her fingers in his hair and pressed her body to his so he could feel her round breasts against his chest. "That's where I like you best, Phil dear."

"Delia," he said in a strangled voice, "don't talk like a tart. I want you forever, not just to bed when I like."

Despite his words, Delia saw the desire kindling in his dark eyes. She loved the powerful feeling that came over her when she seduced him. She placed her lips near his ear and nibbled with soft kisses. Her hands went beneath his coat and stroked his back in ever-widening circles. She brushed her thighs against his rhythmically, until he moaned and caught her up against him.

She could feel the nipples of her breast, hard and spiky against the silken cloth. She leaned back in his arms and opened her dressing gown, offering her breasts to his hands and lips. "See how beautiful they are," she murmured lovingly. She had an irresistible desire to caress her own breasts, to watch her slender, jewelled fingers slip over the white flesh toward the pale coral nipples.

"Delia," Philip said in a hoarse, urgent voice, "tell me you love me, darling."

Delia was caught in a trance of pure desire; her body felt heavy and flooded with it. "I love you," she murmured. She wanted him to take her now, on the floor of the drawing room.

"Tell me you'll never leave me," he whispered, intruding on her pleasure with his demands. "Say it, Delia! *Say you'll never leave me!*"

Suddenly, she felt a rage so great she wanted to scream. She wheeled away from him, clutching her gown together, and half-ran across the room. "Oh you fool," she shrieked. "You great *fool*! With your demands and your snivelling, slavish devotion! I won't be kept in prison any longer, do you hear? I'll go back on the stage and take a hundred lovers if I like. I'll do anything to get away from you! You're ruining my life."

Philip had turned as pale as death. He was trembling visibly. "You don't mean it, Delia. You've given me your virginity; we must always stay together now. Always."

She felt her teeth grinding with anger. In another moment she might explode with it. She reached out and picked up the vase of jonquils. With a scream of rage she hurled it as hard as she could at the mirror above the marble mantle piece. The glass shattered into a thousand fragments, flying about the room. She was looking for something else to throw when Ellen entered, looking terrified.

"What is it, Miss?"

"Go away!" Delia shouted. "Leave me in peace."

And then, because there seemed nothing else she could do, she burst into great, racking sobs. Instantly, Philip was at her side, holding her, anxious and terrified. He thought she was sobbing in remorse and murmured words of forgiveness and love. "What is it, my darling? Something has upset you. Are you ill?"

She laughed at the hopelessness of it. Her laughter mixed with her sobs of rage and produced a hiccupping sound. She beat feebly at his arms, wanting him to disappear from her life forever.

"Is there something you haven't told me, Delia?" Philip asked as he looked at the envelope she'd been holding when he arrived. "Have you had bad news in the post?"

Even through her waves of anger, Delia realized that if ever she should regret this wild outburst, she could always tell Philip a most convincing lie. She could say that she had been grieving over the sad, untimely death of her old friend, Mrs. Throne, and wasn't in her right mind.

* * *

In a saloon not ten blocks away, stood a man who would have been most interested in Delia's quarrel with her lover.

Desmond Patrick Malloy, now in his mid-thirties, had arrived on American shores at the age of seven. The Malloys were a large and quarrelsome brood, and Des was the youngest. His father had eked out a wretched existence hauling barrels for a brewery. His mother had died giving birth to her seventh child, Desmond.

One brother had done well enough in Baltimore but otherwise the Malloys—with the single exception of their youngest child—had fared poorly. One of the little girls had fallen to her death from the window of a tenement; anothed married young and died in childbirth. The eldest son simply disappeared one day, and the second was blinded in a barroom brawl in Brooklyn. The Baltimore Malloy enjoyed a modest success as the proprietor of a popular saloon, but it was Desmond who was fated to succeed in the New World.

He arrived from Kerry speaking only Irish. Although he learned to speak English quickly, he remained illiterate until the age of twenty. None of this mattered, however, because Des Malloy had a unique gift. Nothing he heard, or absorbed in any way, was forgotten. He had a photographic memory and could roll off the names of every winning horse at a racetrack for the past five years. He could also explain the virtues of each horse and the shortcomings of the ones defeated. As a grown man, it was the names of every man in the U.S. Congress, together with their histories and records, which occupied him.

Des Malloy had begun his career as a middle-weight boxer. He had been the favorite contender of the Tammany crowd who recognized, in the compact and ferocious boy from Kerry, an unbeatable combination of physical courage and brains. At the age of twenty-three, he had gone to work as a body-guard for a Tammany official. His employer had learned to rely upon him for political insight as well as protection. Des was sent to Pennsylvania to organize union members. He was hired, on one occasion, to beat nearly to death the enemy of his benefactor. He was neither ashamed nor proud of these activities. They were simply jobs required of him on his journey to the top.

Now, he had nearly reached it. He put men into office, having no interest, himself, in joining the august body of American legislators. He was part owner of two race-tracks, and owner of a most successful bordello in Jersey City. America had taught him corruption, and at corruption he excelled.

In a saloon called Reilly's, off Fourteenth street, Des Malloy stood drinking whiskey with a man who trained fighters. Joe Dunne also frequently played cards at Leary's. He was easygoing and fond of gambling, sport, whiskey, and women—enthusiasms shared by his companion.

"I was wondering," said Des, offering an expensive cigar to Joe Dunne, "have you seen that young lad who used to drop in at Leary's? Called himself Gerry Ryan."

"No, now you mention it. Not for a year or so."

"What do you suppose happened to him?" asked Des, although he already knew the answer. He was more interested in finding out if Ryan's movements were general knowledge.

Dunne shrugged. "He just moved on, like as not. Handsome young devil like that, probably found himself a rich widow."

"Yes, that might be so," Des agreed.

They discussed women for a while, dwelling on the charms of an Oriental showgirl of their acquaintance. Then Des ordered another round and led Joe Dunne into a conversation about the IRB.

"What I can't understand is—who'd be fool enough to risk his life for a country three thousand miles away?" asked Dunne.

"Oh, Joe, that's because you were born here."

"They're not all Irish-born, I'll tell you that. And what about that madman O'Donnell who got himself drowned trying to bomb the old Queen's boat? You remember, it happened when we was just kiddies. He was born here."

Desmond nodded, delighted with the irony of discussing Ryan's father. He would never tell Joe Dunne that Gerry Ryan was Kieran O'Donnell; even though he trusted Dunne more than most. He was sure that Kieran was set on a dangerous course, and he didn't wish to add to the potential perils.

When he'd told Kieran that he had known his da, it had been the truth. He had only neglected to tell the boy he had been nine years old when he had met him. Des had been sitting next to his father at a Fenian rally where Robert O'Donnell was the chief speaker.

Afterwards, O'Donnell had mingled with the crowd, shaking hands. "What's your name, lad?" he'd asked. "Des Malloy." O'Donnell had asked him if he'd understood the purpose of the rally, and Des had astounded him by repeating, word for word, the conclusion of his rousing speech. The man had smiled and patted Des on the head. "You'll make a fine rebel one day," he said. A year later, he was dead.

In any case, he was wrong about Des Malloy. Des wasn't interested in the uprisings in Ireland. He viewed life as a glorious game—the spoils went to those who understood that it wasn't how well you played that mattered, but whether you won. Nevertheless, he was sympathetic to the Organization and wished them luck.

"I've been thinkin' of backin' a play," he said to Dunne.

"Which one?"

"Ah, no play in particular. I thought I'd branch out a bit, and I enjoy the theatre, as you well know." They grinned. Enjoying the theatre, for them, meant bedding actresses. "I'd be very picky about my leading lady, though. There's only one I'd care to back."

"Gladys Partridge?" Dunne winked as he dropped the name of a girl whose favors they had both enjoyed.

"Delia O'Donnell."

Dunne whistled. "She's retired, man. Got herself a society lad."

"She'll tire of him soon enough. That girl was meant for the stage."

When the two men left Reilly's they headed for

Joe's gymnasium. There was a new young lad, name of Kelly, who was making a name for himself, and Des wanted to watch him train. If Kelly looked good enough, he thought he'd drop five notes on his next fight.

As he strolled along, the spring sun shining on his shoulders, he felt a glorious sense of well-being. The sumptuous meal he'd had earlier, and the whiskey, had warmed him to a fine glow. He had spent his earliest years hungry and in rags and he appreciated, more than men who had never known poverty, the simplest pleasures of life. His hand-tailored suits and custom made boots delighted him; the tie-clasp, made of emeralds and fashioned in the shape of a harp, seemed to set a seal on his prosperity. He caught his reflection in the window of a tea-shop and smiled. There went Des Malloy, well-fed and well-dressed, a success. His dark face and black hair shone with health, and more than one lady cast looks of interest in his direction.

"Ah, Joe, it's a great life," he said.

At the gymnasium he watched with professional interest while Kelly sparred with a young Italian. Kelly was a middle-weight, as Des had been, and lightning-fast with his hands. The familiar smell of sweat and leather was nostalgic, and Des let himself be transported back ten years. How it all came together, life, if you waited long enough.

Take the O'Donnells, for example. Who would have guessed that the man who'd patted his head at the Fenian rally so long ago would have importance for him now? The whole O'Donnell family intrigued him, and he knew their affairs to such an extent that they would have been shocked.

Patrick's choice for congress, Lynch, wasn't going to make it. That was one thing Des could have told them. Another was that young Jim wasn't going to make it, either, and not because of Tammany machinations, but because he didn't want a life in politics.

For a long time, Des had been waiting for the younger boy, Terry, to grow up. Des was a patient man, but it was often difficult. He planned to engineer a career for Terry that would place the O'Donnell's in his debt; only by ingratiating himself to that family could he achieve his long-term goal. Now, however, it seemed that a better opportunity had arisen in the shape of Kieran.

He had known immediately who Gerry Ryan was because of his startling resemblance to Delia. They might have been twins. Des was familiar with Delia's face because he went regularly to the theatre and studied her through his opera glasses. He thought it was the most beautiful face he had ever seen, and Delia the most maddeningly desirable creature in the world. His admiration had become a longing such as he had never known, and he did not intend to go unsatisfied. He would have Delia eventually, even if he had to wait five years.

One of the last times he'd seen Kieran, the lad had seriously warned him not to pay court to Delia. "Look, man," he'd said, "the girl is innocent, even though she doesn't look it. If you try to ruin her, you'll have me to answer to."

"Ah," Des had replied with a straight face, "you're her young man, then?"

"We are related."

"Through the O'Donnell's or the Ryans?"

Kieran had flushed, but that had been a long time ago. He'd be twenty-three now, the same age as Delia. Yes, Kieran was his trump card. To put Delia in his debt, he would have to help her cousin, and Kieran, he felt sure, was going to need help very soon.

Kelly had finished sparring and was hanging over the ropes, talking to Joe Dunne.

"You look good, boyo," said Des. "I have a suggestion, though."

"What is it, Mr. Malloy?"

"Here," said Des, unbuttoning his coat, "let me show you how it's done."

Terence O'Donnell began his career at Harvard on a far different note from that of his brother, Jim. Jim had graduated *cum laude*, despite his earlier reluctance to go to the university. He had a reputation among the undergraduates as being shy, studious, and polite. Except for his friendship with Maynard Hill, he had never made any close chums, and nobody could recall seeing him with a girl.

"You're James O'Donnell's brother?" It was a question always asked with incredulity, for no two boys could have been more different.

At nineteen, Terry was exceedingly handsome in a cocky, raffish way that appealed to girls and excited admiration in young men. He was so confident, so sure that he would be welcome anywhere, that he even spoke without fear to the inner circle. If one of them drawled his name, lingering on the "O" in O'Donnell, it never occurred to him that he was being mocked.

He was six feet tall and well built. His dark red hair was thick and springy and had a habit of hanging rakishly over one eye. Before he'd come to Cambridge he had tried to grow a moustache, but the results had been disastrous: a few sparse strands of pale red hair forlornly straggling over his upper lip. "Never mind," Patrick had said, "give it time."

Terry grinned at his reflection in the glass. He was practicing combinations of smiles to see which would be most effective on Walter Brady's sister. Miss Brady was journeying up from Hartford to visit her brother, and Walter had invited Terry to supper at the Ritz-Carlton to meet her. Terry had seen a picture of Miss Celia Brady, and she was very much to his taste.

He decided Miss Brady would prefer an open, frank smile to his dare-devil grin. A frank smile had the advantage of displaying his blue eyes to their best; when he grinned too broadly they crinkled almost shut.

Terry was tired of servant girls and whores. He had enjoyed the favors of six young women of that class—two in Newburgh and four in Cambridge—and thought it was time he moved on. If he impressed the pretty Celia sufficiently tonight, perhaps he could seduce her when he went with Walter to Hartford for a summer visit. He brushed his coat, wishing he had a servant for that purpose, and was ready.

It was too early to go to the Ritz-Carlton. His European History book stared at him accusingly from its position on the table. He was failing European History, but a crammer course and some judicious glances at his neighbor's examination paper might pull him through. He wondered what poor old Jim was doing on his European tour. Probably moping about, pining for stupid Virginia Leonard, who was now Mrs. Jeremy Randall, and unavailable to him forevermore. Terry was fond of his brother, but he thought him a bit of a fool. At nineteen, Terry reckoned, he knew more than Jim ever would about the way of the world.

He thought of taking a nip from his pocket flask and decided against it. He didn't want to be reeking of whiskey when he was introduced to Miss Brady.

He thought of the way Lizzie, the girl who entertained Cambridge boys in her rooms in the South End, admired his body. With any luck, she'd be giving it to him for nothing before long.

There was only one thing Terry feared, and that was venereal disease. Lizzie was clean looking, and she always smelled fresh and sweet, but he wondered how a fellow could know for sure? He pictured himself, blind and raving in the final stages of the disease, crawling home to Newburgh to die. No, not Newburgh. His mother would throw him out and let him die in the streets. Pity Kieran had disappeared. *There* was someone who would be able to advise him. He hoped Celia would fall in love with him immediately and allow him to sneak into her hotel room late at night; only by making love to strictly respectable girls could he solve this most distressing problem.

At the appointed time, he appeared at the Ritz-Carlton in his evening clothes. Walter and his sister were waiting for him near a large potted palm. Celia Brady was even prettier than in her photograph. She had quantities of very fair curling hair, blue eyes as round as saucers, and a promising smile.

Terry sauntered toward them slowly, wishing he'd been able to grow that moustache. Many girls were driven into a state of uncontrollable lust by a really fine moustache.

"May I present my sister, Miss Brady," said Walter. "Celia, this is Mr. O'Donnell."

Terry bent low over her hand, then straightened and gave her the smile he had practiced. "Welcome to Boston, Miss Brady," he said smoothly. "I hope you will find your stay here enjoyable."

The saucer eyes looked into his knowingly. "I hope so, too," she answered. "What would be the point of my coming to Boston unless I enjoyed myself?" She took her brother's arm and squeezed it affectionately. "I dote on Walter, you know. We were always inseparable as children. I miss him so." Walter blushed, and the party of three went into the dining room.

When Miss Brady removed her capelet, Terry was treated to the sight of the upper portions of her breasts, revealed by a rather daringly cut evening frock. All during dinner, he studiously looked away from them, in case she should catch him staring. She made him feel uncomfortable, with her sophisticated conversation and knowing eyes.

With girls like Aggie or Lizzie, he had always been the master, regardless of the difference in age. Celia Brady made him feel like a schoolboy; it would take more than his dazzling smile to capture her interest. He felt a little ruffled, but gradually the feeling passed and was replaced by one of exhilaration.

When it came down to it, Terry loved a challenge!

8

"Sensible and responsible women do not want to vote. The relative positions to be assumed by man and woman in the working out of our civilization were assigned long ago by a higher intelligence than ours."

Grover Cleveland

two years earlier, Veronica had clipped this quote from her copy of the *Ladies' Home Journal*. It had seemed to her so amazingly perverse and wrong that she wished to preserve it. She had never given a thought to voting; with all her concern for the injustices suffered by others, it hadn't occurred to her that she, as a woman, had a cause of her own.

She began to clip many things from the papers and

magazines, and soon the pile of cuttings was so large she had to buy a blank book and paste them in. There were accounts of women being forbidden to swim, hints that if a lady felt she must bathe in the sea, she should progress very slowly.

"It is permissible to close the nose with thumb and finger," quoted *Outing* in a solemn tone.

Male outrage mounted most volubly when ladies tried to take their place behind the wheel of an automobile. The mayor of Cincinnati thundered: "No woman is physically fit to run an auto."

A woman who tried to smoke a cigarette in the back seat of her automobile on Fifth Avenue was promptly chastised by a mounted policeman.

Veronica did not smoke, and she didn't wish to drive an automobile. She had never learned to swim, and Robert never took her to the seaside. Nevertheless, she believed passionately in every woman's right to engage in these activities if she so desired. It wasn't until Grover Cleveland's words made her laugh out loud with contempt and anger that she realized there was something she *did* want. She wanted to vote. More importantly, when Bernadette grew up, she wanted her bright daughter to have a far richer life than she had been granted.

Bernadette, now nearly twelve, was a serious child capable of spontaneous moments of gaiety. She was loving and loyal, but Veronica feared she was also lonely. She had few friends of her own age. This was partly because she had been privately tutored at home, and partly because Veronica, in abdicating her duties as a social wife, had no friends of her own except for the women at the settlement house on Orchard Street.

"Bernadette," she said to her daughter one afternoon, "I am going to show you a book I have kept. It is full of cuttings from newspapers and magazines. I want you to read them, and tell me what you think."

Bernadette took the book solemnly and retreated to a corner of the library. Veronica watched her daughter as she turned the pages, frowning with concentration. The child's face, when she read, was tense with excitement. Her long hair flopped in front of her face and she pushed it back impatiently as she studied her mother's book. Once she looked up and asked: "Mama, what does 'radical' mean?"

"Why, it means extreme, dear. If you are reading about the suffrage movement in England, the author wishes you to read *radical* as *revolutionary*."

"Thank you," said Bernadette, and went on reading.

Forty-five minutes later, she had finished. She shut the book with a decisive snap and came to Veronica's side.

"And what do you think?"

"I think it's a plot," said Bernadette. "If men tell ladies they aren't as good, why, by and by the ladies will have to believe it. Once they commence to believe it, they will act the way the men wanted them to all along. I think girls are just as good as boys. We're just as smart, and brave, only sometimes not as strong, or rich."

"And what is the answer, Bernadette? How does the female half of the race convince the male half?"

Bernadette smiled. "By not behaving the way they want us to, Mama."

Veronica hugged her daughter, pleased, as always, by the child's uncanny ability to accurately state a case. She thought Bernadette would have made, in a different world, a fine lawyer.

"One thing puzzles me," said Bernadette. "Why are the American ladies not more sympathetic? Why are the English ladies so much more active?"

She had obviously read with great care the accounts of Mrs. Pankhurst and her daughter, Christabel, being expelled from a political meeting in Manchester. Mrs. Pankhurst's group, the Women's Social and Political Union, was the most radical Veronica knew of.

"England is an older country," answered Veronica. "I'm afraid it will take America much longer to rise to the cause."

"Do you hate England?"

"Why do you ask, child?"

"Grandfather hated England. You know why; you told me yourself."

Veronica drew her daughter to her, held her hands and spoke very seriously. "That's all behind us, darling. We are Americans, you and I. We have battles of our own to fight. I don't want you to hate anyone at all."

"How can you fight a battle if you don't hate the enemy?"

"You can *educate* the enemy, my love, and then he won't be the enemy anymore. Do you understand?

149

"I think so," answered Bernadette.

The following day, Veronica began to make preparations for a visit to Newburgh. Robert never accompanied her on these trips, but he always gave her a letter, full of elaborate compliments and apologies for his absence, to present to Edith. Outwardly, he preserved the illusion of a well-ordered and harmonious marriage. He spoke to her courteously and even with a sort of affection at times. Veronica thought she knew why: he was grateful to her for allowing him his separate, private life. Some part of him admired her for retreating so completely, when most women would have sought a reconciliation or waged open war.

"Here is a letter for your mother, my dear," he said to her just before dinner. "Please give her my compliments and best wishes." He handed the envelope to her, then stood in the center of the room looking awkward. "When do you and Bernadette leave?"

"At the end of the week. The lilacs should be blooming then."

"I have just been to the nursery to say good-night to Bernadette," said Robert. "She is almost a young lady now." He loosened his collar, fidgeting. "She looks very like you, Veronica. In another few years she will be your image."

"Oh, better, I hope," said Veronica easily. "She is an extraordinarily intelligent child, you know. I am pleased with our daughter."

"I, too." His voice was gentler than usual. "You are an excellent mother, Veronica."

It was the most intimate exchange they had had in five years, and Veronica was not unmoved. When she packed Robert's letter away in her travelling case, she stared at the fussy, neat script on the envelope. *Mrs. Liam P. O'Donnell,* he had penned. It was like him to be so formal, so correct. Veronica sighed. Robert was not a bad man, at heart; he was rigid in his views and bound by generations of conservative Tyrone conventions, but not wicked.

She wondered what sort of person his mistress was, and thought it a pity he had married a woman like herself. She had loved him, once, and was capable still of feeling dim echoes of that love. How different things might have been, she thought. If she had never met Robert Wilson Tyrone at a picnic in 1892, she might at this moment be sharing her lonely bed with a husband who approved her views and encouraged her.

But then, if she had never met Robert, there would be no Bernadette.

"Well, now, would you look who's here?" Des Malloy's face was wreathed with smiles as he pushed back his chair and extended a hand. "Gerry Ryan, isn't it? It's been an age since I've laid eyes on you, lad." Malloy bellowed out a request for a whiskey for his long-lost friend, Ryan.

Kieran studied him shrewdly. The man was far too friendly, and Kieran distrusted him. Beneath the hearty blather and the grin of delight was something cold and mocking. Malloy's black eyes calculated even as they smiled.

"Evening, Mr. Malloy. How's the world treating you?"

"Never better, never better. But tell me, Ryan, where have you been all this time? Leary's hasn't been the same without you, has it, Tim?"

"Indeed it hasn't," said Tim laconically.

"I was taking my grand tour," said Kieran. "Absorbing the culture of the great capitals of Europe."

"Were you now? *Slainte*. Well, that's a grand thing. It will surely prepare you for events to come."

Kieran felt, uneasily, that Malloy was well-aware of his activities. It seemed impossible, but Malloy had a reputation for knowing everything. He was powerful and well-connected, and beneath the stage-Irishman pose lay a ferocious, crude intelligence.

"Deal Ryan in, boys."

Kieran took his place at the table. They played without event for several hands, and then Malloy began a winning streak. A full house followed a flush in diamonds, and then—incredibly—he took Kieran's straight to the queen with one of his own to the ace. There was no question of his cheating. The last man caught cheating at Leary's had been thrown out in the street with four broken ribs. It was simply his infernal luck.

"You know what they say," he chuckled, raking in the huge pile of bills from the pot, "lucky at cards, unlucky at love."

"I'm sure your luck runs in both directions," said Kieran. At the end of two hours he had won back most of what he'd lost. He played a final hand, for courtesy, and then left the table. He drank another whiskey at the bar, passed a few pleasantries with the barmaid, and departed.

It was dark and, except for the melancholy hoot of a tug heading for the harbor, utterly silent. Kieran breathed the briny air gratefully. He was about to walk east and hail a carriage when the door to Leary's opened and Desmond Malloy came out.

"I'd like a word with you," he said. "We'll sit in my motorcar."

"Are you askin' or commandin'?"

Malloy smiled. "Ah, sure an' I meant to request the *honor* of a word with you."

"Better," said Kieran. "I don't like to be told what to do."

Malloy went to his black Packard and spoke to the sleepy driver. "Take a walk, Jack," he said. When the driver's figure had receded in the distance, Malloy beckoned to Kieran. "Get in," he said. "It's more private, like."

"Christ, but you've a sense of the dramatic, Malloy. This is the loneliest spot in New York. We have all the privacy we need."

Malloy scratched his head and looked up to the heavens. "It's private enough for Des Malloy and Gerry Ryan," he said innocently. "I'd even talk to Kieran O'Donnell out in the open. But there's someone else I'd rather not be shoutin' to in front of Leary's, when anyone a'tall could come out and interrupt."

"Who is that?"

"Patrick O'Rourke."

Kieran maintained an impassive expression, but felt a little lurch of alarm. He'd been right; Malloy knew.

"Paddy O'Rourke?" he said. "Where's he, then?"

Nevertheless, he got into the Packard and waited for Des Malloy's next surprise. He stared straight forward, revealing no emotion, while Malloy told him, city for city, where he had been for the past two years. He had some details wrong, but most of his information was accurate.

"You're dead wrong, Malloy. You've been misinformed."

"Boyo, the last time I was misinformed, you was crawling about in your nappies. You're in it up to your neck."

"As I said, you've a real dramatic flair, Malloy. Even if all you said was true, why should you care?"

The older man lit a cigar; in the light from his match his dark face looked Satanic. "Let me tell you a story," he said. "It concerns a lad of nine and a Fenian patriot." He then related the manner of his meeting with Robert O'Donnell. Kieran listened stonily.

"Your da was wrong when he said I'd make a fine rebel one day and you know why?"

"I can think of several reasons, none flattering."

"Feel the leather of these seats, lad. It's the best money can buy. This motorcar even *smells* expensive. I eat the finest food, drink the finest whiskey. When I bed a woman, she's prime goods. I like the high life. I like pleasure. I've arranged my life so's to have as little pain as possible. Now, consider the life of a revolutionary. No joy there, boyo. Always on the run, never knowin' who you can trust, eatin' bad food in low dives. And in the end, what do you get for your trouble? A bullet, if you're lucky. If you're not—years in a British gaol where they'll rip your fingernails out, one by one, just for entertainment."

"I repeat, Mr. Malloy. Why should you care?"

"I like you, Gerry. I like Kieran, too, but Patrick O'Rourke? He'll come to a bad end, and I can't afford to like a marked man."

"Since Patrick O'Rourke doesn't exist, there's no problem."

"Ah, they've done a job on you. You're a proper underground man now, aren't you? Alright, then. Listen and listen well. You may despise me for a corrupt man with no feelin' for your cause, but I'm your friend. You need a friend on the outside, and you can't do better than me. I'm a powerful man, if I do say it. Nothing goes on in this city Des Malloy doesn't know about. I have friends, high and low, everywhere."

"Do they commend you for your modesty?"

"They keep me informed. If ever one of them tells me Bobby O'Donnell's son's been plugged in a back alley, I'll not be surprised. I'll say an *ave* for you, lad."

"Oh, Christ, what the bloody hell do you want from me, Malloy?"

"I want to be your friend; I told you. If ever you find yourself in a tight corner, between a rock and a hard place, you come to me. I'll bail you out. If it's money that's needed, I'll supply it. If it's safety, I can provide that, too. I wish your cause luck, but I'm not daft enough to believe it can succeed."

"You don't offer help without wanting something in return."

"Generally not, but I've made an exception of you, boyo. In memory of your da."

Kieran turned to look Malloy in the eye for the first time. In the dark interior of the automobile he could scarcely distinguish the man's features, but even in the gloom his eyes glittered. Kieran thought that to place his trust in Des Malloy would be like befriending the devil, yet he was touched by the references to his father. Malloy had, after all, heard him speak, had seen his face and even talked to him. He wanted very much to ask for more details of that evening. How had his father looked? What else had he said in his speech? Had the crowd cheered him? But he could not afford to ask these questions or remain in the Packard any longer.

"Thank you for your concern, Mr. Malloy, but I don't warrant it. I'll be going now. Good-night."

Malloy did not try to detain him, but just as he was leaving he said, "There's a man by the name of O'Toole in the Brotherhood. He's gone bad, been dipping into Organization money for his own private use. He's a gambler, you see. He should be out within the week. Watch and see if I'm not right."

Malloy's words echoed in his mind as Kieran walked east in search of a carriage. If he was right about O'Toole, then O'Toole was his informer. The penalty for informing was death, but it was possible that the Organization was not averse to informing if the recipient of the information was Tammany Hall.

He stopped at a saloon in Hell's Kitchen and drank standing at the bar. It was necessary for him to have an audience with the Supreme Council, immediately, and report that his activities were known by Malloy.

"Hello, my pretty boy. Would you stand a girl a drink?"

Plucking at his sleeve was a girl of perhaps twenty. He thought she might once have been pretty, but now her skin was pocked and she had only four top teeth.

"I'd be sweet to you," she said in a murmur. "I know how to please a man." Her eyes pleaded.

"A drink for the lady," Kieran called to the barman. Then he patted her arm. "Not tonight, sweetheart," he said, and left hurriedly.

At ten o'clock the following morning he was shown into a room to meet John Kerrigan of the High Command. The room was over a shop on Bleecker Street in Greenwich Village; the locations of the rooms changed regularly, and they were always bare except for a table and scattered straight-backed chairs. Kerrigan sat looking through some papers, frowning. When Kieran entered he looked up, smiled, and told him to be seated. He finished reading, stoked his clay pipe, and bade Kieran good morning in Gaelic.

John Kerrigan was a mild looking man, almost scholarly. It was said that he could pass for a schoolmaster, or a priest, and that on occasion he had done just that.

Kieran did not know Kerrigan's real name, but it was rumored that he had left Ireland a wanted man. In Galway, county of his birth, a British soldier had been killed by a boy of seventeen, who somehow managed to stow aboard a ship in 1880. The ship had come to New York, and the boy had grown up to be the man called Kerrigan.

"Good morning, O'Rourke," he said in his pleasant, gentle tones. He continued to speak in Gaelic. All conversations at this level were conducted in the Irish language. "What is troubling you?"

Kieran told him of his conversation with Desmond Malloy, omitting only the part about O'Toole. He stressed the uncanny accuracy with which Malloy had recounted Kieran's whereabouts. Kerrigan sat back, nodding studiously. When Kieran had completed his account he re-lit his pipe and puffed in silence for a considerable period of time.

"Not to worry," he said at last. "Malloy is no enemy of ours. In some ways, he is to be considered a friend. In a very limited sphere, of course. I assume you did not admit to any of his accusations?"

"Never. I told him he was dreaming."

"You'll be curious as to who feeds him his information, no doubt?" Kieran nodded. "It's a Tammany liason known as Joe Durkin. Joe's reliable; I'd trust him with my life or yours. But he was never told to mention you, O'Rourke. Our Malloy's been out ferreting on his own."

"What's to be done?"

"I'd like you to lie low for a bit. Not long. Have you anywhere you can go for a spot of rest and peaceful, legal activity?"

Kieran grinned. "Sure, an' I'll go visit me old granny up north," he answered.

"Fine, say three weeks. Come back in three weeks."

The men shook hands and Kerrigan went back to his papers. Kieran stood, undecided. The cries of the men unloading the drays for the Italian bakery beneath drifted up to him and the name O'Toole galloped through his mind. The minutes stretched on and Kerrigan looked up, surprised to find Kieran still in the room. "Is there something else?" he asked.

"Have you seen O'Toole?" asked Kieran awkwardly.

"Why do you ask?" Kerrigan's mild eyes became alert. "Did Malloy mention O'Toole?"

"He only said he had gambling debts."

Kerrigan smiled sadly. "Ah, yes," he said. "Forget about O'Toole. Leave him to heaven."

17 July, 1907
We have been in Newburgh for eight weeks now and are to return tomorrow. I will miss Grandmother and Peg and Rosie and Mrs. Parker, also Uncle Patrick and Michael and Aunt Bridget. I will not miss Aunt Margaret, who is stand-offish to Mama, or Terry, who is horrid. The person I will miss most is Kieran, who came last week. I love him, even though I know it is wrong to love your first cousin. If I were older I would want to marry Kieran. He took me fishing for blue-gills in the river and showed me how to play mumbledy-peg. He says I am a fine Irishwoman and more should be like me! Everyone was very excited to see him, because he has been missing for so long, but Grandmother welcomed him like the Prodigal Son!

President Roosevelt says he is going to send the U. S. Fleet to the Pacific Coast. Uncle Patrick said it was dangerous because the canal at Panama hasn't been finished yet. Uncle Michael said the President was doing it because the Japanese were "feeling their oats."

In the autumn of 1907, James O'Donnell joined the Newburgh law firm of Shanley, Perkins, & Thorne. Although he was the most junior member of the firm, he was also the only man to have a degree from Harvard Law School. In some respects, the older men deferred to him, which embarrassed him greatly. They were all aware that Jim would not be with them for long; it was common knowledge he was destined to practice in New York eventually, and pursue a career in politics.

Jim had done everything expected of him, gratifying his parents and surprising himself. His hard-working years at Harvard, his honors degree, even his grand tour of Europe before settling down, were all part of the pattern required of a second generation Irishman struggling to assimilate.

Except, thought Jim, throwing the brief he had been working on aside, he was still the same boy he'd been the night he lay on the hill above Newburgh, pondering his future. The future might be here, but Jim— despite his new status, despite losing his virginity in Vienna—still felt uncertain and divided.

His job with Shanley, Perkins & Thorne seemed unreal to him. He performed his duties well, writing meticulous briefs and researching cases with care, but his true energies lay elsewhere. In Europe, he had come to life as never before. There he was free to wander at will. Nobody expected anything of him, and if he chose to spend an entire afternoon looking at one picture in the Tait, or lounging at a sidewalk cafe in Paris, there wasn't a soul who cared. Curiously, he had never felt lonely.

He often sought out public houses or taverns where music was played, and listened for hours. On one occasion, in Basque country, he had heard music which seemed to contain echoes of his own beloved Irish tunes. He produced his fiddle and joined the Basque musicians, who welcomed him with glee. All evening they played together, Jim's fiddle sometimes joining in tentatively, sometimes leading the others in a curious, improvised mixture of the music of both cultures. He had heard that the Basques were Celts, and after that evening, he believed it.

The landlady of his *pension* in Vienna had unburdened him of his despised virginity. Frau Bruch was thirty—seven years his senior, and a widow. She had long, fair plaits which she wound around her head by day and took down at night, producing an electric mane of golden hair that reached to her waist. Aside from this glorious hair, she was a plain woman, ample of body and as warm and wholesome as freshly-baked bread. The pleasure she brought to Jim was extreme, but there was no question of love. Frau Bruch was merely lonely and saw in Jim a pleasant means of sexual release. Jim had packed away all thoughts of romantic love when Virginia Leonard married.

He could not see Virginia, even now, without feeling a constriction in his chest. She was especially friendly to him, always going out of her way to cross the street and chat if she saw him in town. Marriage to Jeremy Randall agreed with her, and she had never looked more radiant or beautiful. Jim didn't even have the satisfaction of despising her husband, for Randall was a thoroughly decent sort. He had a slight English accent, and Virginia had begun to affect one, too. Jim, unfortunately, could never hear her speak without remembering Kieran's cruel words about her. He had begun to suspect that Kieran was right, and that was the most painful thing of all.

To have loved and lost was honorable, but to have mistaken an ordinary girl with social ambition for an angel of the heavens was comical.

He sighed and addressed himself to the case of *Graham vs Bollinger*, a dull affair concerning water rights in a pasture on the far end of town. He wrote for a quarter of an hour, and then rose and prepared to go home for dinner. It was his Aunt Bridget's birthday, and there was to be a family party.

Delia, who was back in the theatre again after a short retirement, had sent her mother a magnificent brooch of pearls and diamonds. Bridget wore it proudly, but it was plain she would have preferred a glimpse of the sender, no matter how brief. Terry was back in Cambridge, and Kieran, who had spent a few weeks in Newburgh during the summer, had vanished again. Jim would be the only young person present.

As he put his greatcoat on and left his small office, Jim felt a tremor of elusive sadness. He called goodnight to the aged clerk, who was still bent over his desk, and stepped out into the brisk, cold air of the November night. Winter came early in the mountains, and a fine sprinkling of snow lay on the bare ground.

Jim remembered the day they had buried Liam, and wondered how many more winters would find him in Newburgh. As he walked the short distance from his office to the house on Ridge Street, the sounds of *Road to Sligo* reverberated in his mind.

9

On October 28, 1908, Mrs. William Waldorf Astor, the queen of New York society, died at her Fifth Avenue mansion. Much was written about her passing, and her rivals began to duel to see who would take her place.

The death of Edith O'Donnell, however, merited only a prominent paragraph in the local papers. She had died at the age of seventy-four, outliving her husband, Liam, by eight years. Her surviving children mourned her, and her grandchildren came to see her put to rest on the same hill where they had congregated for the burial of their grandfather. Only Kieran was absent.

"It's likely he didn't know about it," said Bridget.

A large and showy wreath arrived from a man who signed himself D. P. Malloy. No one but Delia knew who D. P. Malloy was, and she did not inform them.

Delia's presence at the funeral was a subject of great excitement in Newburgh—assorted children who watched the funeral party pass by were disappointed that her heavy mourning veil deprived them of a glimpse of her celebrated face. Many had come just to see her.

The wake for Edith was not unlike the one for Liam, except that the party arrived at the house on Ridge Street in motorcars, and the girl who answered the door was named Kathleen, not Rosie. Rosie had married and left the O'Donnells for a life of her own in Albany. Peg and Mrs. Parker had remained behind. Except that one of the O'Shea sisters was bed-ridden and could not attend, the people who crowded into the O'Donnell house to pay their respects were the same as those who had come in 1901.

Virginia Randall, expecting her first child, clung to her husband's arm as she approached the beautiful Delia to offer her condolences. Mr. Finnegan searched in vain for the pretty child to whom he'd given a peppermint at the last wake, but Bernadette was now a tall, glowing girl of thirteen, and had definitely outgrown peppermints. Terry drank openly, rather than snatching furtive sips of others' whiskey; his mother did not drink at all.

Patrick O'Donnell was dry-eyed. He was the head of the family now, and although he mourned her deeply, he acknowledged that she had led a long and rich life. Her death had been a calm one—unlike his da's battle with pneumonia.

"She just slipped away in the night," Bridget told

Veronica. "I came in, in the morning, and she was lying there so peacefully, Vera, she seemed sleeping." Bridget broke down, sobbing in her sister's arms. She was the daughter who had stayed behind, the one who would miss Edith's presence most keenly.

It was Jim who had last spoken to Edith. On the night before she died he had gone into her room to say good-night. Edith was propped up against her pillows, reading an account of the automobile race from New York to Paris.

"Just imagine, Jimmy, they thought they could go over the Bering Sea on the ice! It's just as well they crossed the Pacific by steamer. It's remarkable, isn't it, the appetite some men have for adventure?"

Jim had looked at her fondly, then crossed the room to kiss her cheek as he did each night. She caught his hand and held it, looking up at him with an urgent gaze. "Jimmy, do you ever think of your grandfather?"

"All the time. I think of him oftener than you'd imagine, granny."

"You won't forget him? He loved you, James. In many ways, you were his best companion in his final years. You won't forget?"

"Never."

"Promise me."

"I swear it, granny." And then he had kissed her again, and left.

When Edith's will was read, there was one surprise. As everyone had expected, she bequeathed the house on Ridge Street to her daughter Bridget, and her husband Michael. The small savings she had held in her own name she divided between her children in equal parts. Bernadette was to have her books, Delia her paintings. A beautiful string of pearls was left for Jim, to present to his wife when he married, and a brooch set with topaz and diamonds was bequeathed to Terry, with the same stipulation.

It was the final clause of Edith's will which astounded all present. "I direct that the ring presented to me by my beloved husband, on the occasion of our wedding, be given to my grandson Kieran, in memory of the love I bore his father, who was my first-born child."

Long after arthritis had caused Edith to remove her wedding ring, she wore it on a ribbon of velvet, close to her heart. She claimed it was her most precious possession in the material world, though far from the most valuable. Everyone assumed it had been buried with her, still close to her heart beneath the cloth of her burial dress.

Patrick summoned Peg, who had tended to Edith in her last years, and asked her if she knew where Mrs. O'Donnell's wedding ring was.

"Oh, yes, sir. Madam was most particular about it. She told me if ever she should pass on, I was to take the ring from around her neck and put it in the little drawer next her bed."

"And did she say why?"

"Why, she said it was for Mr. Kieran's wife."

The ring was indeed where Peg had said it would be. Patrick locked it in his safe-box at O'Donnell & Sons, and marvelled at how little he had known his mother.

* * *

Although it was an election year, there was little excitement. Roosevelt had declined to serve a third term, and everyone knew that colorless William Howard Taft would defeat his Democratic opponent, William Jennings Bryan.

Even those who had disapproved of Teddy felt they would miss him. When would there ever be another president who was given to diving into canals fully clothed, or rushing to the bridges of distressed ships, clad only in his white pajamas? He had been unpredictable, robust and virile, and so, by association, had been America itself.

"It'll be a damned dull place without old Teddy," said Elliott Jameson in a slurred and maudlin voice. "Let's have another drink to old Teddy, Delia."

Delia regarded her companion with amused contempt. If Philip Warren had proved intolerable with his intense, possessive ardor, Elliott was unbearable in other ways. It was true that he had no desire to marry her or claim every moment of her time, but he drank too much and was much more stupid than he had seemed at first.

"You have a drink for good old Teddy," said Delia. "I am going home to bed."

Elliott's eyes clouded over; his normally dashing dark moustache was drooping, giving him a lugubrious air. "Aww, Delia, don't be angry with me," he said. He then lowered his voice to a mock whisper. "Take me home with you and we'll *both* go to bed."

"In the condition you're in, my dear Elliott, you'd hardly be any use to me," said Delia sweetly. She clasped her cloak around her and left the restaurant swiftly, aware that many were watching her. Elliott would never be able to catch up with her and by the time he had paid the check for their champagne supper and negotiated his way to the door, she'd be in her carriage and half-way home.

"Miss O'Donnell," the doorman said as he snapped to attention and touched his hand to his cap.

Her private carriage was brought round immediately and Frank, her driver, helped her in. "Will Mr. Jameson be coming along?" he asked.

"Let us hope not, Frank. Drive on."

Delia settled back and breathed a sigh of relief. She was borne away from the restaurant just as Elliott staggered out into the street.

She disliked automobiles intensely, and insisted on maintaining her own carriage, horses, and driver. She felt much more dignified riding in a handsome, gleaming, enclosed carriage, and the rhythmic clopping of the horses' hooves soothed her.

Now, more than ever before, it was important for her to maintain her dignity. She was appearing in a lavish production of Oscar Wilde's *Salome*, and while several critics had found her performance moving and superbly executed, the play itself was highly controversial. It was not the first time *Salome* had played in America, but before it had been stripped of what theatre people laughingly called "the offensive bits." A production had been mounted in wicked San Francisco so stripped of the "offensive bits" that audiences confessed themselves bewildered as to what the play was about.

The clever promoter who had suggested that Delia O'Donnell appear in *Salome* knew exactly what he was doing. People with pretensions to culture would come, to be sure, but thousands more would flock to the theatre to see Delia O'Donnell perform the Dance of the Seven Veils. Invariably there were protestors in front of the theatre. Some shouted that the play was vile and immoral, others that it was sacrilegious. Every night a gaunt, bearded man flourished a sign upon which was printed: AS SODOM AND GOMORROH PERISHED, SO WILL NEW YORK.

Delia entered by the stage door, so she was never obliged to deal with the philistine riff-raff, and Sarah, her dresser, always read the notes sent back-stage before passing them on to her. Most of the notes were still the work of ardent admirers, but there was the occasional condemnation. One had called her an immoral woman. "You are worse than a common prostitute," it had read, "because you are rich and don't need to do what you are doing. God will punish you."

As Delia approached her house near Gramercy Park, she made a promise to herself; she would stop seeing Elliott Jameson. Although he was popular in social circles, he was a gambler and a drinker and not good for her reputation. It would be an easy promise to keep because she was extremely tired of him.

The sense of well-being this modest decision had brought to her began to vanish as she prepared for bed. It had occurred to her that Philip Warren, for all his stuffiness, had given her more pleasure in love-making than the rakish Elliott. She had banished all signs of Philip and returned the jewels he had given her soon after her monumental scene with the vase of jonquils. He had threatened to shoot himself; he had knelt before her, sobbing. She had turned on him a face of stony indifference, knowing his threats were hollow. He hadn't shot himself, of course. After a period of great distress, during which he led a rather dissolute life, he had married a young society girl whom his mother approved of.

Delia had seen them once; their carriages had passed Fifth Avenue. The girl was pretty, young, and artless. Delia had smiled and nodded from her carriage, but Philip Henry Warren and his bride completely ignored her. He hated her, and who could blame him?

The people who protested and sent spiteful, anonymous notes to her at the theatre hated her, too. Their hate was mad, impersonal, but it wounded her. She did not like to be hated. Even the veiled contempt of Mrs. Warren had carried a sting. Sitting before the mirror in her white satin nightdress, she drew the brush through her hair and tried to take comfort in the sight of her perfect face.

Instead, she remembered her mother's face just after she had seen *Salome*. "It's very *advanced*, isn't it dearie?" Bridget had said nervously. "Very European —like a play they'd do in Paris."

"Oscar Wilde was an Irishman, Mama."

"Well, but you know what I mean, darling."

Her father hadn't known where to look, and for the first time Delia had blushed to recall her Dance of the Seven Veils. She wasn't really naked, of course, but the flesh-toned covering, which had been constructed especially for her, gave the illusion of total nudity when she threw away her last veil and presented herself to the mad King Herod. What must her da have felt, seeing his daughter near-bare on a Broadway stage? What must Bridget have thought when she witnessed Delia kissing the lips of a realistic–looking severed head?

If before she had been something less than respectable, she was now approaching notoriety. She went to fetch her book of press-cuttings, and turned to the pages where she was most favorably received.

There is an ineffable brilliance to Miss O'Donnell's performance as Salome, wrote one critic. *She gives the appearance of being utterly reckless in her youthful lust and cruelty, but it is a feat which only an actress of great gifts could accomplish, and it has been executed by dint of the most disciplined work imaginable.*

In the role of Salome, wrote another, *the exquisitely beautiful Miss O'Donnell has found a task worthy of her abundant talents. Mr. Wilde's decadent work, reviled by many on both sides of the Atlantic, assumes the noble mantle of Greek tragedy in the production currently to be seen . . .*

Delia read, then re-read, the most glowing reviews. Then she put aside the book and carefully stripped away her nightdress, as she had done every night since performing *Salome.* She studied her body in the glass with a shrewd, objective eye. She turned in every

direction, appraising her breasts and belly, her buttocks and legs, for signs of deterioration. Her glorious
breasts passed inspection, as always; her round, high
buttocks seemed passable, as did her long, slender
legs. She frowned as she examined the reflection of
her mid-section—was it possible that her months with
Elliott, during which she had consumed prodigious
amounts of champagne, had thickened her tiny waist?
It was a nearly imperceptible thickening, but it was
visible to her.

All the more reason to abandon her current lover!
In *Salome* she could ill afford to gain an ounce, or alter
her magnificently sculpted body in any way. Old-
school enthusiasts might still champion the Edwardian
ideal, the full, plump, body—which looked well
enough in stays and voluminous skirts—but Delia
knew what those women looked like unclothed. Pudding, or lumpy old potatoes.

It was alright for them to eat pastries and gorge
themselves at society suppers—they were not required
to appear almost bare naked on a Broadway stage,
before the admiring eyes of thousands. Delia knew
what it was like to throw off her final veil and stand
in the mellow lights, offering her body to a full house.
It was the high point of her performance, and it never
failed to make her blood race. Sometimes she wondered if an old gent in the first row felt himself gasp
at the sight of her. One night she had imagined a man
in one of the boxes growing hard, uncomfortably hard,
and squirming in his seat, mad with wanting her and
having to conceal it. She had played to that unknown
man, seducing him, firing his lust, seeing in her mind's

eye the moment when he would arch helplessly in his seat, gripped by the pleasure and humiliation of an illicit climax. It had been her best performance, ever. It was for this imaginary stranger that she now re-enacted her role.

Speaking the lines of *Salome*, she went far beyond the usual movements she performed on stage. She allowed her hands to cup her breasts; she stroked her loins and sank backward on the carpet, offering herself to the man, the audience, the world. Dimly, she heard the collective moans of the men who watched her, longing for the right to touch her glowing, vibrant flesh, yearning to plunge themselves into the pulsing heart of her.

Languidly, she snaked from the supplicant position to that of predator. Knees spread, back erect, she lifted her hand to receive the head of John the Baptist from the proffered shield, and hold it aloft for all to see.

"I will kiss thy lips, Jokaanan," she whispered. "I will kiss thy lips." In the production, the curtain fell as the soldiers of King Herod crushed her beneath their shields, but tonight—in her bedroom—she bade them keep their distance. She lowered her head to kiss the bloody and lifeless lips of her beloved, John the Baptist. She looked deeply into his eyes before lowering her lips to his. For a moment she could see the head, as if it were there with her in the room. She thought the eyes were those of her cousin, Kieran, but then she looked again and saw that the eyes and lips were those of Brendan Connolly. The lips of a priest.

She kissed the lips of Father Connolly, shoving her

tongue between his reluctant lips for good measure, and felt her body convulse with an unholy ecstasy so great she sprawled, face down, on the carpet.

When she crept shivering to her bed, it was to sleep deeply, without dreams. She no longer dreamed of crossing the sea in steerage, but of being stoned.

A month before Christmas, Veronica went to hear Mrs. Glendower Evans speak on behalf of Child Labor Reform. Mrs. Evans, a spirited Bostonian from a good family, was in the vanguard of the movement. Five years earlier, she had been appalled to learn that she was—through family inheritance—a stockholder in one of the worst factories in Georgia.

Her audience consisted mainly of women who, like Veronica, were comfortably well-off and therefore had time to devote to the social reform movements. Veronica sat with Mrs. Shipley, of the Orchard Street settlement house, and listened sadly to the dreadful statistics that Mrs. Evans cited. In Tennessee, children worked in mills for twelve hours a day without a break for meals. Despite legislation in many states requiring that children be twelve or over to qualify, violations of the law were numerous, and children ten and under filled the mills and factories. In Pittsburgh, Mrs. Evans had interviewed a small girl whose job it was to roll one thousand cigars a day. In Atlanta, she talked to a little boy who stretched three thousand flour bags in a single shift; she had visited the sweatshops of New York and the mines of West Virginia, where twelve-year-olds slaved for forty cents a day.

"A surgeon I met in the south told me he had

amputated the fingers of more than one hundred children, injured in factory or mining accidents. In his community the mill-owners had what they called a 'gentleman's agreement', claiming it was far more effective than any law. And do you know, ladies, what that 'gentleman's agreement' was?" she asked and then paused with an instinctive sense of dramatic timing. "It was that the employment of ten-year-olds should be limited to *sixty-six hours a week!*"

A rumble of protest swept the hall. "I don't call them gentlemen," cried a member of the audience. "I call them fiends!"

"Ladies! The laws which have been passed to protect the lives of working children are dreadfully inadequate, and they are ignored or willfully overlooked at that. We must continue to fight. We must badger our state legislators, write letters of protest to offending factory and mill owners, and—above all—we must make sure that others are aware of the wretched plight of these most unfortunate children!

"There, but for the grace of God, go our own children. Which of us can hold her head up, knowing she has failed to do the utmost for the suffering children of the poor?"

There was a rousing clamor of applause, and pamphlets which listed factories and sweatshops in Manhattan that violated the child labor laws were handed out. Veronica accepted hers thoughtfully, and turned to Mrs. Shipley.

"Alice, I am a strong woman, but when I hear of such things I want to weep."

"Don't weep, Veronica," answered Mrs. Shipley

briskly. "Act! Good is accomplished through action, not tears."

Veronica returned home and wrote letters to the names listed in her pamphlet. Toward midnight, she was too tired to continue, and went to her room to prepare for bed. Just as she was sliding gratefully between the cool, ironed sheets, she heard her husband enter his own bedroom. The dressing room between them had long been closed and normally she was not aware of his movements, but that night Robert banged about in such a manner she could not fail to hear him. She heard him overturn a chair and when the sounds grew louder, she could ignore them no longer.

She crept to the connecting door and listened. He was mumbling incoherently, as if he had had too much to drink. Veronica, however, thought that was unlikely, as Robert never allowed himself to lose control. Then she heard the unmistakable sounds of weeping.

Veronica felt her heart beating rapidly. She leaned against the wall for support. If Robert was weeping, then the end of the world must have arrived. The sounds filled her with pity, and when she could bear it no longer she pushed against the door, and entered her husband's room.

Robert lay across his bed, half-dressed. One boot lay where he had flung it, the other was still on his foot. His normally immaculately brushed hair was rumpled and wild, and his shoulders shook convulsively. He was indeed drunk.

Veronica walked softly to the bed and touched his shoulder. He gave a cry of surprise and flinched, turning to regard her with reddened and uncomprehending eyes.

"Robert? What is it, Robert?"

"Go away," he sobbed. "For the love of God, go away. You mustn't see me like this."

She sat beside him and gently smoothed his hair. "Tell me, dear. Don't, Robbie; don't grieve yourself so. Let me help you."

"I can't," he said. "You can't help me, Veronica. You are the last person . . ." He broke off, trying to control himself.

"For all our differences, I am still your wife. I am the woman you married. I care for you, Robbie." She knelt and removed his boot. She also removed his trousers, undressing him as she would a child. Beneath her hands he quieted a little, but when she brought him his night-shirt and slipped it over his head he gave a little cry of pain and buried his face in his hands. She kissed his bent head, soothing him, and suddenly he buried himself against her breasts, winding his hands in her hair and sobbing helplessly.

"I did love you," he cried. "Oh, Veronica, I did love you. You should have had a better man than me."

"Hush, hush." She pushed him down and drew the covers over his quaking body. Then she got into the bed beside him and held him in her arms, feeling his sobs subside. Long after he slept, his head heavy on her shoulder, she kept guard over him. It was only when the pale light of winter dawn insinuated its way into the room that she left.

The next morning, in the *New York Times*, an unexpected obituary appeared. Elizabeth Anne Mallory, beloved wife of Thomas Victor Mallory, had died suddenly of a ruptured appendix. Veronica now understood her husband's grief. Elizabeth, her one-time luncheon companion at Childe's—Elizabeth of the fair hair and unappeasable appetite for gossip—had been Robert's mistress.

Her death was never mentioned, nor was the night Robert had permitted himself to weep in Veronica's arms. The entire event was forgotten, by tacit consent, as if it had never been.

13 December, 1908
I have become a woman. Mama explained It to me when I turned thirteen. I was quite disgusted at first, but she told me if I didn't know I might think that I was dying. That is what she had thought, because grandmother did not tell her about It. What shall I do as a grown woman? I think I shall want to go to Barnard College and learn how to change the world. I shall also fall in love, of course, and marry and have children of my own. Perhaps as many as ten. I am reading The Jungle, *by Mr. Upton Sinclair, and find it very distressing and sad.*

10

In his third year as Harvard, Terry's reputation as a rake was firmly established. He drank prodigiously, gambled with an open hand, was never absent at sporting events or parties, and was rumored to be a devil with the ladies. In order to pass his courses with a gentleman's 'C,' he relied on the talents of a bright boy who had lost heavily to him at billiards. Instead of collecting the money owed him, Terry obliged the boy to do most of his work.

Terry was fond of throwing large supper-parties, and organizing weekend trips to New York to see the newest revues or the Ziegfield Follies. His cousin Delia's scandalous performance in *Salome* had truly set the seal on his 'Man of the World' image. *Salome* had, in fact, left Broadway and was touring America, but every undergraduate who had witnessed Delia's dance on stage hungered for a chance to meet her. Terry bathed in her reflected brilliance, often hinting that she would be coming to Cambridge especially to see him.

Although his hopes for a love affair with Celia Brady had never materialized, he had a very active love-life. He was paying court to a socially prominent girl at the Radcliffe Annex for Women, and when she retired to her chaste bed he would nip round to see one of the lively South End girls for a bit of fun. He had long ago learned not to fear venereal disease. Once, tipsy from too much brandy and champagne, he had confided his fears to a whore named Violet.

"Old silly," said Violet fondly, stroking the moustache he had at last managed to grow, "you'll never get a disease from working girls like me and Lizzie. Why, don't you know you're more likely to get clapped by one of them society women? They're ignorant, you see. We know what we're about."

And indeed they did. He had developed a great fondness for having two girls in bed at once, and could imagine no more pleasant way to pass an evening. He even had hopes of tumbling Julia Sommers, his Radcliffe bluestocking, from her pedestal of chastity. All in all, life had never seemed more full of pleasure and promise than in the early spring of 1909.

Of course, all of Terry's pursuits required money, and without a steady supply of cash, none of the high life would have been possible. His father regularly sent him a check for what he quaintly called "pocket money," and it was a respectable sum if a fellow wanted only to live decently, but for a *bon vivant* like

Terence O'Donnell it fell far short of what was needed. Fortunately, in this respect, his mother showed perfect understanding.

Margaret Fitzhugh O'Donnell knew that a gentleman could not excell at college without spending lavishly. Accordingly, Terry made periodic raids on Newburgh to wheedle money from her. He also knew that it was best to approach her when she had had a bit too much to drink.

"Mother," he would say, "I don't mean to be beastly, but I've run short again. Father does keep me on such a tight string."

"Your father has not had your advantages, Terence. He does not understand the expense of maintaining friendships with people of the upper classes."

Sometimes he would bait her with a line like; "Whit VandeVeer has had me for supper at the Ritz twice now, mother. I really must have enough at my disposal to reciprocate."

Margaret would agree, once more stating her views on the importance of remaining socially active. In the end she would withdraw sums from her private account and give them to Terry, warning him to keep their transactions from his father.

It wasn't until near the end of the spring term that life got hard for Terry. He was failing his course on torts and might have to repeat it the following year, and he had foolishly agreed to participate in a wager with a Virginia boy named Ford Lanier.

Ford was from Charlottesville, where he had been captain of the Virginia fencing team. As fate would have it, fencing was the only sport at which Terry truly excelled, and he enjoyed annoying the Virginian by pointing out flaws in his technique. Terry didn't much like Ford Lanier. He had all of Terry's rakish charm and none of Terry's drawbacks. He was an effortless scholar and very, very rich. He even had a better moustache, and a beautiful fiancée in Virginia.

One day he turned to Terry in front of four onlookers and drawled, "If you think mah technique is so poor, O'Donnell, let's see if you can best me. Ah'll wager you two hundred dollahs on it."

There was nothing Terry could do but accept. If he backed down, the four eager listeners would spread it all over Harvard Yard before the day was out. Already, they smiled slyly at his discomfort.

"Make it five hundred, Lanier, and I'm your man," he said.

Gratifying sounds of admiration came from the group, but Lanier merely smiled and asked if O'Donnell would prefer foil or epee?

"Oh, foils I should think," said Terry carelessly.

It was agreed that the match would take place on the following day, and since students were forbidden to gamble on sporting events, Lanier proposed a field some three miles north of Boston. The four who had witnessed the challenge would come along to referee.

"Christ," muttered Terry to Violet on the evening before the great event, "who does that bloody Virginian think he is?"

"But you're the one who pushed the stakes up," said Violet reasonably. "I think it's thrilling, sweetheart! It'll be almost like a duel!"

The admiration in her eyes soothed him temporarily, but he couldn't help but wonder what would happen if he lost. He didn't have five hundred dollars. He had precisely eighty dollars, and even if he pawned his watch and cigarette case he would not be able to scrape together more than two hundred. There was nothing for it—he would simply have to win.

The following afternoon Terry arrived at the field in Walter Brady's Packard with two of the referees. Lanier and the other two were already there, grouped around Lanier's Silver Ghost, drinking from flasks and having a fine time. Terry hoped that Lanier might choke on his brandy and perish before the match began, but there was to be no reprieve.

Under a brilliant sky, the field stretched vast and lonely. Far to the west, corn and alfalfa had been planted, but where they stood it looked unused. One of the referees went to scout out the most level ground.

"Cut when you have to, old man," Lanier said imperiously as he handed him a scythe.

Fifteen minutes later, the five other boys went to examine the chosen site. Lanier made many ferocious, mock-lunging motions to test the ground's springiness, but Terry disdained such effort and merely said, in his most laconic tones, "It'll do." Nothing remained but for the opponents to don their protective doublets and masks.

Terry took as long as he could to complete these tasks, but soon he was standing, foil in hand, facing Ford Lanier at the end of the scythed strip. Ford was fussily weighing two foils, tossing them lightly up, and snapping his agile wrists. At last he motioned that he was ready, and the chief referee read the rules they had agreed upon.

The object was to disarm the other man completely, but if neither man had achieved it at the end of a quarter of an hour, the winner would be the man who had made the most touches. Two referees would keep score of touches on each side of the strip, another would be the time-keeper, and the fourth—a senior man on the Harvard Fencing Team—would be the final adjudicator.

"Does that meet with youh approval, O'Donnell?" asked Ford Lanier. Terry nodded. "Good then. May the best man win. *En guard.*" He saluted.

Terry assumed his position, crouching uneasily. Always before, he had seen himself as a romantic figure when he fenced, but here—in a deserted field with visions of financial ruin dancing in his head—he felt merely ludicrous. Lanier was coming toward him, using the swift, mincing footwork he was famous for, and Terry marshalled his wits. He was best at attacking, possessing a lightning-quick lunge of exceptional depth and elasticity. At defense, however, he was less accomplished. He would let Lanier make the first few touches, convince him the match would be over in moments, and then stun him with his offense.

Lanier was cunning as well as skilled. When their foils engaged, his celebrated wrists flicked like clockwork so the clash of the metal sounded like a speeded-up metronome. Terry parried once, twice, and found there was something hypnotic in Lanier's technique; he felt like the proverbial snake being mesmerized by the mongoose. Lanier retreated, drawing Terry back with him and forcing him into the offensive position.

They continued their delicate tapping, the slender shaft of each weapon seeking to find the vulnerable point·of entry.

"*Hah!*" Lanier cried as he lunged and scored a touch beneath Terry's left shoulder. "*Hah!*" Another touch, before Terry had time to re-plot his offensive.

It seemed that the Virginian was toying with Terry; he could imagine indolent eyes mocking him behind the mask. They engaged again, and by this time Terry's anger had mounted to a fine, warlike pitch. He went flying down the strip as soon as he had parried; he forced Lanier's foil into a clashing confrontation which was satisfying to hear but accomplished little. He feinted again and again and was warded off almost lazily. His rage continued to mount, until he felt as if he would prefer to be fighting a real duel, with sharpened blades. He touched Lanier once and his confidence mounted. His opponent called "*touché*" in his infuriating drawl and Terry summoned up every ounce of skill he possessed.

Craftily, he retreated just enough to bring Lanier toward him, and then charged in for the kill. At just the right moment he would catch his opponent unaware and plunge deeply toward the earth so that Lanier would parry awkwardly. Then he would disarm him. His muscles tightened in a joyful anticipation of that moment.

When he lunged he gave a little shout of pure glee at the perfection of it. He felt his body propelled by a force so great it seemed almost magical. He brought his foil up in a powerful, sideways motion intended to frustrate Lanier's protective parry, and felt it close on air. Ford Lanier had executed a perfect Italian three-point landing—his feet and one arm on the stubbly ground—and Terry was deprived of his target. Lanier popped up with infernal speed and knocked Terry's foil from his hands. It went spinning off, catching the sun on its spinning blade, and the match was over.

"Match to Mr. Lanier!" shouted the adjudicator. There was a spate of applause. "In nine minutes, fifteen seconds," said the time-keeper. "Well done, Ford!"

Lanier dragged his mask back and advanced on Terry, grinning. He thrust his gloved hand out to shake hands, and Terry took it like a gentleman. "No hard feelings, O'Donnell," said Lanier. "Well played, old man."

All five of them watched while Terry wrote a check to Ford Lanier, drawn on his bank in Cambridge, for the sum of five hundred dollars. Terry smiled as he wrote it, hoping his hand would be steady, and suffered being clapped on the back. He maintained his composure until he was safely behind the wheel of Walter Brady's automobile and then he pounded his fist and cursed with every colorful phrase he had ever learned. The check, of course, was worthless. Unless he managed to find the money over the week-end, his career at Harvard was over.

The referees remained behind in the field with Lanier, whose Silver Ghost was commodious enough to accomodate them all. They preferred to ride home with the victor. Terry imagined them laughing at him;

to lose and be the object of ridicule was bad enough
—to pass a bad check would mark him forever. He
would never be able to show his face in Cambridge
again.

Schemes roiled in his brain. He could not hope for
support from his mother this time. She would be
appalled. He toyed with the idea of breaking into the
safe-box in his father's office, stealing the brooch left
to him by his grandmother, and pawning it, but this
seemed impossible to achieve without being caught.
He would have to borrow the money somehow.

Three hours later, he was on the train to New York.
He had vague notions of throwing himself on his Aunt
Veronica's mercy. She was soppy and easily preyed
upon. He would tell her he had befriended a poor
tavern-keeper's son in Cambridge, say the boy was
dying of tuberculosis and needed to move to a more
healthy climate. He would tell her—oh, Jesus!—if
only Delia hadn't gone off touring in *Salome*. She was
rich as Croesus, wasn't she? She hadn't even touched
the sum left her by their grandfather, whereas Terry
had squandered his in one year.

When he got to his aunt's house, rehearsing his
speech about the tubercular boy every step of the
way, a maid informed him that Mr. and Mrs. Tyrone
had gone to Baltimore. Feeling that everyone and
everything beneath the sun had conspired to defeat
him, Terry went to a saloon in the theatre district and
ordered a number of double-whiskies. When he
stumbled from the door into the street, he noticed a
bright poster advertising a musical revue. It featured

a montage of long legs and smiling female faces, so he went into the theatre, purchased a ticket, and took his seat. More than anything, he wished he were thousands of miles away, with Admiral Peary, say, on his voyage to the North Pole. Terry wondered why he'd ever thought he could lead a gentleman's life at Harvard. The Laniers of this world would always triumph.

In this mood of inebriated self-pity, he watched a dark-skinned man wearing a vulgar tie-pin approach him. The man was smiling, as if he knew Terry, and moving through the crowds with assurance.

"And how are you keepin', Mr. Terence O'Donnell?" he asked, bending down and addressing Terry deliberately. "You won't remember me, but I'm an old family friend. Ye're at Harvard now, aren't you?"

"I don't believe we've met," said Terry, in the tone of an aristocrat addressing his social inferior.

The man studied him with amusement, his black eyes calculating. "Here's my card," he said, handing Terry an embossed, expensively-printed calling card. "If I can ever be of any use to you, don't hesitate."

Terry studied the name, and remembered the large wreath at his grandmother's funeral.

"Why should you want to be of use to me?" he asked.

"I told you," said Mr. Malloy. "I'm a friend of the family." The curtain was about to rise and Malloy turned back, but before he did, he drooped one eye in a sly wink. "I'm a most resourceful man," he whispered, and vanished.

* * *

At first, the novelty of going on the road was pleasing to Delia. She had demanded, and received, certain privileges from the company manager. Her own dresser, Sarah, travelled with her and was given a raise in salary. In Delia's compartment on the train there were always fresh flowers, and in her dressing room at each theatre a bottle of imported champagne. Most importantly, the manager agreed that a bodyguard should stand outside her dressing room in case some frenzied zealot tried to accost her.

Cleveland and Chicago loved *Salome*, but in Kansas City someone threw an egg at the stage and was removed by the police. St. Louis was guarded in its response, Denver riotously approving. Delia learned how to temper her performance according to the city. If the morning papers told her the police were considering shutting the theatre down, she gave them a very mild version of the *Salome* she had performed in New York; if—as in Denver—the audience clamored for more, she seduced them all.

In October of 1909, two-thirds of the way through the tour, she was thoroughly sick of the play and of travel. She resolved that the next time she accepted a job outside of New York, it would be across the Atlantic. It was her dream to perform for that noted connoisseur of female beauty, King Edward VII.

Although Delia was often invited to be the guest of honor at various civic dinners, and was once presented the keys to a city by its mayor, she led a chaste and uneventful life on the road. Most of her time was taken up by riding on the train, and she was far too tired at the end of her performance to seek adventure. Only two unusual occurrences marked her private life.

The first was that flowers arrived, quite steadily, from her admirer Desmond Malloy. Initially, she thought he was following her, but it soon became clear that he knew her itinerary and had instructed florists across the country to send her their best on the appropriate evening. The energy and enterprising nature of such a scheme amused her, and she became intrigued.

The second was far more important. When the company arrived in San Francisco, she saw, in the crowds at the station, her cousin Kieran. He was standing alone, hands in the pockets of his coat, with one foot propped on a battered–looking valise. The line he stood in was waiting for a train heading back east.

Delia broke away from her escort and ran toward Kieran. The station was thick with people, and they blocked her way. Many turned to stare at the beautiful, expensively-dressed young lady who so rudely pushed her way past men and women. Someone recognized her and called out her name, and soon dozens of strangers were buzzing excitedly. "It's Delia O'Donnell! The actress!"

Kieran's line was moving toward the gate and he was still fifty feet away from her. Desperately, she called his name, but he did not turn around. She made one last effort to reach him, dodging the press of people as nimbly as an athlete. "Kieran!" She shouted his name so loudly he could not fail to hear. "Kieran O'Donnell!" The man just behind him was staring in her direction. She called to him, asking him to get the attention of the next in line. He plucked at Kieran's sleeve. Delia could see him explaining, gesturing toward her.

Kieran turned and looked straight at her. It was the first time she had seen him in five years. Like Delia, he was now twenty-six, and like Delia he was still as beautiful as he had been at eighteen, but he had altered in some strange frightening way. There was a hardness, an impenetrable, steely edge to him which had not been there when he'd bade her farewell in her dressing room.

His blue eyes stared at her but registered no recognition; Kieran might have been looking at a stranger. Anyone comparing their two faces would think they were identical twins, yet Kieran shrugged slightly and said: "There must be some mistake, Miss."

Delia wanted to scream at him, or run to his side and strike him in the face, force him to admit that he knew her, but the line had begun to move again. When he turned his back on her she cried out, "You broke your promise to me, Kieran! You broke your word!"

He seemed to flinch at her accusation, but he walked steadily toward the gate, never turning back. When he vanished through the door she found, to her surprise, that she was close to tears.

Three days later, a note arrived addressed to her in care of the *Salome* company. It had been posted from Sacramento, no doubt on the platform during a stop. It said only: *Forgive me, Dee. I had to catch a train. As for the other, I'm sorry. I wish you luck always. Forgive, and forget.*

It was unsigned.

* * *

Bridget counted off the months; if all went smoothly, the baby would be born in August, 1910. It would be a good year to be born; the child would always be able to count its life out in fine, round decades.

It was an amazing thing, a gift from God, that she should be pregnant again at the age of forty-three. When the twins had been born, she had felt herself a glorious and powerful creature—a fecund Earth Mother capable of giving her husband a dozen children if she so desired. She was barely eighteen, and was about to give birth to not one child, but two. All during her long labor, her cries of pain were somehow jubilant.

Delia was born first and gave a lusty yell immediately, but her twin had been less fortunate. The little boy, who was to be named Thomas, after Michael's father, had lived for only an hour. He was weak, pale and silent, a tiny thing whose lungs had not formed properly. Bridget's grief was real enough, but diluted by the triumphant glow of having produced a perfect daughter.

In those days, she had assumed she would be able to give Michael many sons, so when the doctor told her, at age twenty-three, that it was unlikely she would be able to bear more children, she sank into a black depression which had lasted for nearly a year. Michael had held her in his arms and insisted that it didn't matter; he loved her, and they didn't need any more than their beautiful Delia. Gradually, she emerged from her sorrow and began to lavish on her daughter all the love she had intended for many children.

While Delia was growing up, Bridget was gripped with a morbid and insistent fear—something would happen to Delia, because she was too beautiful and extraordinary to survive. Some terrible accident would take Delia from her; if she let the child out of her sight for even a moment, God would punish her.

God had once before punished Bridget for being careless, and although her parents had never once— even in their extreme grief—blamed her outright, she would always blame herself. Another luckless Thomas, Tommy, her little brother, had drowned when he was five and she was twelve.

Now, at the age of forty-three, she was being given another chance. The childish carelessness that had resulted in Tommy's drowning; the mysterious workings of her womb which had not properly nourished her own son, Tommy; the vigilance in raising Delia, only to have her run off at seventeen—all these mistakes would be rectified miraculously in August of 1910.

Bridget did not tell her husband of her pregnancy until Christmas Eve. Michael was so astounded she had to repeat the joyful tidings three times before he understood what she was saying.

"Are you sure, love? How can it be?" He wrapped his arms around her and laid his head against her belly. "When, Bridget? Did the doctor say you'd be alright?"

His questions flew at her so rapidly she laughed.

"In August," she answered. "I haven't seen the doctor. I don't need a doctor, Michael. I know."

She promised him she would see Dr. Randall in

January, when she would enter her second month of pregnancy, and all during the last days of the old year, she went about with a secretive, dreamy smile, wrapped in private thoughts.

Only one thing marred her happiness: she wished her parents could have lived to see Tommy re-enter the world and join them once more.

11

delia was never to fulfill her dream of performing before Edward VII. He died in May of 1910 and with him, as everyone repeated sadly, an era. America sent ex-President Roosevelt to the King's funeral as their official representative and once more 'Good Old Teddy' made the country proud.

Margaret O'Donnell mourned the King by wearing black until he was buried. Her husband, who was not partial to English monarchs, mourned his sister instead.

Bridget lay in her bedroom on Ridge Street all day, staring at the ceiling with blank eyes. The doctors had assured her, first gently and then with force, that she was not pregnant, but Bridget had refused to believe them. Michael related these facts to Patrick, locking the door of his office and speaking in a hoarse, fearful whisper. When he told Patrick how Bridget had appeared at dinner one night with a pillow strapped beneath her dress, he broke down and wept.

"Now, man," Patrick soothed, thumping Michael's back awkwardly, "don't take on so. She'll be alright. It's her time of life, Mike. They get that way, sometimes."

But the doctors had told Michael that Bridget had not yet entered upon her change of life, and that the problem was a mental illness. He was advised to be patient and loving, but avoid humoring his wife's delusion.

Michael knew that Delia's presence would help, but she had earlier sailed for Europe. In desperation, he wrote to Veronica and begged her to come to Newburgh. Veronica agreed and promised to arrive within the week.

Jim had moved to New York and was temporarily living with the Tyrones. He had left the Newburgh law firm for a junior, but promising position with the Wall Street firm Briggs, Clay & Clay (the senior Clay had changed his family name from Clancy twenty years before).

The move to New York made Jim feel even more lonely and anxious, despite his aunt's kindness. He wondered if his rise in the legal profession had driven yet another nail in his coffin.

Only Terry was happy that spring. A year from the day of the ill-fated fencing match, he was able to laugh at his visions of being a social outcast, ruined and despised. Meeting Des Malloy seemed to be the best thing that had ever happened to him. Malloy had sought him out and encouraged him to confide his sorrows. He had smiled at the mention of five hundred dollars, and had produced a roll of bills so large Terry's eyes nearly fell out of his head.

"Here's five to make the boyo's check good, and one for yourself," he said paternally.

Now, whenever Terry needed money, he had only to contact Malloy—and he did so frequently. He was in his last year at Harvard, and he wanted to go out with a flourish.

Terry knew Malloy was crooked, but he admired him as he had never admired his decent, hardworking father. Des Malloy owned a fabulous brothel in Jersey City, where Terry had enjoyed himself *gratis* on one occasion, and the girls were so stunningly beautiful that they made Vi and Lizzie look like kitchen drabs. There were Chinese girls and statuesque Africans as well as the more typical blondes and redheads, and Terry had wondered how to choose from such a bevy of temptresses.

The beauty of it was that Malloy granted Terry so many favors and wanted nothing in return! It never bothered Terry, because he was very good at taking. It seemed only right to him that people should wish to make him happy. He was handsome and lucky—and the world was his oyster!

In a village in County Mayo, on the western shores of Ireland, stood a public house that was run by a man named Sean Rafferty. Rafferty's place was far from elegant, being a one-room cottage roofed with sod, but he sold the potent, illegal *poteen,* which he manufactured himself, and the place was always full.

To this cottage, late in the year 1910, came a travelling man called O'Rourke. O'Rourke was making his way up to Sligo on a personal errand, and had decided to stop at the village in Mayo for several reasons. For one thing, it was a cold, damp autumn, and Mayo, warmed by the Gulf Stream, offered a refuge for a time. For another, his business in Dublin and other parts of the country had been extensive, and he was weary. When he had asked a local if he might find a room in the village, he was directed to Rafferty's.

He entered the low room, stooping under the lintel, and was confronted by a dozen pair of watchful, not altogether friendly, eyes.

"God save all here," he said in Irish. He asked for Rafferty and stated his business. Rafferty, a short, stocky man in his fifties, scratched his head and thought. Eventually he nodded, asked Kieran to wait, and sent a grubby urchin out into the night. Kieran drank a jar of poteen, sipping slowly, and covertly studied the men in the room.

He had learned not to make instant judgments. Ireland had been a revelation to him, and had taught him a great deal. He was stunned by its beauty, saddened by its poverty, and perpetually surprised by the contradictions which lay everywhere. These people, who seemed to be concerned only with eking out a miserable existence, ought, by rights, to have no time for politics. But Kieran had been taught, by Clarke and others, that beneath the guise of a wretched, broken man, there might be the poesy and ardor of a revolutionary.

The urchin had returned, and was beckoning to him. "My sister will show you," he said. "Go with her."

Kieran left the cottage and found himself staring at a ragged girl wrapped in a shawl. Her head was shyly lowered as she started walking along the lane without having said a word to him. He noticed that her boots were broken, and revealed one small toe.

"Are you Rafferty's daughter?" he asked.

"One of them," she replied. "There's six of us, and the four boys." Her voice was muted, but there was a sweetness to it. "It's just along here," she said, gesturing vaguely. "It was my aunt's place, but she died."

When they arrived at the cottage, Kieran saw it was little more than a hut. There was a great slash in the roof, and the door hung loosely. The girl went in ahead and ushered him inside.

The room contained a low pallet, a square table and two broken-down chairs, a basin and ewer. She lit the lamp, letting her shawl fall about her shoulders as she did so, and turned to face him.

"Da would be askin' five shillings for the week," she said defiantly.

Kieran was silent. He was not concerned with the wretchedness of the place, nor with the price Rafferty wanted. He was silent because the girl, revealed to him at last, was so lovely he could not speak. The shawl had hidden hair of a bright, fiery red-gold which sprung in unruly curls from her small head and spread itself over her shoulders in brilliant points. From within the hood of her hair, the girl's heart-shaped face was lifted to him in a mixture of appeal and pride. She was very pale, so pale her skin reminded him of snow, and great, hungry eyes burned from the little face, almost golden in the glow from the oil lamp. He thought she was sixteen, perhaps.

"Would you be stayin' the week, sir?" She refused to try to sell him the place by discoursing on its non-existant merits; she held herself very straight and maintained a peculiar dignity. "If you decide you'd like it, I'll cook and clean for you," she offered.

"What is your name?"

"Maureen."

"The place'll do fine, Maureen. There's no need for you to cook, or clean."

"But that's a part of it, sir." She seemed distressed. "I must."

"You'll be wantin' the rent now," he said, confused and unable to think what to say to her. He withdrew the money and held it out to her, but she stood where she was, her huge eyes hanging on his face. Then she lowered her lashes and repeated the list of amenities available to him. "There's peat cut for the fire, and a stream out back for the water," she said. "I'll be by in the morning to bring you bread and tea."

She accepted the five shillings which he pressed into her hand, and left quickly. Kieran went to the door and called goodnight to her, but she was walking swiftly up the lane, her bright hair concealed once more beneath her shawl. She did not answer him.

Kieran stayed a full week in the hovel in Mayo. In the normal course of events, he would have tired of the refuge there in two days, but something strange and unforeseen possessed him. He found himself hungering for his daily encounters with Maureen Rafferty, in a way so powerful it caused him to feel pain when she left him. He preserved, outwardly, a purely friendly and casual attitude, but inwardly he marvelled at the emotion she stirred in him. Their conversations were brief, at first, but after the second day she seemed to look forward to seing him.

"Are you from Cork, then?" she asked one morning, setting a pan of soda bread down on the table and going to stir the fire.

"Cork? Do I sound it?"

She was silent, and he realized it had only been her way of asking where he was from. "I was born in America," he said.

She turned, kneeling by the fire, the poker still in her hand. There was a smudge of black across her knuckles, and another on her cheek. "Never," she said. "You were not, surely?"

For the next quarter of an hour he told her stories about America, watching her eyes as she listened. Sometimes they shone with interest, but when he mentioned New York they clouded.

"That's where I shall have to go," she said. "My older sister had a position there, in service with a family."

Kieran felt his heart contract at the thought of Maureen crossing the Atlantic to work as a domestic servant. "Do you want to go?" he asked gently.

She shook her head, folded her hands and looked down. Then, as if rejecting such monumental self-pity, she smiled at him and said briskly: "Well, it can't be helped. There are too many mouths to feed here, and I've my living to earn."

She rose and began to sweep out the little room. Watching her, Kieran yearned to take the broom from her hand and kiss the sooty knuckles. He thought of the terrible things that could happen to a girl like Maureen, alone in New York. Her beauty would not go unnoticed, and he imagined her fighting off the attentions of the master of the family where she worked or worse—the attentions of unscrupulous men who might seek to turn her beauty to their profit.

"How old are you, Maureen?"

"Seventeen, Mr. O'Rourke."

"Can you read and write?"

Her pale face blushed deep red. "Only a little," she said, "but I'm not stupid."

"I never thought you were. I think you are very intelligent." His longing to touch her was a torment, now. "Please, Maureen, don't be offended."

"I'm not, then," she said, returning to her sweeping.

Alone, on his hard pallet that night, he was visited by images of her so vivid that he could not sleep. He imagined bathing her face and hands, brushing her tangled, lovely hair until it glowed like a river of fire, buying her pretty dresses and fine boots, and teaching her to read and write. He thought he knew exactly how she would feel, held close in his arms; he could taste the sweetness of her lips, feel her heart beating beneath his own.

It was the first time in his twenty-seven years that he had felt this way. He had bedded many women with enjoyment, lusted greatly for a few of them, and even liked one or two; yet, he had always supposed that his cousin, Delia, was the woman he loved best. He saw how wrong he had been. It was not his desire for Maureen which overpowered him—although it was strong enough to deprive him of his sleep—but his feelings of tenderness.

One day she consented to walk with him on the strand, which lay only half-a-mile from the edge of the village. The wintry sea was leaden and grey, and the waves humped in upon themselves like the backs of dolphins at play. Maureen shivered in her shawl, but he did not dare to put his arms around her. It would alarm her, and be his undoing.

He talked to her of trivial things, making her laugh. He wanted to ask her if she would miss him, but would not allow himself. In the life mapped out for him, there was no place for Maureen. He could not take her with him, on his secret and dangerous travels, nor could he remain behind with her in Mayo. He could not even write to her. It grieved him, and since he was not accustomed to feeling sorrow of a personal nature, he felt bewildered and angry as well.

Over the crashing of the sea he heard her voice ask him the one question he could not answer. "What is it troubles you?" she asked shyly. He could only shrug and reply that nothing troubled him, and watch her retreat back into her native reserve. Head held high, she walked back with him to the village in silence. They parted in front of his cottage.

He knew what it was he had to do. He must leave the village before he saw her again, even if he had to walk all night to reach the next town. He collected his things and banked the fire carefully. In less than an hour she would be at his door with his supper, and he wanted to be miles away. He looked around the miserable little room, realizing it as the place where his life had nearly been jogged from its inevitable course. More than anything, he wished to leave something for Maureen, something which might improve her pitiful condition. Hoping it would not offend her, he placed a five pound note—all he could spare—on the table, beneath the ewer. She had said she could read a little, so he left a note beside the money. He printed, in capital letters, the words: *FOR MY TRUE FRIEND MAUREEN*. He added, in Gaelic, a thank you.

Then, feeling as if a stone were lodged uncomfortably in his breast, he left the cottage and began to walk north, toward the Sligo border.

1 January, 1911

I have so many wishes for the New Year I scarcely know where to start. First, I most sincerely hope it will be a happier year for my family than the one just past. Mama says poor Aunt Bridget is better now, but it is only (I think!) thanks to Mama's staying with her in Newburgh for above two months. For Jim, I wish a young lady who is intelligent and good. He is lonely, I know, and it seems unfair that he should be so. Why must girls always lose their heads over men like Terry, when anyone with an ounce of sense can see Jim is a hundred times nicer? Delia is coming home from Europe, where a count is said to have fallen madly in love with her. For Delia, I wish a play that will make people ad-

mire her, instead of whispering scandalous things behind her back.

Mama and I both hope for female suffrage, of course, and better conditions for the poor. If it is not too selfish, I also have a personal wish for myself. I am to go to a school for young ladies this year, since Mama believes I have been privately tutored long enough. I will still live at home, but I am anxious about making friends. My wish is this: a girl, my age, like me, who will be my best friend, and in whom I can confide!

Veronica had missed the Womens' Suffrage parade in the spring of 1910—she had been at her sister's bedside. Now nothing would prevent her. Mrs. Blatch had announced that they would try again, and Veronica intended to walk up Fifth Avenue with the others of her sex who were brave enough to ignore the jeering crowds.

Harriot Stanton Blatch, daughter of Elizabeth Cady Stanton, stressed the importance of being on time. The march was scheduled to begin at 3:30. Any lateness would only cause their enemies to chuckle and remind the world that "women were never on time."

"But why can't I go, too?" Bernadette cried in outrage.

"Because, darling, I would fear for your safety."

"But if it's dangerous, someone should go along to look after you," said Bernadette reasonably.

"I am well able to look after myself."

"And so am I. What good does it do to teach me

things, Mama, if you won't let me act on my principles?"

Veronica sighed. Her daughter was looking especially fierce. She stood in the middle of the room, coltish legs planted well apart with her hands on her hips. She was becoming a handsome young woman, and her argument had merit.

"Bernadette, listen to me. I want you to act on your principles, but at fifteen you are too young to join a parade which could end disastrously. I promise you that you may come along next year, when you are sixteen."

"But what if we win this year? There won't *be* a parade in 1912 if we're triumphant now."

"We won't be," Veronica answered grimly. Seeing her daughter's crestfallen expression, she crossed the room and put her arms around Bernadette's slender shoulders.

"It's only that I'd like to be a part of history," Bernadette said in a small voice.

"And so you shall," Veronica assured her. "When the time is right."

Three thousand women assembled for the march. Despite Mrs. Blatch's warning, they were half an hour late getting started. Veronica carried one edge of a large banner which proclaimed: *Men Have The Vote—Why Not We?* Fifth Avenue was lined with shouting, hooting crowds who had assembled to ridicule them as madwomen and zealots.

"Where's your trousers?" screamed a red-faced man over and over, as if it were the most original joke in the world. "Where's your trousers?"

"Shame!" shouted others. "Go back home where you belong!"

The ninety four brave men who marched together under the banner *Men's League for Woman Suffrage* were the targets of the worst jeers. "Lizzie!" the crowds shouted at them, and as they passed the Waldorf Hotel someone threw a wet Turkish towel down on the group. Some of the by-standers shouted oaths and obscenities. Veronica heard words she had never heard spoken, and was glad she had forbidden Bernadette to join her.

Near Thirty-seventh Street, she saw a couple in the crowd who were observing the march with quiet amusement. Like many she had seen, they were society people who turned out for the event as a form of amusement, but unlike the others, they were people Veronica knew personally. Mr. and Mrs. Van Sickle had been the host and hostess at the long-ago dinner party during which she had publically opposed Robert. She saw Mrs. Van Sickle nudge her husband, smiling cynically. Veronica walked on.

"Can you do a man's work?" shrieked a working-class woman from the crowd. "Where's your trousers?" shouted her husband.

A reporter from the *Tribune* approached seventy year old Emma Butterworth Danforth.

"Young man," she cried, "if you do anything to make this parade look ridiculous, I'll never forgive you."

The reporter retreated. "One cannot ridicule one's grandmother," he confided to onlookers.

Near the end of the parade, someone threw an egg

into the group. Nobody was hurt, but the open hostility of the crowd had begun to daunt Veronica. The exhilaration she'd felt at the beginning of the afternoon was beginning to fade. She wondered what Edith would have said, if she had lived to see this day, and decided her mother would, all in all, be proud of her. Someone, surely, had to suffer the ridicule of the public in order to accomplish change, and she was hardly alone. She was one of three thousand. She squared her shoulders and walked on, proud to be in the vanguard.

The next day, the *New York Times* guardedly admitted that the women "did not lose but gained respect." It was tepid praise, but welcome. Veronica carefully clipped the article, and pasted it in her book.

Now that her younger son was ready to graduate from Harvard (though not so triumphantly as Jim), Margaret believed her life in Newburgh was over. It was time, as she told her husband at dinner one night, to move to New York. When Patrick politely asked her where she thought the money would come from to finance such a move, Margaret closed her eyes in pain. It was so like Patrick to mention money, when she had been discussing something as important as her sons' careers.

Patrick was happy in Newburgh, happy enough, and had no wish to go to the city. He vaguely thought of schemes whereby he might transport his wife to New York and yet remain behind. Nor was he pleased with Terence. Where Margaret saw a handsome socially adept young man ready to take the world by storm, he saw only a garish, dissolute boy without moral principles. He loved his younger son and would have unquestioningly given his life for him, but he did not like him.

Of Liam's grandchildren, he thought his own Jim and Veronica's Bernadette the finest. Delia might be the one to be remembered, but he felt there was something missing in her. Something was also missing in Kieran, but how could it be otherwise?

Patrick still felt grief for his misguided brother, Bobby, and for Bobby's orphaned son he had always felt a special affection. If all of Kieran's passion and intelligence could have been channeled in another direction, he might have achieved greatness, but Kieran would, he feared, come to a bad end. Patrick was not ignorant of events on the 'Other Side,' and he was fairly sure that Kieran was involved with them.

In Ireland, there were men like O'Donovan Rossa and Thomas Clarke who were waiting for England's misfortune to turn into Ireland's opportunity for freedom. O'Donovan Rossa had organized the dynamiting in England in 1883. He promised he would employ "dynamite, Greek fire, or Hell fire . . ." to get the English out of Ireland, and his promise continued for more than twenty-five years, until a new generation of Irish patriots had sprung up to heed his rallying cry.

Thomas Clarke, jailed by the British for treason, had served the cause in America under a false name until general amnesty was granted in 1898. He then returned to Ireland as an American citizen and had founded a new paper, *Irish Freedom.* The paper was one of the leading separatist voices in Ireland and Clarke and O'Donovan Rossa along with countless others were waiting for the perfect moment to stage a Rising. Such men foresaw a war between England and Germany, and during a war their perfect moment was bound to arrive.

Kieran, thought Patrick, was with these men. Whether here or on the 'Other Side,' Patrick knew that his nephew had joined the ancient battle, just as his father before him had done.

Kieran was so much in Patrick's thoughts the last months of 1911, that Patrick was astounded when he appeared at O'Donnell & Sons in December. Patrick had not seen Kieran for four years but still he felt compelled to shake his hand rather than clasp him in an avuncular hug; something about Kieran forbade any show of affection.

"It's good to see you, lad," said Patrick. "What brings you up this way?"

"I thought it was past time for a visit. How is grandmother keeping?"

"She's dead, Kieran. It's been over three years now." Patrick hadn't meant the words to emerge so bluntly, but the fact that his nephew had cut himself off so completely from the O'Donnell family angered him.

"I'm sorry. I didn't know, uncle." He had colored at Patrick's words. With his black lashes cast down, he might have been the Kieran of twenty years ago, caught climbing too high in the maple tree or frightening Mrs. Parker with a mouse.

"Kieran, boy—how could you know? You've been a stranger to us these many years."

His cold, brilliant blue eyes regarded Patrick steadily. "I have," he agreed flatly.

"Mother left you something in her will. I don't know what you'll make of it, but the fact is, she bequeathed you her wedding ring. It is for your wife, if you choose to marry."

"If I marry?" Kieran repeated the words as if they were a strange new language. He smiled oddly, and passed one hand over his eyes.

"It seems unlikely, doesn't it?" asked Patrick softly.

"What do you mean?"

"Do you think I'm deaf and blind? Do you imagine I don't know what goes on in the world? I was twenty-two when your da died, Kieran. Christ, boy, how much does history have to repeat itself? At least I credit you with some compassion. You'll not take an innocent woman down with you, Kieran. You'll leave the life you're living, or you'll not marry."

"You know nothing about my life," said Kieran. "Nothing."

Patrick sighed and poured out two glasses of whiskey from a bottle he kept in his desk. "To your return," he said. "*Slainte.*"

"*Slainte,* uncle."

"Be careful, boy. I'm beggin' you."

"That I will."

Kieran stayed for nine days in the house on Ridge Street. He was so perfectly charming and sympathetic, so amusing and courteous, that even Margaret was impressed. He coaxed giggles from Bridget and applauded Veronica, when she came up from New York, for her work on behalf of the suffrage movement. Bernadette fell in love with him all over again, and even Terry was forced to admit that he was a damned fine fellow. When Jim arrived for the holidays, Kieran requested that he play his fiddle, and listened by the hour. Yet through it all, Patrick watched uneasily, an ominous thought unfolding in his mind.

The day before he left, Kieran went to the church-yard on the hill where his grandparents were buried and stayed there for an hour. Then, on the day of his departure, he made a request which confirmed Patrick's suspicion. He asked if he might have the ring his grandmother had left him.

Patrick unlocked the safe-box and handed it to him wordlessly. For the past nine days, all during the festive Christmas season spent in the bosom of his family, Kieran had been saying good-bye.

Patrick was sure, now, that he had come home for the last time.

part three

12

In the company of other girls, Bernadette discovered that she was old for her age in some ways, but young in others. Her learning in a wide variety of subjects made her academically superior to most of the young ladies at Miss Eden's School, but in worldly matters she was woefully behind. Having passed most of her childhood in the company of her gentle, dedicated mother, Bernadette had never learned to flirt with boys or develop what one of her new friends called her "womanly wiles."

"What you do when you want a man to notice you, Bernadette, is *this*," Alice Mary Gardner said as she rolled her eyes. Then she started, as if she had seen a ghost, and dropped her lashes shyly, turning her head to a becoming angle on her slender neck. "You let them see you've taken notice, and then you pretend it didn't happen. That way you attract them without seeming too bold."

Bernadette thought the "technique" looked foolish, but politely refrained from saying so. Aside from her cousin Kieran, she had never seen a man who made her want to behave out of character.

"Perhaps Bernadette doesn't want to flirt," pointed out Louise Wolfe.

"She has to learn some time," said Alice Mary.

"Even if I wanted to, I don't know any boys," said Bernadette.

"Not boys—men. Call them *men*, Bernadette. You're sixteen years old," Alice Mary said sternly. "My brother is coming home for the weekend soon. He's twenty-one, and quite presentable. If you like, I'll invite you home with me and you can practice on him."

"It's awfully kind of you, but . . ."

"Think nothing of it. He's engaged, so you mustn't expect anything to happen, but it will be good practice."

Louise Wolfe's shoulders shook with silent laughter. Of all the girls at Miss Eden's, Louise was the one to whom Bernadette felt closest. She was an intelligent, witty girl with immense dark eyes and a sympathetic nature. Louise was Jewish, and her father was intent on marrying her off to a rich gentile so she could, as he put it, 'assimilate.'

"Poor Papa," Louise confided to Bernadette one afternoon, "he doesn't understand that I haven't the least interest in marrying to suit him. Is your father like that?"

Bernadette thought about it. "I don't think so," she

said. "To tell the truth, I don't think Papa notices me much at all. My mother is wonderful, though. She wants me to do exactly as I like."

What she had said was true; however, she had failed to add that her father would do doubt disown her if ever she married a Jew.

"Is your father anti-Semitic?" Louise asked, as if reading her mind. She smiled wickedly. "You can tell me, it's alright. Mine hates the Irish."

"Yes," said Bernadette, biting her lip, and then they both burst into laughter.

For over a year now, Bernadette and Louise had considered themselves best friends. Bernadette sometimes wished that Louise were older, because she thought she would be the perfect girl for her cousin, Jim.

Jim was escorting a young lady named Clair Trumbull to concerts and the theatre, but he did not look happy, and Bernadette was afraid that Jim was destined, at twenty-eight, to be a bachelor all his life. She worried about her cousins, having no brothers and sisters of her own, and confided their affairs to Louise. She envied Louise her large family—an older, married brother, a brother at medical school, and two pesky small sisters still at home.

Louise envied her the freedoms and privileges Bernadette's mother bestowed on her only child. More than anything, Louise envied her friend's soon-to-be realized dream of marching in the Suffrage Parade that May.

"But what will your father do? Won't he forbid it?"

"My mother is not someone who takes orders," said

Bernadette loftily. Privately, though, she had been worried about just this point. Her father had been conveniently out of town last year, and never knew that his wife had marched down Fifth Avenue with a group of fanatical women.

However, two nights before the parade, Veronica looked across the table at her husband, drew a deep breath, and said, "Robert, I shall be participating in the parade for Women's Suffrage on the fourth. I thought I had best tell you. I know you don't approve, and I'm sorry, but it is something I must do." She paused, watching the anger mount in Robert's face, and then added, "And I shall be taking Bernadette with me."

Bernadette watched fearfully as several things happened. Her father's face became very red while her mother's grew pale. Robert put his napkin down decisively, narrowed his eyes, and stared at each of them in turn.

"Veronica," he said, "I think you should understand something. I have never been able to control you, and I gave up trying to do so many years ago. You are a grown woman, and if you want to make a fool of yourself you are free to do so." His tone was conversational, deceptively bland, but when he turned his gaze on Bernadette the words emerged with precise, bullet-like force, as if bitten off. "My daughter is a different matter. There is still hope for her to grow into a normal, gentle woman of reason and respectable habits. I will not have her in the company of hysterical, dangerous, subversive women. I will not have it, do you understand? *I will not have it!*" He shouted these last words, then controlled himself with effort and spoke again with cold authority.

"I forbid you to go, Bernadette."

"Papa—"

"That is all I have to say."

"Robert—"

"Be quiet, Veronica!" He brought his hand down on the table so forcefully the water goblets jumped and tinkled. "Bernadette is my daughter, and she will do as I say."

"Bernadette is also my daughter. If I may say so, she is much more my child than yours. It is I who have raised her all these years, I who have loved and cared for her. She is sixteen, and well able to make up her own mind. You have never taken the trouble to educate her or show her much tenderness, Robert. Why should you now reserve the right to forbid her to do what she wishes to do?"

"Because you are a madwoman," he spat out. "You are not right in the head. Your whole family is tainted. Your brother was a felon, your sister is unstable. Your niece is no better than a courtesan! And you?" He laughed bitterly. "You are a cold, hysterical fanatic of a woman. You aren't a woman at all, Veronica."

Bernadette saw her mother flinch under the cruel words as if Robert had taken a whip to her. Veronica's hands trembled; her lips quivered. In a moment, Bernadette feared, she would cry. Her own throat was thick with tears and she felt a terrible sadness mix with her rage. She stood up from the table and faced her father.

"Don't ever speak to her like that again," she said. "I have heard more words from you tonight than ever in my life, and every one was cruel and untrue. I intend to go with Mama to the march and you will not prevent me. You have no right to forbid me anything."

Robert stared at her. The silence stretched on and still he did not speak. At last he rose and left the dining room. A moment later they heard the front door slam shut. Bernadette went to her mother and knelt by her side. Silent tears were coursing down Veronica's cheeks and she shook with an emotion Bernadette did not understand.

"Don't cry, Mama," she said, putting her arms around Veronica. "We have each other."

"Yes, we have each other." It was a whisper. And then, for the first time Bernadette could remember, her mother sobbed as if her heart would break. She gasped one phrase over and over again. "I am not cold," she cried. "I am not cold!"

"I wouldn't want the *responsibility* of voting," Clair Trumbull said thoughtfully. "Women ought to have different concerns, Jim. Politics and world affairs don't interest us, so how can we vote responsibly?"

Jim turned to look at her, seeing her neat little profile with the usual mixture of amusement and irritation. Much as he had liked Clair at first, her pronouncements on every subject under the sun were invariably vapid.

"And what concerns would you allow women, Clair?"

She pressed his arm lightly with her gloved hand. They were strolling in Central Park. It was a fine, balmy day and Clair wore a fashionable bonnet with blue streamers. "Women have *tremendously* important duties, Jim. We must run our homes efficiently, look after our husbands and children, provide a stable life for our families."

"Even when you're not married?" Jim instantly regretted his little jest. Clair gave him a wounded look and withdrew her arm from his. He had been distinctly ungallant.

"An unmarried woman is even less qualified to vote," she said distantly. "She does not have a good man to advise her."

They walked on in silence, past the lake studded with little boats. Jim knew Clair expected him to propose marriage to her, and it was this expectation which allowed her to accept his kisses, even though they had never exchanged words of love. Clair was eminently kissable. When her rosy lips were not spewing forth absurdities, Jim felt she was so lovely he would forgive her anything.

Clair Trumbull was twenty-two years old, the daughter of a Professor of Classics at Columbia University. Her mother was a scholar also, and Jim sometimes felt Clair's determined anti-intellectual stance was a protest against her formidable parents. He had met her through the senior partner, Clay, who was the Trumbull family solicitor. She had auburn hair and sparkling grey eyes, a tiny waist and dainty, fascinating hands. And, although she looked nothing like

Virginia Leonard, something in her self-satisfied, girlish femininity had reminded him of Virginia the moment he laid eyes on her.

"Then, too," she said, breaking the silence, "so many of the women are simply fanatics. Did you know what Mrs. Adams said when word came about the *Titanic*?"

"No, Clair, what did Mrs. Adams say?"

"She actually said that the rescue boats should have contained an equal number of men and women! Now, surely, Jim, you see why that is wrong?" Receiving no answer, she said triumphantly, "It makes the gallantry of those poor men who died meaningless. It mocks their courage and degrades everyone."

Jim thought of what his Aunt Veronica had said to him the last time he'd seen her. "It's most discouraging that so many women are against their own best interests. I can understand men fearing the Suffrage Movement, but women? They can be their own worst enemies."

When he took Clair home to her parents' brownstone in the Upper West Side, Mrs. Trumbull engaged him in a lively conversation about the relative merits of traditional and classical music. Mrs. Trumbull was withered and sported a few grey hairs on her chin, but Jim found he enjoyed conversing with her far more than with her daughter. Clair sat on a horsehair sofa, sipping her tea and waiting for her mother to withdraw.

When she and Jim were finally alone, Clair pouted a little. She knew how charming she looked, with the late afternoon sun streaming through the windows and striking lights from her hair, and it seemed to Jim that her awareness of her beauty was an open invitation.

He came to sit beside her on the sofa. He was aroused and despairing at the same time. Where, in all the world, was there a woman who combined Clair's attractions with Frau Bruch's sexual appetites and the fine, fiery consciousness of, say, his little cousin Bernadette? He doubted that such a woman existed, and as Clair offered her soft lips to him with a kittenish tilt of her head, he thought he could feel himself being gently thrust behind iron bars. Clair would put him in a marital prison, where he would be free to make love to her in exchange for a lifetime of her platitudes. He shuddered, half in horror and half in desire, and then lost himself in the delight of her soft, eager kisses.

Later, he was to think how odd it was that Clair had marshalled the *Titanic* tragedy to her arguments. Upon returning to his lodgings, he found a letter waiting for him with a Philadelphia postmark. He opened it with some puzzlement, since he knew no one in Philadelphia.

The letter came from Mr. Joseph Morgan Hill, who wanted Mr. O'Donnell to know that his late son, Maynard, had directed in his will that Mr. O'Donnell be the recipient of all his personal writings and journals in the event of his death. "My son was living abroad," wrote Mr. Hill, "for the past five years. After his disappearance from Cambridge, my wife and I did not have news of him for some time, but gradually Maynard began to write to us, and in 1908 he visited us in Philadelphia and told us he was going to the Continent. You will be gratified to know that Maynard looked well and seemed extremely happy when last we saw him. He married a Frenchwoman in 1910, of whose whereabouts we have no knowledge. Last month, in April, he embarked from Cherbourg on a journey home."

Maynard Hill, who had confessed that he felt himself a ghost, sitting on the verandah up in Newburgh —Maynard Hill, the golden boy and consummate musician who had befriended Jim at Harvard—was dead at the age of twenty-eight.

Maynard Hill, of all people, had gone down with the *Titanic*.

On May 5, 1912, the *World* declared:
Woman Suffrage marched yesterday in the most significant demonstration ever attempted by it in this country.
The *Press* observed:
The march stirred the minds of the beholders as no other pageant seen in the city streets has done.
The *New York Times* warned:
The situation is dangerous. We often hear the remark nowadays that women will get the vote if they try hard enough and persistently; and it is true they will get it, and play havoc with it for themselves and society, if the men are not firm and wise enough and—it may as well be said— masculine enough to prevent them.

"It's about time to give them the vote," said Inspector McCluskey of the police. "I wish to God they would. I'd be with them."

Fifteen thousand marchers had walked from Washington Square to Carnegie Hall. Five hundred thousand spectators cheered them on their way. It was the greatest demonstration by women in this country's history. No one could ever call them a small band of fanatics again, and no one could slyly insinuate that the Suffrage Movement was the pet project of women in Society. Society had turned out, all right—even Mrs. O. H. P. Belmont, whose daughter Consuelo was married to the Duke of Marlborough, had marched this year—but the parade contained thousands of shop girls, factory workers, and ordinary housewives. It had proved, said Mrs. Blatch, "the solidarity of womanhood."

Margaret read the accounts of the march with distaste. Mrs. Belmont and the other upper-class women who participated slipped many notches in Margaret O'Donnell's esteem. Bridget, however, thought of her sister, and smiled. Good for Vera.

Veronica and Bernadette returned, tired but triumphant, to their house on Thirty-eighth Street. Robert was not at home, which was just as well.

"And now do you feel you are a part of history?" Veronica asked her daughter.

"Yes," said Bernadette, "I do." That night she wrote the longest entry ever in her journal.

Des Malloy had retreated to his Jersey City house of pleasure, where the women were not concerned with suffrage. They did what women were intended to do, and were paid very well for their efforts. Malloy often compared the working conditions in his brothel to those in the wretched factories and sweatshops, and wondered why more women didn't choose to become prostitutes. If a girl was good-looking, and willing, she could earn enough in five years in a place like his to comfortably retire.

"Tell me, Lilli," he asked, clapping a hand on the bare thigh of the girl who shared his bed. "What in the name of God do those women want?"

"They just want to rile the men," answered Lili in her syrupy drawl. She turned over and placed a hand on her employer's chest. It amused her to compare their skin colors, for Lilli was a light-skinned black girl from Louisiana, and scarcely darker than Malloy. "Why does it trouble you, sweetheart?"

Malloy laughed at such naivete. He drew Lilli up until she was lying over him, toe to toe. Then he flipped her over and performed the act of love in record time. His technique as a lover was rather like the technique he had displayed as a boxer—fast and hard.

"I'll tell you why it troubles me, darlin'," he said some moments later. "The first thing the bloody women will do if they get the vote is close down places like this. Then they'll be closin' the saloons, and soon they'll outlaw pleasure of every kind."

"Oh, Lord," said Lilli, "I never realized!" She toyed with his dark hair thoughtfully, her brow furrowed. The thought of a world in which there would be no pleasure was very grim, indeed.

Desmond waited until it was decently possible to leave Lilli, for he liked to be polite to women. Then he bathed and dressed and went downstairs, where he joined a Tammany chum for a drink. The two of them speculated on the character and flexibility of Woodrow Wilson, who was almost sure to be the next president, while the gramophone played *Oh, You Beautiful Doll*.

Whenever Malloy heard the song, he thought of Delia O'Donnell. Sometimes he thought she was almost in his grasp, but always she proved slippery, elusive. His floral campaign, when she had been on tour in '09, had provoked her interest, but then she had gone to Europe and remained there for an unforgivably long time. It had only been in the past six months that he had begun, slowly and with discretion, to make her acquaintance.

Although Delia was still the most beautiful woman he had ever seen, she was no longer a girl, and certainly not innocent. He amused her, which was more than the society lads seemed capable of doing, and their easy friendship, he hoped, would lead inexorably to bed. Some things were worth waiting for, and Delia, he believed, would be the sweet culmination of a lifetime dedicated to the twin gods of power and pleasure. Malloy even thought, after his third whiskey, that it would be pleasant to marry her.

Delia dreamed that she was drowning, and woke gasping and crying out for her mother. She lit the lamps and wrapped herself in a costly maribou-trimmed robe, and went to the kitchen to make herself a cup of tea. She was not aware, as she ladled sugar into the cup, that she was doing exactly what her mother would have done in the same situation.

The dream reminded her, horribly, of those she had had as a young girl. As a child, she had imagined herself suffocating in the hold of a ship, in steerage. Now she dreamed she dwelt in a glass house, high on a hill above a blue sea. At one moment all was peaceful and serene, and then suddenly the sky darkened and huge waves formed. She sat watching, paralyzed with horror, as the waves reared up, reaching the window and hurling themselves on her with vengeful fury. At the last moment, the glass broke and she was sucked down, down into the boiling sea, choking and unable to scream for help.

Delia knew she would not sleep again that night, so she carried her tea to the sitting room and read a new script. It was a clever piece of froth about a young girl of simple origins who accepted a job as governess in a great and monied family in England. The young girl managed to solve the problems of everyone, from the Dowager Duchess to the rustic, good-hearted gardener, and ended by marrying the son of the house and becoming a titled lady.

Delia threw it on the floor, sighing. She sighed not because she disapproved of the play, but because the heroine was eighteen, and she was now twenty-nine. Her mirror told her that she was more beautiful than ever, but she disliked approaching the age of thirty. She felt restless and anxious, despite her success, and wondered if she should get married.

She never lacked for suitors, but each of the men

who swore undying love for her was flawed. One was handsome and rich, but dull. Another was rich and amusing, but ugly. Yet another filled all her requirements, but was married and did not believe in divorce. Unfortunately, she had lately begun to enjoy the company of Desmond Malloy, who was a thoroughgoing scoundrel. He made her laugh, with his colorful phrases and frankly corrupt way of life. She admired the way he thumbed his nose at the world and feared nobody; she also marvelled at the extent of his knowledge. She sometimes thought there was nothing in the world he didn't know something about, and this air of knowledge gave him a Satan-like power she found exciting.

Poor Malloy, she thought. He didn't know he was the last man on earth she would allow in her bed. He was far too much like the older men in her family—an evil version of her father or grandfather or Uncle Patrick—for her to ever feel desire for him. But, so long as he thought he might become her lover, he would remain her friend, and Delia didn't want to lose his friendship, both because he amused her and she thought, rightly, that he would make a very dangerous enemy.

When the sun had fully risen, she went to dress for the day. The horror of the drowning dream had receded, but it hovered at the borders of her mind like a dark bird just out of sight. She decided to accept the role in *Daisy's Triumph*, and also to ask her personal physician for some laudanum—she thought it would help her to sleep without dreaming.

That night, at Delmonico's, she saw Malloy across

the room with a party of his male cronies. Her escort was boring, so she sent a note asking Mr. Malloy to join them. Gleefully, she watched the look of incredulity on her companion's face as Malloy approached them.

"You can't expect me to share a table with *him*," he murmured.

"Whyever not, John? He is an excellent friend of mine. Do order another bottle of champagne."

"Good evenin'," said Malloy, his face wreathed in smiles. "As a rule I don't enjoy surprises, but this one is grand."

"Mr. Malloy," said Delia, suppressing laughter, "this is Mr. Middleton. Won't you sit with us?"

Malloy thrust out his dark hand, his diamond rings flashing in the candlelight. Middleton took it with supreme reluctance, his lips thinning visibly. Delia was glad Malloy was wearing the supremely vulgar, harp-shaped pin in his cravat, for it only deepened her escort's disapproval.

"Are you interested in the horses, Mr. Middleton? If ye like, I've just had a fine tip." Malloy's dark eyes sparkled with jovial good-humor.

"I think not," said Middleton, spacing the words so that the rebuff was unmistakable.

Malloy's eyes continued to sparkle, but with malice rather than joviality. "Suit yerself," he said mildly, then turned to Delia. "I've been thinkin' of backin' a play, Miss O'Donnell. It's called *Daisy's Triumph*."

Delia laughed. "I'm rather sure I'm going to *be* Daisy," she said. "What a splendid coincidence."

"Indeed." He drooped one eyelid drolly. Middleton gave a snort of disgust, and the waiter brought more champagne.

"To Daisy!" cried Delia and Des Malloy.

Middleton drew himself up. "We really must be leaving," he said. He stood waiting for Delia to rise from the table, but she stayed where she was.

"Oh, dear, John, have you a headache?" she asked solicitously. "You must go straight to bed. I shouldn't dream of prolonging your discomfort."

Middleton turned very red. "I will see you home," he said.

"That won't be necessary. Mr. Malloy and I shall be talking business for some time, I fear."

Middleton stalked off, muttering, and Delia sputtered with laughter. Malloy called good-night to the man who had snubbed him, and then said: "Ah, ye're a wicked thing, aren't ye? Thoroughly heartless. The poor, thick boyo is havin' apoplexy."

Delia drank more champagne than she usually allowed herself. Malloy's company cheered her, and the prospect of a new play, backed by her amusing, Satanic friend, seemed a cause for celebration.

"I had to get your rascally cousin out of a scrape," said Malloy casually. "Young Terence should know not to bet more than he has in his pockets."

"Terry isn't so young any more," said Delia. "He's going to be twenty-six this month. He'll never amount to anything. All he ever does is make trouble." She felt suddenly saddened. "We're a troublesome lot, we O'Donnells," she said. "Except for Jim, and my little cousin Bernadette, we thrive on trouble."

Her tongue had been loosened by the champagne, but she thought what she said was true. A sudden image of Kieran, as she had seen him in San Francisco, filled her mind and saddened her further. She was the only one, of all the cousins, who had not seen Kieran in Newburgh last Christmas. Sometimes she thought she would never see him again.

"I had another cousin," she told Malloy. "Many years ago, he said he knew you."

"Why, yes—Kieran." He spoke the name softly. "A good-looking, fiery lad. Your double, in the male form."

"I don't know where he's gone," said Delia.

"Why do you want to know?" Malloy's eyes were suddenly alert. He leaned forward and poured some more champagne into her glass.

"I liked him best. We were very close, as children."

"And would you like to see him?"

Delia nodded. She thought of the note. *Forgive, and forget.*

"I'll see to it, then, when he comes to New York."

Delia stared at him. Earlier, she had thought there was nothing he didn't know, and now it seemed she had been right. "You know where he is?"

"Yer cousin's over on the Other Side," said Malloy, "but he'll be back."

"The Other Side?"

"Ireland."

"And what is he doing there?"

"Ah," said Malloy, in the manner Kieran himself had perfected, "this and that. Nothin' much to speak of."

* * *

In the autumn, as she was pinching dead leaves from the asters in her garden, Bridget grew dizzy and faint. She told herself it was from stooping for so long, but when she got to her feet there was a great roaring in her ears.

She did not tell Michael, not wishing to worry him, but when it happened again a few days later, Peg was with her and called the doctor. Michael came home to find his wife in bed. The doctor had ordered complete bed rest for at least a week. He had listened to Bridget's heart, and did not like what he heard.

Michael wanted to summon Delia, but Bridget wouldn't let him. "I'll be fine, Mike," she said. "It wouldn't do to bring poor Delia up here now. She's just starting a new play."

Michael looked at his wife as she lay against the pillows, her hair streaming untidily about her. Even sick she seemed robust and vital. The frailty of her heart disturbed him far less than the terrifying frailty of her mind. He could not believe that anything too serious could be wrong with his darling Bridget.

He sat by her bedside and read her the newspaper accounts of Mr. Wilson's campaign for the presidency. Nothing would happen to Bridget, because he would not allow it.

13

"Beware four things in life—
The bite of a mad dog,
The kick of a horse,
The horns of a bull,
And, last but not least—the smile of an English-
man!"

The man who sang these lyrics, in an ancient bitter, mirthless laugh. He had lost two of his sons in the sectarian rioting in Belfast in 1912 and now, a year later, he was a staunch supporter of the Dungannon Clubs.

"Ah, if I were forty years younger," he said to Kieran, "I'd go to Dublin and make me presence felt."

"You're needed here in Belfast, Mr. Sweeney. You can be of great help."

"How's that, then?"

"Many men of your generation, and younger, resent the Dungannon. You can set them right. Sinn Fein's all very well, but action's what's needed. Men like Clarke and MacSwiney support us. Can you ask for better?"

"I'm your man," said Mr. Sweeney. He had never learned to read, but he had been raised in the bardic tradition, and within a half-hour he could repeat, quite stirringly, the speech which Kieran had written. It was intended to convince recalcitrant members of the IRB that the more radical Dungannons could serve the best interests of northern and southern Irishmen. The speech was framed on the words of the Quaker, Bulmer Hobson, and the young Belfast businessman, Denis McCullough, who had founded the organization.

"God bless, O'Rourke," said old Mr. Sweeney when Kieran took his leave.

Kieran left the backroom and trudged to his temporary lodgings, weary and bone tired. He lay on the narrow bed and contemplated the cracked ceiling. In four days he would be back in Dublin, and in a month God knew where. He went where he was sent, and generally this pattern of happenstance living was pleasing to him, but tonight he suffered from a melancholy conviction that he would never arrive at the end of his interminable travels. Like the Flying Dutchman, he was condemned to move eternally, without rest.

Such thoughts would never have come to torment him if he had not been daft enough to try to find the girl, Maureen Rafferty. Before reporting to Clarke, in Dublin, he had journeyed up to Mayo to the little village where he had stayed in the autumn of 1910. He was driven there as if by demons, and went without volition or thought. He had believed if he could see her face once more, something would be resolved for him forever.

The village had not changed, and sly Rafferty still sold *poteen* in the hovel by the road-side, but when Kieran inquired for the girl, he was told she'd gone.

"Maureen's gone to America," said young Brendan. "She left this past year."

Kieran visited the site of the cottage where he had lived, and found the place more run-down than ever. The door was completely severed from its hinges, and the North Atlantic wind blew sadly through the room where he had lain and been visited by images of Maureen Rafferty. The fire-place where she had knelt and plied her poker had fallen in upon itself in a heap of rubble. The place was a ruin.

Kieran knew that he could ask Rafferty the name of the family who employed Maureen, but he decided not to. The fact that she had gone to America seemed an omen to him; if he had been intended to see her again, their paths would have crossed. The following day, he presented himself at Clarke's modest tobacconist's shop off Sackville Street in Dublin, and resumed the life he felt he had been born to lead.

Now, in grey Belfast, he groped about on the floor

for the bottle of whiskey he'd left there. He found it, and drank from the bottle, wishing to sleep, but an odd thing happened—the more he drank, the more old voices from the past buzzed in his brain and deprived him of oblivion.

He heard his Uncle Patrick say: "You'll not take an innocent woman down with you, Kieran." Patrick's voice was joined by Delia's, accusing him of breaking his word to her. She was drowned in the quiet, urgent tones of Patrick, begging him to be careful, and supplanted by the voice of Grady, in the backroom in Chicago, telling him of the British soldier who had crippled his arm for life.

Old Mr. Sweeney joined in, singing *the smile of an Englishman,* and was replaced by Desmond Malloy. "Consider the life of a revolutionary," said Malloy. "No joy there, boyo."

Kieran thrashed about, willing the infernal voices to be gone, and was visited by the most disturbing voice of all.

"*What is it troubles you?*" asked Maureen Rafferty.

There were so many answers to her gentle question that he fell asleep, pondering them.

Four days later, in Dublin, something happened which provided an unexpected answer. Because Clarke's shop was always watched over by political detectives, Kieran reported to the IRB in Ballybough, outside Dublin. Sean MacDiarmada received him there, still limping from the polio he had contracted the year before, and warned him to stay away from Sackville Street. Smiling, as usual, MacDiarmada told Kieran that many British soldiers were patronizing the tobacconist's shop. This was, he explained, due to the fact that the soldiers, together with the Dublin prostitutes, were confined to one side of the street. They were free to walk down the side of Sackville allowed to them, so long as they did not penetrate fashionable Grafton Street. The result was that Clarke's shop swarmed with the enemy, who had to purchase their tobacco somewhere. Both men laughed over this unlikely turn of events, and returned to Dublin separately.

At twilight, as Kieran was crossing the Liffey near Trinity College, he heard someone call his name. "Kieran!" cried the voice. "Here—*Kieran!*" He reacted involuntarily, turning at the sound of his name, only to see a child of twelve answer the summons. The boy ran over the lumpy bridge to his sister, who cuffed him.

Kieran remained where he was, staring after them, feeling that the child had stolen his true name. With all the Kierans in the world, he had not heard his own name spoken for over a year. He was Patrick O'Rourke, or Gerry Ryan, or—on his travelling papers —Rory Quinn. He no longer had a name of his own.

Others could go home to their wives, or families, and hear their true names spoken and know they existed, but for Kieran there was no such contact with the real world. He was whoever they said he was. His identity was known only to the Brotherhood. This, he thought, was as it should be, but as he crossed the bridge over the Liffey he could not help but feel that he had become a ghost.

* * *

In the summer of 1913, Robert Tyrone became convinced that his wife had a lover. He had not slept with her in over a decade, but long ago she had been the wife of his heart, and he knew. A man knew such things.

Veronica was now forty-four, a delicate age for a woman. Instead of fading gracefully into a muted copy of her earlier self, Veronica grew younger daily. Robert thought she seemed more desirable now than she had been as a very young woman, and was infuriated by this unnatural turn of events.

So long as he could attribute her glowing appearance to the unholy zeal which prompted her to champion Women's Suffrage and Child Labor Laws, he was easy in his mind. He had long ago accepted that Veronica was neurotic. Elizabeth Mallory, his late mistress, attributed Veronica's "Do-Good" nature to guilt. Veronica, according to Elizabeth, suffered from the everpresent knowledge that she had more than she deserved. Robert's wife ought by rights to have married an Irish contractor and had eight children, but luck and fate had made her rich and idle instead. Robert had never agreed with this analysis of his wife's character, and had despised Elizabeth, just a little, for describing her so.

On an evening in August, he entered the house on Thirty-eighth Street to find his wife and daughter at the piano, laughing as they attempted to play *Down By The Old Mill Stream*. With their slender figures and downcast heads of pale, red-gold hair, they seemed to be sisters. Even their profiles seemed identical to him—strong, well-cut, full of character, and yet lovely in a womanly way they seemed bound to deny.

He stood speechless, watching them as they leaned against one another in helpless laughter. Veronica's color was high; her pretty smile flashed in a way it had not for him in many years. Bernadette seized her mother's hands and returned them to the keys sternly. They played on for a moment, but gradually they became aware of his presence and looked up, chastened. All the merriment drained out of them, and they were his dutiful wife and daughter, silenced because he had entered the room.

Robert cleared his throat. "Don't stop on my account," he said. But Veronica and Bernadette had become self-conscious. They rose from the piano like guilty children caught in some mischief, and for the first time in his life, Robert saw himself as the bleak and chilly dampener of high spirits he had always been.

By all reckoning, it was a small moment of revelation, but it changed the lives of Robert and Veronica Tyrone dramatically. Robert did not go out that evening, but remained with his wife and daughter in the sitting room. Bernadette was reading a play by Ibsen, of whom Robert blessedly knew nothing, while Veronica wrote letters. From behind his newspaper, Robert watched them covertly. Bernadette was to enter Barnard College in the autumn, and no one could now mistake her for a child. Occasionally, though, she pushed a strand of her hair back impatiently, as she had done as a little girl, and Robert wondered how the years could have passed so swiftly. Veronica, head bent over her desk, continued to seem mysteriously desirable to him.

He wondered if she had chosen a man sympathetic to her causes to share her bed, and felt an unreasoning black jealousy sweep over him. Even worse—what if she had taken up with some muscular, working-class fellow? He imagined brawny Italian stonemasons, hulking Irish longshoremen. He saw them take slender, lissome Veronica Tyrone into their sweaty arms and tumble her on a squalid bed in a tenement. His wife.

It was very quiet in the room; all he could hear was the scrape of pen on paper, the pages of Bernadette's book rustling as she turned them, the ticking of the clock. Robert rattled his paper.

"I see that the Georgia State Senate had voted down the Child Labor Bill," he said in an unnaturally loud voice.

Veronica looked up, as startled as a doe in the lamp light. "Yes," she said.

"Seems a pity," said Robert. "Massachusetts passed it two months ago."

Veronica laid down her pen. "I didn't know you followed such matters, Robert."

"I like to keep well-informed," said Robert. His tone was mild enough, but inwardly he was shaking with indignation and excitement. He would show her he was not the monster she made him out to be. "No sane man can approve of miserable working conditions for children," he said.

"Bravo, Papa!" said Bernadette.

He looked to see if she were mocking him, but her eyes, though speculative, were affectionate. Veronica's gaze was unreadable.

A little later, Bernadette went to her room. Veronica wrote for a bit longer, and then rose. She bade him a pleasant good-night and went upstairs. Robert poured himself a glass of sherry and sipped it slowly. Ten minutes later, he followed his wife upstairs.

When he appeared at the connecting door of their dressing room, Veronica was standing in her nightdress, her hair flowing down her back. She was holding a photograph in her hand and looking down at it lovingly. She jumped with alarm on seeing him, and put the photograph, face down, on her dressing table.

"Whose image were you looking at so intently?" Robert asked, and although he had meant the words to emerge casually, his voice was unexpectedly rough, almost brutal.

Veronica looked up at him in confusion.

"I do not wish to know his name or see his face," said Robert. "What you do is your business, but this is my house. I will not have you mooning like a schoolgirl over another man in *my house*." He was breathing rapidly, relishing the look of astonishment in her wide eyes; her lips had parted as if to deny what he had said, and he wanted to kiss them.

"Robert, what are you saying? I don't understand." Veronica picked the photograph up and held it out to him. "I have been so worried about her," she said. "She hasn't been really well for almost a year."

The face in the photograph was that of Bridget Flynn, her sister. It had been taken several summers ago, up in Newburgh. Bridget and Veronica stood near the rose bush, arms around each other, laughing. Robert examined the photograph, hands trembling with shame.

"Did you think I had a secret lover?" asked Veronica. "How could you—who imagine me so cold—have such strange thoughts?" Her astonishment had turned to anger. She rose and confronted him, her color high. "Sadly enough for me, Robert, the only lover I have ever had has been you. I have learned to live with loneliness, accept it as my lot. If I had met a man I could love I would unquestioningly have become his mistress, but it never happened. I have been all too faithful to you, Robert, and if you don't believe me—" She cast about for a sufficiently strong conclusion, but her anger had passed. "I don't care," she said. She sat down on her bed abruptly, as a child would do.

Robert found himself walking toward her. It was only a distance of six feet, but he thought it the longest distance he had ever travelled. He sat beside her and drew her into his arms, gently smoothing her hair. Her body was stiff and resisted him at first, but as he stroked her she fell against him a little, relenting. Her head lay helplessly against his chest, and he could feel her trembling.

"Our daughter is grown," he murmured. "Can't we try to be good to each other? We have only each other, now. I am lonely, too, Veronica."

He raised her chin and saw tears filming her eyes. When he kissed her, they spilled over and he tasted salt on her lips. Slowly, her arms came around him. Her hands clasped his back; timidly, they touched his hair. When he bore her back on the bed she trembled like a virgin, and he was as gentle and careful with her as he had been on their wedding night.

He was not a passionate man, but his mistress had taught him not to make love furtively, like a thief in the night, and he loved his wife tenderly and well. In the old days, he would have crept back to his own room in the dark, but now he remained beside Veronica, happy and fulfilled. She slept with her head on his shoulder, and Robert thought of new beginnings.

Veronica was strong-willed, troublesome, defiant— but she was his wife, and he loved her still. At the age of forty-six, Robert Tyrone was at last ready to admit that the woman he had married was his equal.

When Margaret O'Donnell's father died, she inherited a great deal of Fitzhugh money. She was, as Patrick knew, financially independent. Sitting in the morning room at the house on Ridge Street, Margaret worked out her plan of action. That evening, she presented it to Patrick at dinner.

"I should like to go to New York for the fall season," she told him over the soup. She looked him straight in the face, which should have alerted him, since Margaret avoided her husband's countenance when he ate soup. Patrick tended to click his spoon against the bowl in a manner she found trying. "I know it is a particularly busy time of year for you," she continued, "so I should not expect you to accompany me."

"Well, Margaret, you're free to take a little jaunt, aren't you? It will be pleasant for you to see the boys, and you can go to the theatre and opera." Patrick spoke self-consciously, sensing that his wife had a master plan.

"Someone must look after their futures. I am particularly anxious to see that Terence meets the right sort of people."

"Terry's a big lad, my dear. He's bound to have sorted it out for himself by now."

"Then," said Margaret, "he will have to un-sort it. You have never understood that Terry needs guidance and encouragement. His instincts are fine, but he is high-spirited and likely to overlook important opportunities."

Patrick laughed softly, thinking of Terry's fine instincts. He was afraid that Margaret would be greatly disillusioned if she could know even a tenth of what her younger son was up to, and began to see her proposed trip to New York as a disaster.

"Jim's right enough," he said to change the subject.

"James lacks backbone. He is a good, steady man without the slightest sense of ambition. It is high time he married."

Peg came in to clear away the soup dishes and Margaret did not speak again until the lamb and potatoes made their appearance. "I shall take rooms at the Waldorf, and I shall make inquiries about a suitable house in New York. I see no reason why we should not have two establishments, Patrick."

By the end of the meal, he understood her master plan completely. With her new fortune, Margaret would settle herself in New York for a part of each year. There, she would storm society—in a sedate, Fitzhugh manner, of course—and provide important contacts for Terry and a socially acceptable wife for Jim. She would be in control at last. He thought it a highly unlikely scenario, but Margaret was firm and sober. Her drinking, never acknowledged between them, had tapered off when she inherited her father's money and Patrick understood that she was in training, like an athlete, for the major event of her life. She had waited nearly fifty years for this moment.

He studied her curiously. It never seemed to occur to her that she was insulting him greatly. By announcing her intentions as a *fait accompli*, she was repudiating him as a husband—even as the token husband he had become. This amused him, because it was so typical of her arrogance. For two years now he had been carrying on a most satisfying affair with Gertrude Beach, a Newburgh widow, and Margaret's contempt for him no longer rankled.

"Why do you not stay with Veronica?" he asked over coffee. "It would be nicer than staying in a hotel."

Instantly, he regretted the words. Why should his sister be forced to tolerate Margaret's slights and whims? He needn't have worried, though, for Margaret had no intentions of going anywhere near her sister-in-law.

"It pains me to say it, Patrick, but Veronica is not someone I wish to know socially. Robert Tyrone is a fine man, but your sister has placed herself beyond the pale." For the next ten minutes she lectured him on the vulgarity of women who involved themselves in politics.

"Is Mrs. Belmont vulgar, then?" he asked.

"Mrs. Belmont will surely come to her senses," said Margaret. "Any sympathy gained for the Suffrage Movement was lost when that madwoman misbehaved so badly on Derby Day last June."

Patrick remembered. Emily Davison, an English suffragette, had "misbehaved" by throwing herself beneath the king's horse. It had been her final protest, since she died of her injuries a few days later. For Margaret, an insult to the king was the ultimate crime.

"Veronica isn't about to throw herself beneath a horse," he observed drily. "My sister has convictions, but she is quite sensible."

"I must disagree."

"And now, if you'll excuse me, I am going to visit my other sister. In case you'd forgotten, she may be dying."

"I hope you find her in good health."

Patrick left the house. Drunk or sober, the woman made no sense. She was too utterly absorbed in herself and her unrealistic dreams to care for anything which did not touch upon them. Right now she was no doubt picturing a rosy future in which Jim was married to an Astor and Terry, that creature of fine instincts, had just won a seat in the U. S. Senate.

Terry was leaving the theatre, after a most enjoyable evening, when a rough-looking young man jostled him rudely, calling him by name.

"Damn it, watch where you go," said Terry haughtily. There was something vaguely familiar about the chap's face, but his grimy fingernails and working

man's clothing did not belong to anyone of Terry's
acquaintance.

"No," said the ruffian. "*You* watch where *you* go,
hear? I've come to bring you a message."

"What message can you possibly have for me?"

"This," said the man, and hit Terry full across the
face with the back of his hand. It was a soft blow,
meant to insult rather than injure, but Terry reeled
back. The streams of people leaving the theater quickly drew away, not wishing to become involved. Terry
regarded his assailant with loathing and some fear. A
gentleman did not engage in fist fights on the streets—
at least not with complete strangers who looked muscular and dangerous—but he could not allow this
thug to get away with hitting him.

He assumed the approved Harvard boxing stance,
advancing warily. "Who the devil are you?" he
snarled. He knew he made an odd picture, attired in
his evening clothes, preparing to box with a demented
stranger, but what could he do? He knew of no proto-
col for such a situation.

"Come on," said the man. "Hit me back."

Terry tried a quick jab, but it glanced lightly off
the man's shoulder. The man laughed and came toward
Terry with murder in his eyes. "Here's the second part
of my message," he said, and drove his fist into Terry's
stomach with a sickening thud. Terry sank to his knees,
gasping with pain. He made a feeble attempt to grasp
his tormentor's ankles and bring him down, but the
man was suddenly straddling him, forcing him to the
pavement. Strong fingers fastened on his neck and
ground his face into the cement.

"You stay away from my sister. If you ever come near her again, I'll kill you."

Terry felt blood in his mouth and grunted to keep from crying out. The blow to his stomach, the pain of it, was nothing compared to the humiliation of being forced to rub his face in the filth of the streets. The man kept going on about his sister, and Terry felt sure he was a lunatic.

As suddenly as it had started, the incident ended. Terry felt the fingers loosen, and heard the footsteps echo in the street as the man ran away. Moments later, he heard a voice which reminded him of his father's.

"Are you alright, sir? Easy, there, I'll help you up."

He found himself confronting an Irish policeman. He wanted to shake the man off, but he could not stand straight and had to accept his arm.

The constable was asking him questions, but Terry had recalled who it was the thug had resembled. Her name was Betty; she was a shop girl he had fancied briefly. He'd met her while purchasing a dozen handkerchiefs, and managed to seduce her three days later.

"It was a private dispute," he told the policeman.

In the cab going home, he pieced it all together. At the beginning of the summer, a tearful Betty had confessed she was pregnant. Terry was far too wise to tumble for such a timeworn scheme. Betty had not been a virgin. The child might belong to anyone. He refused to see her again, and returned her letters.

Stay away from my sister! No fear. She was the last person he wanted to see. He hadn't even thought of her from that day to this. Shaking his head at the unfairness of a world in which Betty's ape of a brother would dare to touch him, he paid the cab and limped up the stairs to his rooms on Barrow Street.

It was a very comfortable place, and Terry lived in it rent-free because it belonged to a friend of Des Malloy's. He looked at himself in the mirror and cursed. His opera cloak was soiled and ripped, and his face looked like a piece of raw beefsteak. The skin was scraped away around his cheeks, and his nose was swollen and bruised. He tried to bathe it, wincing, and pondered schemes of revenge.

He could ask Malloy to send someone to break the thug's legs. This solution pleased him, but a nagging voice told him it wouldn't work. Malloy might laugh at him. Betty's brother had meted out primitive justice, and that was a concept Malloy understood all too well.

He slumped on the bed, feeling humiliated and extremely sorry for himself. It would be days before he looked presentable. He was about to invent a plausible excuse for his appearance, when he noticed the day's post lying on the mat. A pale blue envelope addressed in his mother's hand interested him, but only because he thought it might contain a check.

He had fabricated employment of a very noble nature to appease his mother. He had written glowingly to her of his job as aide to an aristocratic old Judge named Hammond. Justice Hammond—who did not, in fact, exist—was retired and needed someone to help him in the writing of his memoirs. The work was fascinating and would lead to splendid opportunities, but Terry was woefully underpaid. "I am sure you will agree it is better for me to struggle along in such a worthy position than to earn more at a vulgar one," he'd concluded.

He hoped she'd risen to the bait. Grinning, despite his pain, Terry lifted the letter from the mat and slit it open. He was dismayed that it contained no money, but even more dismayed when he read the contents of the letter. Incredulous, he read it again, hoping there had been a mistake, but it was all there, in black and white. Or, he thought crazily, like his own face— black and blue. Margaret was descending on New York to meet Judge Hammond and help him to make the "proper social contacts." She would arrive tomorrow.

Terry slumped forward and uttered an oath more appropriate to his father. *"Oh, Jesus, Mary and Joseph,"* he groaned. "The old *fool!"*

3 October, 1913
It is feared there will be a civil war in Ireland over the issue of Home Rule. The Protestant Loyalists in the North claim they will fight rather than accept it, and poor Mr. Asquith is having a very rough time of it. Uncle Patrick always said Ireland could never be free because the bloody Orangemen would prevent it, even if England agreed to Home Rule, which it would do when hell froze over. I raised this question with my History Professor today, and she said it was an ancient and insoluble problem. "The Irish are a very contentious *people, Miss O'Donnell," she said. Then she blushed and added, "And a coura-*

geous and poetic people." I am going to write a theme-paper for her entitled: How a Nation's History May Serve to Make its Citizens Contentious.

Teddy Maitland, a young man I met at Alice Mary's coming-out last spring, has written to ask if I will attend a dance with him when Columbia and Yale play football in November! I rather think I will accept. Louise is in love with a friend of her brother's. She says I must learn to dance the tango.

14

America, divided on so many issues, was able to agree on one important fact in 1914. Everyone loved to dance the tango. The Bishop of Nashville had forbidden it, and certain killjoy elements continued to decry it, but nobody was listening.

Delia O'Donnell tangoed divinely, and with the assurance of one who knows exactly how to preserve the correct mixture of arrogance and sensuality. Terry tangoed quite well, and what he lacked in style he made up in enthusiasm. Bernadette, with the help of her friend Louise Wolfe, learned not to be embarrassed and, by the beginning of the year, discovered she quite enjoyed tangoing with Teddy Maitland. Even Jim was called upon to tango occasionally, and because he understood most music instinctively, he performed creditably.

The older generation of O'Donnells reacted to the craze as might have been expected. Margaret sided with the Bishop of Nashville, unaware of the fact that Patrick's mistress had taught him to tango in her bedroom one night. Bridget watched others tango wistfully. It was a dance she might have performed very well, but her doctor had forbidden it. Veronica came for a visit to Newburgh, bringing Robert with her. Robert could not bring himself to tango, but he smiled benevolently when his wife laughingly tangoed with Michael Flynn.

The beauty of the spring was so intense that year it encouraged wild behavior. A daring new fashion for men, the armless bathing suit, threatened to appear when the weather grew warmer.

Margaret, shuttling back and forth between Newburgh and New York, began to drink heavily again. She told herself the perfumed air had made her giddy, but the truth was she drank to forget a number of unpleasant things.

Her assault on society had met with not so much as a ripple. The friends of the Fitzhugh family living in the city were not nearly so distinguished as she had thought them to be, and received her courteously but without fanfare. Her plans for setting up an "establishment" in New York had to be abandoned when she found prices ten times higher than she'd remembered. She could afford to stay at the Waldorf as often as she liked, but to maintain a distinguished residence in a good neighborhood was far beyond her means.

But dwarfing all these concerns was the matter of her son, Terence. When she'd arrived in the fall of

1913, he had not been at the station to meet her. He sent a note saying he was travelling to Virginia for Judge Hammond and would not return for a week. The note had been delivered by a low man with dark skin and diamond rings on his fingers. He had told her, in his peasant brogue, that Terry had a fine career in politics ahead of him, but that Margaret must be realistic. In effect, he warned her that political circles in New York were not the proper sphere of dignified ladies. Margaret, mortified and repelled by the man, had nearly gone back to Newburgh that afternoon.

Soon after, Judge Hammond had died, and Terence was out of a job once more. Although he was continually badgering her for money, he already lived far beyond his means. Whenever Margaret tried to imagine where the money came from, she ended by pouring herself a large glass of whiskey. The whiskey enabled her to ignore the persistent voice which whispered that her handsome, charming son was a 'ne'er-do-well.'

James had involved himself with a young lady who displeased Margaret mightily. She was a serious, dark-browed girl of dubious ancestry who wanted to be an opera singer. Margaret was sure she was partly Italian. The thought of grandchildren who might have Italian blood sent her to the whiskey bottle too, so that the spring of 1914 passed for her in a haze of drunken anxiety.

Bernadette, too, felt drunk, but for different reasons. Teddy Maitland came nearly every weekend from New Haven, and she had begun to believe she was in love with him. The flaws she had seen in him fell away, one by one, until he was revealed to her as a perfect man. A certain lack of maturity became, instead, dashing and mysteriously male. His tendency to agree with everything she said, which had once seemed annoying, now seemed a proof that they were perfectly matched. His soft brown hair and myopic eyes represented the ultimate in masculine beauty.

Bernadette needed to believe she was in love with Teddy Maitland because she wanted, desperately, to have him make love to her. When Teddy kissed her the world spun dizzily, and parts of her body she'd never thought much of sprang to life with alarming urgency. Her body felt as if it were too large for her confining clothes, yet she was as slender as ever. When she walked down the street and felt men's eyes on her, she wondered if they would like to make love to her and then was ashamed and confused. She spent many sleepless nights in her room on Thirty-eighth Street, and longed for the weekends to come, for each time Teddy ventured down from New Haven, she hoped he would divest her of the virginity which had become so painful.

The trouble was Teddy himself. Always, after kissing her until they were both panting with lust, he would spring to his feet and pace about, muttering. Then he would apologize to Bernadette for "forgetting" himself. These encounters took place in the Maitland house on Fifth Avenue. The Maitlands were in Europe, and nothing prevented Teddy from taking Bernadette to his room and having his will with her but his conscience.

Bernadette finally saw she would have to be the

aggressor. If she waited for Teddy to end her torment, she might be an old woman before she tasted love. So, on an afternoon in April, while she lay on a *chaise*, panting and writhing while Teddy Maitland apologized for touching her breast, she seized his hands and pressed them to her.

"It's alright, Teddy," she gasped. "I want you to make love to me."

"You don't know what you're saying," Teddy gasped back. "I mustn't forget myself, Bernadette."

But she was determined. What was the use of believing in Free Love if she couldn't experience it? She imagined she was Delia—sensuous and awesomely beautiful. She pulled Teddy Maitland back to her and moved against him—duplicating Delia's movements in *Salome*. She didn't have to work at it very long, for Teddy was so astonished and aroused he actually forgot himself and took her, right there on the *chaise*.

It didn't last very long, and it hurt, but Bernadette sensed a vague echo of pleasure to come. When Teddy had stopped apologizing, they went to his bedroom and presently made love again.

"I'm going to like this very much, I think," mused Bernadette afterward, as they lay in each other's arms. Teddy looked shocked.

"Will you marry me?" he asked.

Bernadette closed her eyes. Marriage had never entered her mind. She wasn't even sure she believed in it as she once had. "Oh, Teddy," she whispered. "Let's not speak of marriage now. We have to finish our schooling."

He protested, but Bernadette detected a certain note of relief in his voice. Later, when he brought her home, she felt her blood singing with triumph. Veronica looked at her oddly, and she wondered if her mother could tell. Was it possible that mothers were endowed with mystical powers where the matter of their daughter's virginity was concerned?

Bernadette, who thought of her mother as her friend, at last had a secret she could not reveal to her. They were both women, now.

In the same April in which Bernadette explored the secrets of love, the Ulster Volunteers landed 35,000 rifles at Larne, County Antrim, and Kieran returned to America. The provisional government in Ulster had scored an enormous gain, and it seemed Home Rule had once more been defeated. Home Rule was of no concern to Kieran or the IRB—they wanted nothing less than total freedom.

While the British government turned a blind eye to the illegal activities of the Ulster Volunteers, it was likely that any gun-running on the part of the Nationalists would be punished by death. A feeling of reckless exhilaration prevailed among Kieran's comrades —surely, at last, the Rising was at hand.

Kieran reported to a man named Mangan and was sent to see a sympathizer up in Buffalo. The sympathizer's price for 10,000 rounds of ammunition was much inflated, and Kieran was instructed to return to New York and bide his time.

America felt alien to him now, and as April gave way to May, and the sun grew hot and dazzling, he felt almost as if he had ventured to the tropics. He was more at home in cool, green Ireland; here, in the land of his birth, he felt exiled. Streets and buildings once familiar to him were as exotic as the pyramids of Egypt might have been.

His old haunts were no longer available to him. Leary's was dangerous because of Malloy, and he could not chance seeing his family. He found himself standing, one day, outside the house of his Aunt Veronica. A tall young woman emerged, and it took some time for him to realize that she was his cousin, Bernadette. He turned away so she could not recognize him.

On Broadway, Delia was appearing in a play called *Daisy's Triumph.* Kieran studied the photograph of his cousin outside the theatre, and remembered the time they had all stood beneath the mistletoe and made wishes for the new year. He remembered them as they had been, without nostalgia, much as he might have remembered an incident from some other person's past.

He had no trouble finding female companionship, when he felt the need, but he never slept with the same woman twice, and never felt anything beyond the brief, mechanical spasm of sexual release. They called him Gerry, or Patrick, or Rory, and if they asked him about himself he invented whatever story sprang to mind. Sometimes he was a travelling journalist, sometimes a merchant seaman, and sometimes they didn't ask.

If he was lonely, he accepted it as his natural state. While other young men danced the tango and discussed the need for a Great White Hope to trounce the boxer Jack Johnson, Kieran bargained for guns and ammunition. It was not a pastime to be shared.

Toward the end of May, on a hot, fragrant day of utter perfection, Kieran met a man called Hogan near the boat house in Central Park. They sat quietly together on a bench and discussed a consignment of Mauser rifles, and parted soon after. Kieran walked west swiftly, toward Seventy-second Street, oblivious to the beauty of the day. He had just left the park when he saw, standing near the grey wall, a slender figure clothed in a plain cotton jacket and frock. She was turned away from him and he could not see her face, but something in her stance was familiar. Her proud carriage, the tilt of her head, her bright hair pinned up beneath a straw boater—all belonged to someone he both longed for and dreaded to see.

He stood, paralyzed, knowing he should walk away before it was too late. Moments passed during which the only sound he could hear was the accelerated beating of his heart, and then the figure seemed to sigh and shake itself, as if preparing to leave. Her head turned slightly and Kieran could see her profile, and it was as he had known.

She was staring wistfully out at the park, in the manner of a child who has been forbidden to play. The heat of the day had brought a faint color to her pale cheeks. She was still a delicate creature, but she no longer looked half-starved.

"Maureen!" He called her name. He could not prevent himself. The terrible joy he felt at the sight of her rendered him weak and helpless.

She turned to him, and started as if she were seeing a ghost. Her enormous eyes grew wider still and she seemed unable to speak.

"Do you remember me?" he asked.

"I do," she said. "I thought never to see you again, Mr. O'Rourke."

At the sound of her voice, something broke in him. The hard dam which walled his heart seemed to crumble and fall away, and he wanted only to walk in the sunlight with Maureen Rafferty, and listen to her voice, and keep her close to him.

"You are quite grown-up," said Kieran. "I shall have to call you Miss Rafferty now."

"No one has ever called me that but you."

"They should." He could not have enough of looking at her face, turned up to his in the golden light. Although there were no smudges on her face now, although the once matted hair was smoothly brushed and coiled, there was a wildness to her beauty which could never be subdued. "Will you walk with me, in the park?" he asked.

She caught her lower lip in her teeth and looked distressed. "I cannot," she said. "I must go back to the house where I'm employed. It was my half-day off, you see."

"Then I will take you back." He offered her his arm, and after a little hesitation, she took it. The touch of her small hand was more exciting to him than all the passionate acrobatics practiced by the women he had lain with.

Maureen told him the family she worked for was called Lifson. They were German Jews, and very kind

263

and good. Dr. Lifson was a surgeon, and his wife had two small daughters. Kieran was relieved to discover there were no hulking sons in the menage.

"And are you happy here?" he asked.

Maureen considered. "I am content," she said.

Kieran thought of how homesick she must have been in her first weeks in America, and of how she must miss the little village in Mayo. "I saw your da last autumn," he told her. "And your brother, Brendan."

The look in her eyes was so eager he racked his brain for things to say. "Brendan is very big now. Your da is well." He thought of the ruined cottage, the mournful wind. That place was home to Maureen, and she had resigned herself to never seeing it again.

"You were passin' through, then?" He remembered her indirect way of asking questions. They had arrived at the Lifson's house, a well-kept brownstone just off Central Park on Seventy-sixth Street.

"No," he said. "I went out of my way to go there. I wanted to see you."

"You left me a message," she said, her voice low and uncertain. "You said I was your true friend. And the five pounds, Mr. O'Rourke—you shouldn't have done it."

"Why not, Maureen? You had more need of it than I did. True friends don't stand on pride."

"But," she persisted, "you went away without sayin' good-bye."

"I had my reasons." He found it almost unbearable to stand conversing with her on the street, unable to touch her or speak his mind. In a moment she would vanish through the servants' entrance, and he would be deprived of her again. Tomorrow he would be on his way to Utica, and Maureen would be sweeping grates and making beds.

"I can read quite well now," she said proudly. "Mrs. Lifson has been teaching me. The writin' is harder, but she says I'm a good pupil."

A child of about eight suddenly threw open an upper window and called down. "Maureen, Maureen! Come see the picture I made for you!" She was pulled away from the window by her nanny, and Maureen smiled. "That was Clara, the youngest," she said. "They're lovely little lasses."

Kieran asked if he might see her on her next half-day, a week in the future, and Maureen agreed. She gave him a last questioning look, and ran down through the servants' entrance.

For the remainder of the day, Kieran could think of nothing but Maureen Rafferty. He was glad she dwelt with kind and generous people, glad that the children of the house were fond of her and made her a part of their family. She would be safe with the Lifsons, until the time when he could take her away.

That he must take her away and care for her himself seemed inevitable. He had denied himself the happiness of caring for her once, but the fact that he had encountered her in New York, when he least expected it, could only be attributed to the hand of Fate. His own destiny, the grimness of his daily life, was forgotten for a little while. That night he drank a great deal of whiskey to blunt the intolerably sweet pain she caused in him, and in the morning he boarded a train for Utica.

Within twenty-four hours, he saw the truth of things clearly. He had no right to twine his fate with hers; it had been madness to imagine it. He would write her a letter at the brownstone on Seventy-sixth Street, and explain that business would detain him elsewhere.

He wrote the letter, but did not post it. On the appointed day, he waited outside the Lifson house. Maureen came out, attired in the same respectable domestic servant's plain brown frock, and together they walked into the park like any other courting couple. Kieran rented a boat and took her rowing. Maureen trailed her hands in the water and confessed that she had never been in a boat, except for the one that had conveyed her to America. He bought her an ice-cream, and watched with delight as her little pink tongue dipped into the treat avidly. They sat on a grassy knoll and Maureen said that Ireland was more beautiful than America, but that it was nice to be in a place where the sun was always shinin', even in May.

On the way back, he pulled her behind a thick stand of chestnut trees and caught her in his arms. He kissed her then, and held her close, and her alarm receded and she put her arms around his neck and gave him her sweet lips. "I love you, Maureen," he said. "I love you so."

She hid her face against his chest and asked a question. "What is your Christian name?" she whispered. "I never knew it, O'Rourke."

"Kieran."

"Well then," she said, looking him in the face with

determination, "I love you, Kieran. I've always been lovin' you, right from the first."

Delia allowed Des Malloy to come to her dressing room after a performance of *Daisy's Triumph* one night in late June. She had not seen him for several weeks, and missed him, after her fashion. She was also annoyed by the tremendous popularity of *The Perils of Pauline* and wondered if her future might lie in the movies instead of on the stage. The world was moving quickly in new directions, and Delia did not want to be left behind.

"Do give yourself champagne," she called out. She stood behind a folding screen, slipping out of her Daisy costume and into a Japanese kimono embroidered with pearls. The desire in Malloy's eyes fed the ever-hungry need for admiration which burned in Delia's breast, but tonight he seemed subdued and preoccupied.

His black eyes flicked over her splendid form, when she emerged, without their customary reverence. Only the lust was there, and it made her uneasy. Delia sat opposite him, chastely smoothing the kimono over the arc of her lovely thigh. "What is it, Malloy? Did your horse lose?"

"Have you read the newspapers today?"

"I have. *The Perils of Pauline* is drawing millions. Mrs. Belmont is planning to convert Marble House into a replica of the Imperial Palace at Peking next month. Did I miss something?"

He ignored her question. He lounged in his chair, holding his champagne glass idly in two fingers, and regarded her with the unwavering gaze of a horse trader. "You're a marvelous creature," he said. "Nothing touches you."

"Unless I wish it to."

"Tell me, beauty. Do you still want to see your cousin?"

Nothing could have surprised her more. She remembered the promise Malloy had made her at Delmonico's. "I wouldn't mind," she said. Idly, she toyed with a strand of her hair; it wouldn't do to seem too eager—not tonight, with Malloy so peculiarly insolent.

He rose and came toward her, and she felt his fingers on the cloth of her kimono. They crept up her back, under her hair, until he was toucing the soft nape of her neck. She could call for the stage manager, or simply order him out, but for the first time he seemed to be in control. She was a little afraid of him, and the experience was novel and not without its pleasure.

"And what will you do for me, if I produce your cousin? What will you give me in return?"

"My heartfelt thanks," said Delia sweetly. "And my friendship, which you already have."

He pulled her to her feet so swiftly she had no time to protest. His hands pinioned her wrists and he held her captive, laughing softly. "That's not enough," he said. "Not any more."

"Des, dear—who do you imagine you are speaking to? I am not one of your Jersey City whores, you know. You ought to be grateful to be seen in my company. Better men than you would be satisfied with what you have."

"But not this man, Missy. This man has devoted a great deal of his valuable time to helpin' your family when they stub their toes. This man was the one who said he'd back bloody *Daisy's Triumph* only if Miss Delia O'Donnell would appear in it. This man bails worthless Terry O'Donnell out of every stupid trap he falls into, and gives him a livin' besides. In a few years time, I could put him in the State Senate, useless though he may be. I could also save your cousin Kieran from makin' an early exit. Do you understand, beauty? There may be better men, but *this* man is the only one who counts."

With each phrase, he had shaken her lightly, effortlessly. Delia stared at him defiantly. In his entire diatribe, the only thing she'd really heard was his assertion that she had been hired to play Daisy because of him. Didn't he know she was considered the finest young actress in New York?

"One day," said Malloy, "you'll be old. You'll always be beautiful, but there'll be others who are beautiful too, and young. Do you imagine, darlin', they'll be beatin' down your door to play Daisy then? You're not Sarah Bernhardt, Delia O'Donnell, and that's a fact."

"Get out," said Delia, forcing her voice to remain languid. "You're beginning to bore me, Malloy."

"This man is the only one who won't desert you," he said. "We're two of a kind, you and I."

"Never." She was nearly blind with rage, but she sensed the best way to repay him for his cruel words was to cut him with scorn. "At least," she said, "I've never forced myself on anyone who didn't want me."

"What a glorious bitch!" said Malloy, as if speaking to the heavens. He released her hands and shook his head in amusement. "Ah, girl, y'think all life is acted on the stage. What does it matter if you want me or no? I want *you*—that's the thing."

He collected his hat and walking stick and stood at the door. "Remember. If you want to see Kieran, let me know."

"Get out, you old devil."

"Don't wait too long, though. You may not have much more time."

"Because I am so elderly, you mean?" His remarks had enraged her. Now that she was thirty-one, the prospect of aging was a real terror.

"Because," he said grinning, "there's to be a war."

"Nonsense."

"Within six weeks all Europe will be at war." He pointed his walking stick at her in a jaunty salute. "I said it first, and I'm never wrong." He tossed his newspaper on her dressing table, winked, and left the room.

Delia fled to her mirror, searching for signs of small lines, treacherous wrinkles, but there were none. She thought she could detect a subtle hardening—so slight no one but she could notice—in the face which was her only true friend. Otherwise, she was as beautiful as she had been at eighteen.

Satisfied, she turned her attention to the *Sun*, which Malloy had folded back to a particular item.

There had been an assassination at Sarajevo, in a place called Bosnia. Archduke Franz Ferdinand and his wife, the Duchess of Hohenberg, had been shot by revolutionary Slavs. Delia re-read the article, frowning. How could the death of an Austrian Archduke, in a place nobody could pronounce, be of any consequence? Malloy had said all Europe would be at war within six weeks, but she could make no sense of it. Even stranger was his warning that she must not wait too long to see her cousin.

What had a war in Europe to do with Kieran?

Austria did not take kindly to the murder of Franz Ferdinand, and delivered an ultimatum to Serbia which was designed to be unacceptable. Serbia, backed by France and Russia, did not reply in time. On July 25, all Europe seemed on the brink of war, just as Des Malloy had predicted.

"Unthinkable," said Americans. How could countries ruled by men who were related by blood possibly go to war? After all, the Kaiser and the Czar called each other "Willy" and "Nicky."

Three days later, Austria, backed by mighty Germany, declared war on Serbia. Bridget, lying in bed and listening to these sad accounts as her husband read them to her, said: "The Kaiser seems so silly, doesn't he, Mike? That spiked helmet and those uniforms—doesn't he make you want to laugh?"

No one laughed when Germany declared war on Russia on the first of August. It seemed Willy and Nicky might fool them, after all. Willy went on to declare war on France two days later, and on August Fourth the unthinkable happened—Germany invaded

Belgium, and at eleven o'clock that night, Britain entered the war.

America still danced the tango, but nothing seemed the same. "The lamps are going out all over Europe. We shall not see them lit again in our lifetime." This remark of Sir Edward Grey's crossed the Atlantic, and all Americans, along with Woodrow Wilson, shuddered at Europe's misfortune.

Another, smaller war was taking shape, of which most Americans knew nothing. The IRB's search for arms, in Germany and America, met with success in early August. Three yachts slid into Howthe and Kilcoole, carrying 1500 Mauser rifles and 50,000 rounds of ammunition. Erskine Childers sailed a consignment straight through a British squadron. At Howthe, the army fired on a jeering crowd, killing three and wounding thirty-two. The message was clear: if Ulster gun-running was tolerated, gun-running on the part of the Irish Volunteers was to be met with bullets. The old theory—that England's trouble would be Ireland's opportunity—was about to be tested.

Kieran, who had waited years for history to turn this particular corner, was caught in a diabolical dilemma. There were now two passions in his life instead of one, and he knew they could never be reconciled.

Jim, aware only of the larger war, felt strangely exhilarated. The casualty lists had not yet begun to appear, and he saw the conflict as something idealistic and grand, which would eventually touch him personally. He had read the journals bequeathed to him by Maynard Hill, and found in them a message. He read it clearly, but he knew he did not have the courage to uproot himself, as Maynard had done. It would take some cataclysmic event to free him from a life he did not wish to lead. In the European War, Jim sensed his freedom approaching.

When the endless, frightful casualty lists began to roll in from the fields of Belgium, Veronica read them and wept. She was not alone. The dreadful roll-call of the dead sobered all of America, and put an end to a certain brand of American innocence forever.

Up in Newburgh, Michael Flynn began to censor what he read to his wife, Bridget. He had a premonition of what would happen in a year or two, and for the first time in his life he was glad she had never given him a son.

15

Teddy Maitland and Bernadette quarrelled frequently about the war. It was Teddy's dearest wish to whip the Kaiser personally. Since everyone knew that America would never enter the war, Teddy schemed and day-dreamed. He wondered if it might not be possible to join the British Army as a volunteer.

Bernadette thought him foolish, and war in general wicked. Like her mother, she was a pacifist. Her friend, Louise Wolfe, was going through a Marxist phase, and took Bernadette to an interesting *salon* in Greenwich Village. Here she met poets and anarchists and iconoclasts of every description. Many of them were as foolish as Teddy, in different ways, but Bernadette was thrilled to be a part of the bohemian life. She bobbed her hair for the first time.

Robert Tyrone and Margaret O'Donnell were proud

of the loyal Protestant Ulstermen who flocked to join the British war effort. Margaret went so far as to suggest that the entire Irish populace should be conscripted.

"If that ever happened, Margaret," said her husband, "the blood would run in the streets."

Although he had been born in America, Patrick could not imagine himself fighting on the side of the British, and the thought of native-born Irishmen joining the British was absurd. He wasn't for the Kaiser, and wished for a speedy end to the war, but the thought of the British as allies was grotesque to him. He was well aware that there were Irishmen even now bargaining with the Germans for help in their cause. A part of him, long-buried, wished them luck.

Maureen Rafferty lived in a state of double confusion. She had imbibed a hatred of the British with her mother's milk, but it was quite an impersonal hatred. She had nothing against the Germans—hadn't the Lifsons, who thought of themselves as German first and Jewish second, been kinder to her than almost anyone? Dr. Lifson was deeply disturbed by the war, and Mrs. Lifson feared that anti-German sentiment would surface in America.

It all seemed very far away to Maureen, in any case. For the first time in her life, she knew what it was to be truly happy. Her love for Kieran seemed a miraculous thing, for it flowed in two directions. There was the love which stood in awe of him, of his learning and his beauty, and could not believe he loved her in return. Then there was the sweet knowledge that she could, by a word or a touch, bring him happiness. His troubled nature, so moving to her from the first, was something she did not understand, but she could soothe him, and bring a smile to his eyes and lips.

She was pulled between the two extremities of her love—her desire for him, over which she had no control, and the power of her tenderness, which was hers alone. More than anything, she wanted to become his wife. He had spoken to the Lifsons, and they were content to let her see him often. Maureen knew it was because he was a gentleman, and imagined they were surprised that such a man should be paying court to her.

In his company, she saw a part of the world entirely new to her. He took her to the theatre, and once to an opera, and seemed to derive most of his pleasure from her reactions. He bought her little presents, which she had learned to accept without shame, and a lovely picture-book showing scenes of western Ireland which she looked at endlessly.

What he did not do, and what she longed for him to do, was to hold her in his arms and kiss her as he had that day in Central Park. Sometimes he held her hand, or pressed his lips to her forehead, but never again had he shown her what his love might be like if he allowed it.

In the second month of the war, she sat with him in the kitchen on Seventy-sixth Street. She was mending a singlet of Clara's, and he sat across from her at the big deal table. She told him of the Lifsons' misgivings, hoping he would volunteer an opinion, but, as usual, he refused to be drawn into a discussion of the war in Europe.

"Are you not political, then?" she asked. "Doesn't the war interest you?" He did not answer, and she looked up. There was such a strange look in his blue eyes, such a strangled, hopeless look, she put down her sewing and went to him. "Why will you never tell me anything about yourself?" she asked. "Is it that you think I'll not understand?"

For an answer, he pulled her down onto his lap and held her so tightly she could scarcely breathe. She caressed the black hair and felt him tremble. "Kieran," she whispered. "Oh, love, what is it troubles you?" She wound her arms around him, as she had dream of doing, and felt his heart beating against hers. "Do you have to go away again?" she asked, her voice pleading. "Don't go, or take me with you. Please take me with you, Kieran! I'd go anywhere with you. I'd go to the ends of the earth; only don't leave me alone."

He raised his face to her and she thought she had never seen such torment. Then he shuddered, and said in a quiet voice, "I'd never leave you, Maureen, but I can't take you with me."

"Make sense, man!" She heard her voice become ragged, hysterical. She wanted to beat him with her fists, or pull the hair from his head, in order to understand what was happening. She, who never cried, felt sobs of grief battling in her breast. "I don't care if you won't marry me," she said. "It doesn't matter to me, Kieran. I'll be whatever you want me to be, only take me with you!"

He shook her then, so violently she felt he would tear her apart. His rage spent itself, and he caught her close and kissed her with a hard, male passion she had never felt before. She opened her lips and drank him in gratefully, feeling his tongue like a sword in her mouth. Her body seemed to want to force its way into his own, though she knew it should be the other way around. Her timidity was gone forever; she felt she could kill him with the force of her desire.

When he lifted her in his arms she thought he would at last make her his own, but he placed her on the table, like a queen, and knelt at her feet. Formally, he asked her if she would be his wife, and when she said yes he buried his head against her thighs and swore that he would love her forever.

Two days later, Maureen Rafferty became the bride of a man she thought was called Kieran O'Rourke. They were married in a church on Carmine Street, with an elderly woman as witness. Kieran placed upon her finger the ring his grandmother had left to him, and took her to his lodgings on Eighteenth Street directly after the ceremony.

There, he undressed her with reverent hands and made such love to her as she had never known existed. From all she had heard as a girl in Mayo, the act of love was brutal, short, and frequently painful. She had known it would not be so with Kieran, but she was unprepared for the pleasure he brought to her. He overcame the shyness which prompted her to hide her body from him, and with his hands and lips he adored her until she cried out in ecstasy. When he entered her, she welcomed the pain, because it meant she would be his true wife at last. From the moment she had seen him, on that chilly night outside her da's place in Mayo, she had wanted to feel him deep inside her. At last she had her wish, and so soon did the pain become pleasure, that she threw her legs around him and willed him to stay within the heart of her, forever.

"My wife," he called her, lying against her breast. "My darling wife."

She had no way of knowing that the priest who had performed the ceremony was sympathetic to the IRB. He had married her to a man who did not exist, because that was the only way Kieran could marry her at all. Yet if she had known, she would have realized that her husband considered the marriage to be as binding, sacred, and true as any performed within the law.

Bridget dreamed that Delia was a little girl again. Delia and Kieran were hard at play in the garden, running and shouting. Bridget looked down at them from the window of her bedroom and smiled. They were so beautiful, like twins they were, and the sunlight struck blue light from their coal black hair, and their eyes shone like sapphires. She called to them, and they waved at her. She saw then that they were not normal children, but angels of light, and a terrible sadness crept into her breast. Then a dark cloud rolled across the sun, and when she peered down into the garden, they were gone, and it was winter.

Bridget awakened from the dream and felt tears hot on her cheeks. She wanted to see her daughter, and felt there was not much time left. Her tears dried, and she slept again, but in the morning she told Michael to send for Delia.

Delia arrived a day later. During her mother's sickness, Delia had been told only that she needed rest. She was ignorant of her mother's condition, because Bridget had insisted that she was not to be worried.

"Mother," she said, coming into Bridget's bedroom like a fantastic apparition from another world, "I came as quickly as I could." She unpinned her stylish bonnet and advanced in a cloud of scent. She sat on the bed and tilted her exquisite face toward her mother.

Bridget guessed the mournful look was something Delia had learned during her years in the theatre. It was appropriate, in Delia's world, to lift the brows slightly and part the lips in an exaggerated mask of concern. Delia took her mother's hand in her own and pressed it. Bridget felt the cold bulk of the jewels on her daughter's hand pressing against her still warm flesh.

"Are you very ill, Mother?" Even the timbre of Delia's voice suggested the need to project emotion to the back of the house.

Bridget looked into her daughter's face and wondered where she'd gone wrong. Her lovely Delia, who might have grown to womanhood in a blaze of glory, was now a self–absorbed creature whose only defense against the cruelties of the world was her beautiful face. She remembered how, in the dream, she had thought Delia and Kieran were angels of light. Delia was a fallen angel, and Bridget pitied her with all her heart.

"What is it, Mother?"

"I am dying, dearie," said Bridget. "It's as simple as that."

Delia shook her head, smiling in protest at this overstatement, but when she saw the truth staring back at her in her mother's eyes she grew very pale.

Bridget reached up and stroked her cheeks, smoothed her hair. "It's alright, darling," she said. "I've been very happy with your da all these years. I wish you could be as happy."

Tears poured from Delia's eyes and she began to shake. Her grief was not the pretty, mannered kind she simulated so well on the stage, but the strident, ugly grief of real life. She sniffled and gulped, as she had done as a little girl, and finally gave way to racking sobs. She lay beside her mother and cried, and Bridget soothed her.

"There, there, my Dee," whispered Bridget. "There, my poor girlie. Mama loves you."

Comforting her daughter, holding her in her arms once more, Bridget felt perfectly happy. Two nights later she died peacefully in her sleep, as her mother had done. Patrick and Veronica were desolate, but it was Michael Flynn who suffered most. At fifty, he had been a handsome man, strong and youthful looking. Standing by his wife's graveside he appeared old and crushed. The death of his wife had aged him many years.

1 January, 1915
It seems the war will not end so soon, after all.
There are rumors of terrible new battle weapons
—boats that dive under the sea and release depth
charges, Zeppelins capable of crossing the channel
and bombing London. It is a sad beginning to a
New Year. Mother's heart is still sore because of
Aunt Bridget, and I am feeling melancholy too.
I think I shall see less of Teddy and devote more
time to studying. This is the year I will turn
twenty, and it is time to make something of my-
self.

Six Zeppelins did cross the channel and bomb England in the early weeks of 1915. The Island Kingdom, which had always relied on the sea to repel her enemies, was no longer safe. In Ireland, there were rumors that a sinister body, far more dangerous than Sinn Fein, had come to life again and authorities suspected that a treasonable element existed within the Irish Post Office.

What the authorities could not know was that Sir Roger Casement, a patriot in the service of the Irish Cause, had visited Germany and signed a ten-article pact with the German government. It provided for an Irish Brigade to be equipped and fed by the German government, and promised—in the event of a German naval victory—that German transports would convey the Irish Brigade to attempt a landing on the coast of Ireland.

Clarke, MacDiarmada, and Padraic Pearse forged

on, planning the Rising from their humble quarters in Dublin.

Jim O'Donnell was concerned with revolution, too, but the risings that occupied him were events from other centuries. In the late, cold spring he sat at his desk surrounded by papers. They were not legal briefs or law journals, or anything to do with the career which earned him his bread and butter, but he was much more absorbed in them than in the affairs of his law office.

From time to time he consulted the pages of a large book, then shuffled his papers and made notations. He had begun a large file, which grew daily until it was bursting from its drawer. The name neatly inked on the file was: 'Irish Music', but there were scores of subdivisions for airs, marches, jigs, reels, hornpipes, long dances, polkas (found only in County Kerry) and the music of O'Carolan, the greatest of the Irish harpers.

The book he referred to was the monumental collection compiled by Captain Francis O'Neill of the Chicago Police Department. O'Neill's collection was the most extensive Jim knew of, but he also referred to books by P. W. Joyce, George Petrie, and Edward Bunting. The latter two were of the nineteenth century. Bunting, a Belfast organist, had collected the music of the last of the harpers. Dr. Petrie was more eclectic, and Joyce had included songs as well as instrumental music.

It was Jim's great dream to write a book which would be a collection as well as a history of Irish music. It was a project which could take years, since he might discover a dozen different versions of a single air or reel. It had occurred to him that songs of revolution, an area which had not concerned him, would occupy a large place in his book, and he was making a new division for the file. His grandfather had been fond of *The Croppy Boy*, which he had sung in Gaelic, but Liam, like Jim, had cared most for the music itself.

Jim felt he had much to learn, and wished there were more hours in the day. He wasn't seeing his lady friend, the aspiring opera singer, any more. If he had broken with pretty Clair Trumbull because she was too frivolous, he had severed connections with the singer for the opposite reason. Adela had been an ardent lover. Unlike Clair, who had never permitted him more than a teasing kiss or two, Adela had come to his bed with a vengeance. She performed the act of love with operatic intensity, which was all to the good, but this same intensity pervaded every action in her life. He had rarely seen her smile. She liked to hear him play, but listened to everything he played for her with the same scowling expression, whether it was a lament or a wild reel. Gradually he came to see that she was as stupid, in her own way, as Clair had been.

Jim was a kind man and hated to cause grief in the hearts of decent young women, but there was one trap he had vowed he would not fall into. It was enough that he had allowed his mother to force him into a career at the bar; nothing would force him to give up what little freedom remained to him.

At his Aunt Bridget's funeral the previous year, he had seen Virginia Leonard Randall. She had four children now, and had grown plump. She was still a lovely woman, although she harmlessly dimpled and flirted in a way unbecoming to a matron of thirty. He had talked to her without feeling the slightest twinge of the pain which had once threatened to destroy him with its intensity, and he remembered with a smile the night he had played *Bright Love of My Heart,* weeping in his rooms at Cambridge.

He took up his pen again and scrawled a fragment of a song Liam used to sing:

> *We drink the memory of the brave,*
> *The faithful and the few—*
> *Some lie far off beyond the wave,*
> *Some sleep in Ireland, too;*
> *All, all are gone—but still—lives on,*
> *The fame of those who died,*
> *All true men, like you, men,*
> *Remember them with pride.*

Jim had forgotten the name of the song, but he remembered all too well why his grandfather had sung it, although it had always saddened him. It had been in memory of his son, Bobby, that Liam paid tribute to the faithful and the few.

The old Fenian, O'Donovan Rossa, died in New York in July. His body was shipped back to Ireland to lie in state at City Hall. Kieran read the accounts of O'Donovan Rossa's funeral in the *Gaelic American* to Maureen.

On August 1, tens of thousands filled the streets of Dublin to mourn him. The British soldiers and Dublin police wisely stayed away. Padraic Pearse, in his funeral oration, warned those who thought Britain had purchased half of Ireland and intimidated the other half: *the fools, the fools, the fools—they have left us our Fenian dead, and while Ireland holds these graves, Ireland unfree shall never be at peace.*

"'Tis true enough," said Maureen. She was moved by the accounts of the tributes to O'Donovan Rossa, but something was troubling her. It had lately begun to occur to her that her Kieran had mixed himself up in something dark and dangerous. She was no stranger to plots and secret societies. No one who had grown up on the west coast of Ireland was oblivious to such things, but that the spirit of rebellion might have rooted itself on the other side of the Atlantic was a new thought for her.

She and Kieran were now living on Twelfth Street. They occupied the top floor of a brick building, and Maureen could see the tops of plane trees from her windows. To her it seemed like unbridled luxury—her own gleaming pots and pans, the large brass bed in which she and Kieran slept and made love, the fireplace with its design of pineapples worked into the marble, were all things she had never dreamed of possessing. Kieran had taken money from a legacy left him by his grandfather to provide her with these objects. He had bought her new clothes and shoes and a proper warm coat for the coming winter, and now she feared that he had used up the remainder of his legacy. He was often away, at his business, but what his business was he would never reveal. He spoke vaguely of being a journalist, but she knew he earned much of their money gambling at cards.

"I could take work in a shop," she told him once. "I don't mind." But his face had darkened. "My wife will not work in a shop," he had said haughtily. "I will care for you, Maureen."

She passed her days keeping their rooms immaculate and gleaming, shopping in the markets, and cooking. Occasionally she visited the Lifsons, and played with the little girls. She practiced her reading. Mainly, though, she waited for him to come home to her, and worried.

Once, missing him, she had gone to the wardrobe and held one of his coats in her arms. The familiar garments soothed her; she lay her cheek against the tweed and wool, loving him, and then, industriously, she looked to see if anything needed mending or tidying.

A button was missing on a jacket he rarely wore in the warm weather. She thrust her hand into the pocket to see if the button might be there, and found instead a small key. She stood for some time, the key in the palm of her hand. She hated the image of herself as a prying woman, but Kieran's secrecy was a threat to her happiness. She would do anything to keep him from harm.

What had she expected to find in the box at the bottom of the wardrobe? Vaguely, she imagined papers of some sort—papers that would show Kieran was being blackmailed, or had been in jail once. Her heart beating with dread and guilt, she unlocked the box and opened the lid.

The revolver was large and oily looking. Beside it lay a box of shells. She picked the gun up, not knowing whether it was loaded or not, and held it with revulsion in both hands. It was marked Smith & Wesson; she had never seen such a weapon before, and she felt a hatred for it, as if she had come upon a rattlesnake in the wardrobe. At last she locked it up again, and replaced the key in Kieran's pocket.

Normally, when she heard him at the door, her entire being sang with happiness. She could imagine no greater joy than the feel of his arms around her after hours of separation. On that night, however, when he came home, her joy was mixed with terror. She kept her questions to herself, not wanting to ruin the peace and tranquility she alone seemed able to bring him.

They sat by the fire, and Kieran brushed her long hair. She caught his hand, and kissed it. The memory of the hideous gun began to recede, become less ominous; it was dwarfed by the reality of his presence. Nevertheless, from that day on, her happiness was marred.

On the day he read about O'Donovan Rossa's funeral, she detected something in his blue eyes she had come to read so well. Something in his expression went beyond the emotion he might feel at the death of a great Fenian, or at Pearse's stirring words. It was a look of longing which had nothing to do with her. Kieran, she saw, wished that he could be in Dublin with the others.

"Kieran," she said quietly. "Are you in the Organization?"

He put the paper down and stared at her, as if she had changed into a supernatural form. "What did you say?" he asked. She repeated the question, speaking in Gaelic, as befitted the discussion of such a topic. He answered her in Gaelic.

"I am not," he said.

"I am your wife. There must be no secrets between us."

He came to her then, and circled her face in gentle hands. "Whatever I may have been," he said, "I am not the same man now. Whatever I was, I am no longer."

And that was how she knew her happiness was not just marred, but shattered. She remembered what her da and the men in Mayo had always said of the Organization. *Once in, never out.* She lay against his breast and told herself that if her husband was outside the law, then she must follow him there. It was the only way they could remain together.

Desmond Malloy knew almost as much about what was going on in Dublin as the IRB did. Through his informant, a traitor in the employ of the New York Fenian John Devoy, he learned that a Military Council formed within the Organization was recognized by the Supreme Council in September. He knew that $100,000 had been raised, in America, and that Sir Roger Casement had visited Devoy to collect and raise funds.

He was interested in these details because, if he was

to prevent Kieran from joining the rebels, time was running short. He had not heard from Delia since his encounter with her in her dressing room. One word from her, and he was prepared to arrange to save Kieran's life.

There were many ways in which he might carry off such a *coup*. He could arrange to have Kieran beaten badly enough to require hospitalization, without permanently injuring him, or he could have him jailed on some petty charge for a year or two. Kieran now lived on Twelfth Street. He had had him tailed there and was satisfied that it was his true address. The shadow man had reported seeing a very pretty young girl go in and out, but her presence didn't worry Malloy. He knew Kieran was fond of the ladies, and he knew he never stayed with one for long.

He had always told himself it was for Delia that he bothered with Kieran, but one of the whores at his Jersey City place set him to examining his true motives. She was a lissome blonde called Kitty, one of his favorites, and she loved nothing better than to climb into his lap and tease him, calling him a pagan, evil, old devil and asking him if there had ever been a time when he could go to confession without blushing for his wickedness. Such play was an aphrodisiac for Kitty, and normally Malloy enjoyed it too, but on a night late in the year of 1915 he had a vision.

"Wicked old Des," Kitty was crooning, straddling him with her bare thighs. "Such a bad, bad, black Irishman he is! I'll reckon he was a wicked one when he was just a little boy," she said as she nipped at his ear and giggled. It was then he had the vision.

He saw himself with his da, at the Fenian rally in Brooklyn. He saw the face of poor Bobby O'Donnell —younger then than his son was now—and felt O'Donnell's gentle hands tousling his hair. Even at nine he had sensed the futility of Bobby O'Donnell's cause, but he had admired him whole-heartedly. At the age of nine, he had been capable of boyish enthusiasm; he had not been entirely wicked then.

He pushed the startled Kitty from his lap and decided, then and there, what he would do. For Bobby O'Donnell's sake he would have his son kidnapped. He would not harm Kieran, or have him imprisoned. He would simply remove him for a period of time until the danger was over. That the Rising would fail, he had no doubt. British agents would be aware of it, the Germans would betray the Irish; it would all end tragically, but he would at least have the satisfaction of seeing that history did not repeat itself.

Accordingly, he sent two men to the house on Twelfth Street on a dark night in late November. He instructed them to take "O'Rourke" at gunpoint, not harming him, and bring him to Malloy in Jersey City. The plan had a beauty to it. Surely Kieran, when he had time to think it over, would not object to being kept prisoner in a choice bordello until the troubles were over.

It was past midnight before his deputies drove up, and one look at their faces showed Malloy that something had gone wrong.

"Has our pigeon already flown the coop?" he asked.

But it was worse than that. Stumblingly, in dread of

his employer's wrath, Finn, the more intelligent of the two thugs, told him what had happened. They had waited until light appeared in the windows of the top-floor flat on Twelfth Street, to be sure their quarry was at home. Then, according to plan, they had climbed the stairs and knocked, guns drawn. When their knocks were met with no response, they kicked the door down and entered. The flat seemed to be deserted, though a lamp was burning, and they began a systematic search of the rooms.

In the center of the kitchen table, they had discovered a train ticket for Newburgh, together with two letters. The first was in Gaelic, which neither Finn nor the other could read, and they had not bothered with the second but continued their search.

It was when they were about to enter the last room, the bedroom, that they heard a movement within. The figure rushed at them so quickly they had no time to do anything but act. It was dark and the figure held a pistol aimed at them. Finn had fired at the assailant's arm, but the frightened quarry had flung herself, in desperation, to one side. The bullet had gone cleanly through her heart.

"It wasn't O'Rourke," said Finn with an air of helpless dejection. He handed Malloy the train ticket and the letters, together with the revolver, a Smith & Wesson, which had proved to be unloaded. "The other's in the boot of the automobile," he said. "It was easy. Nobody was about."

The other, when the boot was unlocked, was a small corpse, hastily taken from the flat on Twelfth Street, wrapped in a quilt to stanch the blood from the gun-shot wound. Malloy easily lifted the burden in his arms and turned it over. The face was that of a young girl, the eyes wide with terror. Her red hair streamed wildly over her breast, and was stained a deeper red by the blood which blossomed there. She was, Malloy thought, very beautiful.

Gently, he closed the eyes. Tenderly, he crossed her hands on her breast, noting the ring she had worn on her wedding finger.

"This is a fine night's work," he said to Finn. "Ye've killed a little girl."

"What will we do with her?" asked Finn.

"Dump her," ordered Malloy. "And the gun. In the river."

Before they drove off, he had another thought. "Mind," he said to them, in an unmistakable note of authority, "mind ye leave that ring where it belongs!"

The letter which had been written in Gaelic he read alone, feeling that a goose had walked over his grave. It was a love letter, telling the recipient that Kieran had been called away, but would return. He was sending his love to a place where she would be safe, and cared for. She must go there immediately, and he had provided her with a ticket for that purpose.

The second letter was even worse. It was addressed to Kieran's uncle, Patrick O'Donnell of Newburgh, and begged Patrick to look after the bearer. "Please keep her safe, and treat her with all tenderness," Kieran had written, "for she is my true wife, the woman I love, and the mother of our unborn child. Her name is Maureen, and she has given me the only true happiness I have ever known."

Malloy burned the letters, and the train ticket, and felt, for the first time in thirty years, the burden of his immortal soul heavy in his breast. History would repeat itself after all, and he was powerless to prevent it. Indeed, with the best intentions in the world, he had hastened it on its damnable course.

A week later, his informant told him that the Military Council had set the date for the Rising. It was to take place on Easter Sunday of the following year, the 23rd of April, 1916.

Patrick O'Donnell was named Man of the Year by the Chamber of Commerce in Newburgh. The Newburgh Club held a gala dance in honor of the event, just before Christmas. Patrick's wife was ill in bed, which only made the event more cheerful. His son, Jim, came up for the festivities, and watched with pleasure while Patrick danced with the attractive widow, Mrs. Beach.

Jim had written a joking reel for his father, which he played for the assembled company. It was called, of course, *Patrick O'Donnell's Reel,* and his father received it with red-faced delight.

In a lull during the party, Jim asked his father a question. "Do you recall the song grandfather used to sing about the faithful and the few?"

"I do," said Patrick.

"What was it called?"

"It was called," said Patrick, *"The Memory of the Dead."*

16

Delia found the war in Europe very tiresome. Songs like *There's a Long, Long Trail* and *I Didn't Raise My Son to be a Soldier* failed to move her. The people who tried her patience most were those who thought America would enter the war, eventually, and discussed what would happen in endless detail. When a handsome young man she knew joined a Canadian regiment to help fight the allies, she thought it a terrible waste.

On Valentine's Day, she was presented with a pretty trinket—a heart studded with tiny rubies and diamonds and mounted in white gold. The man who gave her the trinket was Walter Brady. He had been at Harvard with Terry, and was some four years younger than Delia. He was also married, and the father of two children. He had been infatuated with

Delia ever since he'd ventured down from Cambridge with Terry to see her on stage.

"How pretty, Walter," said Delia, holding the little heart aloft and admiring the way the rubies caught the light. "How amusing of you."

"It isn't half good enough for you. I wish I could give you black pearls."

"Ah, but your wife might not approve," said Delia, watching him blush. He always blushed whenever Delia mentioned his wife, who would certainly not have approved of the heart, either. He was really, thought Delia, a very nice young man. She doubted that he had ever been unfaithful to his dull little wife. Except for his steadfast and rather expensive devotion to her, which she had never rewarded, Walter led an exemplary life.

"I shall be going out in an hour," said Delia, "but you're welcome to stay for a bit, as long as you don't discuss the wretched war."

Walter seated himself, devouring her with his eyes. Delia appreciated the reverence in those eyes. It warmed her, and she was beginning to feel an inner chill these days. Walter asked her if she had chosen a new play, and Delia replied airily that nothing but rubbish had come her way. She was thinking, she said, of writing Mr. George Bernard Shaw in London, and asking him to write a play for her. The truth, however, was rather different. Since *Daisy's Triumph* had closed its triumphant run, she'd been offered only one play. It had been unsuitable because although Delia would play the central role, there was a juicy part for an ingenue who could conceivably steal the scene. She wouldn't risk appearing with a young girl. The idea made her furious, and she had instructed her manager on no account to submit plays for her consideration in which younger women appeared.

"How is Terry?" she asked idly.

Walter mumbled something about not seeing much of Terry these days. He was actually blushing again, and Delia found herself charmed by him. How young he seemed!

"I suppose Terry's in trouble again," she said. "Doubtless your wife disapproves of him. Most decent women do."

Walter was much too gentlemanly to comment on Terry, and Delia didn't want to know, anyway. Terry's troubles were always of two varieties—money or women. She had heard he was scarcely more than a glorified errand boy for Tammany.

"I wish you wouldn't mention my wife," Walter said suddenly.

"Whyever not?" Delia's lips curved with scorn. How dare this hypocritical pup forbid her to mention his silly wife's name? "Let me guess," she said sarcastically. "Your wife is a good, respectable woman, and you love her dearly. You are drawn to me, but you love her, and it wounds you to hear her name on the lips of a notorious woman like me."

"No," said Walter with surprising firmness. "That's not it. You do it to make yourself seem wicked, and you're not." He sat forward in his chair, his eyes burning. "It's you I love," he said. "I've always loved you. I know I'm not half good enough for you. I'm content just to be near you, now and then. Please don't spoil my happiness by mentioning my wife. I want to think only of you."

Delia felt her body warming, slightly. It was as if the temperature in the room had actually risen. She held the little heart against her white throat and closed her eyes. "Go on," she whispered. "Tell me. I want to hear."

Stumblingly, Walter poured out his adoration. He told her he could hardly sleep, sometimes, for wanting her. He spoke of her beauty with a trembling voice.

"Ah, yes," sighed Delia, "describe me, Walter. Do you really think me beautiful?" She was growing warmer and warmer; his words acted on her as caresses might on another woman—they teased her nerve endings and made her shudder with delight.

Head swimming, she rose and beckoned for him to follow her. Outside the door to her bedroom she told him to wait, and to enter only when she called for him. She left the door ajar, and bade him to continue talking. His voice was trembling with desperation now, but he was too aroused to do anything but obey.

Delia slipped out of her tea gown and stood in her lacy chemise and stockings, regarding herself in the mirror. His voice flowed in, continuing to excite her, stoking the warmth and making her ache with desire. She wrapped her arms around her body and squeezed herself, smiling at her image in the glass. Walter was right; she was, truly, the most beautiful woman in the world. She freed her breasts, imagining the look on his face when he saw them and when he was commanded to describe them. Clad only in her stockings, she lay on her bed with her arms clasped behind her head. "Come in, now, Walter," she cried.

As she had known, his eyes nearly started out of his head at the sight of her. "Look at me," she murmured.

"Delia—oh, God!" He lurched toward her, half falling to his knees beside the bed.

"Talk to me," she pleaded. "Ah, don't stop."

A stream of words burst from him now, and Delia let them bring her to a peak of sensation maddening in its intensity. She lay, shuddering in the aftermath of ecstasy, while Walter struggled out of his clothing, still gasping with desire. It was only fair to give him his pleasure, now that she'd had hers. She lay beneath him, thinking of the pretty little heart.

It lay beside her on the table, winking gaily. Suddenly she was reminded of Desmond Malloy's harp-shaped pin. She had seen him the month before, sitting with a group of men at a new supper club. She had been prepared to cut him dead, but there was no need. Malloy had given her a quick, furtive look and turned away, almost as if he felt guilty.

The look Walter Brady gave Delia as he was leaving was something else again. However rapturous he had been while making love to her, his departure was hasty. He seemed almost sad!

Oh, men, men, thought Delia—the funny creatures! They never know what they really want, do they?

Jim had gone to see the great piper, Patsy Touhey, play at a theatre on Forty-seventh Street. Touhey, a genial leprechaun of a man was a great popular favorite. The theatre-goers who packed a house to see him accompany George M. Cohan sensed only the appeal of his music. Few of them knew enough about music to realize that Patsy Touhey was a genius.

Jim was still whistling *The Steam Packet* when he returned to his lodgings. He was surprised to see a female figure sitting dejectedly on the steps of his house, and for a moment he was afraid it might be his discarded love, the opera singer. Then he saw that the head, cupped in her hands, sported bobbed hair of a familiar, pale red-gold. She looked up at the sound of his whistling. It was his cousin, Bernadette.

"Wee Bernie," he called. "Come in, girl. You'll freeze, sitting there."

Bernadette followed him up the stairs, saying nothing. Safely inside, she slumped in a chair and asked if he had a cigarette. Jim gave her one, lighting it and noting that her hands shook as she inhaled fiercely. Bernadette did everything fiercely, and with a youthful intensity which he found both amusing and appealing.

"You're half-frozen," he said. "Shall I make you some tea?"

Bernadette shook her head. "There's no time," she said. "I came to you because you're the only one who can help." She seemed close to tears. Her distress was genuine. Jim took her cold hand and chafed it in his own. She'd tell him in her own good time; you didn't hurry Bernadette, who knew exactly where she was going.

"The thing is," she said, puffing sternly on her

cigarette, "Mother's been arrested. She's at the Greenwich Village Police Station."

"Arrested?" Jim knew his Aunt Veronica was active in various movements, but they had always seemed to him to be safe circles. Bernadette's anxiety disturbed him. "What for?"

His cousin explained that she and her mother had gone to a Pacifist Meeting at the home of a Jane Addams disciple on Bleecker Street. Afterwards, when they were leaving, a group had suddenly appeared in the streets, jeering and carrying signs with messages such as: HUNS KILL CHILDREN AND RAPE WOMEN and DOWN WITH THE COWARDS WHO SIDE WITH THE KAISER!

A particularly large and vocal man had singled Veronica out for abuse, shouting that she was a traitor and a German-lover. He had become obscene and threatening. Finally he had pushed at Veronica, causing her to lose her balance and fall in the gutters of Bleecker Street.

"I think she hurt her knee, Jim. She looked so frail, lying there, it made me see red. I ran at him and kicked him, hard. I wanted to kill him." Bernadette spoke wonderingly, as if the force of her anger amazed her. She was, after all, supposed to be a pacifist.

"He turned on me, but I wasn't afraid. He was stupid, *stupid!* The others were trying to restrain him, and they were all ready to creep away, but suddenly Mother got to her feet and came at him like a lioness. 'Don't you dare touch my daughter!' she screamed, and then she threw a big stone at him. He ducked, and the stone went through the street-floor window."

The destruction of property, thought Jim, would do it. Property was more valuable than human life or dignity. He was not surprised to hear that the police had taken his Aunt Veronica away, and booked her on disturbance of the peace. What surprised him was the degree of Bernadette's distress.

"It's alright," he said gently. "I'll come with you to the station. She'll be out in no time. Didn't you have the bail?" Bernadette shook her head. "Your ma's a real firebrand, girl," he said. "It runs in a part of the family."

Bernadette caught at him desperately. "What if Father finds out?" she said. "That's why I came to you, Jim. Father mustn't know."

Jim looked at his cousin with new respect. He had long understood that the marriage of his Aunt Veronica mirrored the unhappy union of his own parents. Robert Tyrone and his mother had much in common, but whereas Margaret and Patrick had long ago sundered any pretense at marital happiness, Veronica and Robert had lately grown closer. Bernadette sensed this closeness, and was afraid it was about to be severed again.

"Come, Bernie," he said gently, "we'd best go to the police station now."

The police were all too happy to have Veronica taken away. Red-faced and apologetic, they treated Jim with the utmost respect and called Veronica "Mrs. Tyrone." In the cab going to Thirty-eighth Street, Veronica thanked Jim and leaned, exhaustedly, against the window. She held Bernadette's hand in her own and shook her head with remembered disgust. "Shall I have to go to trial?" she asked.

"No," said Jim. "It's a mere formality."

"Do you know," said Veronica with an air of wonderment, "I wonder if I am a pacifist, after all?"

He delivered her home, to Robert, with an expert ploy. "There was some unpleasantness at the Pacifist Meeting," he said. "Aunt Veronica distinguished herself by remaining aloof. The police took her into custody, temporarily, to explain matters. The interlopers were ruffians."

Robert Tyrone put a protective arm around his wife and thanked Jim excessively. Bernadette squeezed his arm and winked. Jim went home and pondered the intricacies of married life. How was it possible that such opposing forces as Patrick and Margaret, Veronica and Robert, could have chosen to cast their lots together?

In the morning, the *Sun* carried an article which read: BANKER'S WIFE ARRESTED IN WAKE OF ANTI-PACIFIST VIOLENCE! It portrayed his Aunt Veronica as a dangerous radical, with violent tendencies, who heaved bricks through windows on the slightest provocation.

Terence O'Donnell, like Delia, found the war a great bore. When he read that over a million French soldiers had died to gain three miles of territory, he thought men must be mad to fall for all that patriotic stuff. Patriotism was just a false emotion invented by government officials to maneuver less fortunate men to their deaths.

The item about his Aunt Veronica amused him, and set him to thinking. If America ever did enter the war—it seemed unlikely, but a fellow had to look ahead—perhaps he could pretend to be a pacifist.

Malloy had cut him in on a new saloon in the Chelsea district. Terry was a partner in the enterprise, bankrolled by Malloy, and had certain duties. He saw to the saloon's books and bargained with liquor distributors, but mainly he spent long hours on Twenty-first Street, glorying in his position of owner. It pleased him to invite friends to come to "his" place and give them drinks on the house. He enjoyed bullying the barmen and organizing the gambling in the back room. Something else gave him pleasure, too, although he didn't acknowledge it—it was for *this* that his mother had sent him to Harvard, believing he would mingle with the upper crust! If she could see him now, old Margaret would throw a fit.

Terry had discovered he was never meant to be a gentleman. It was all very well to swan it up in Cambridge, it had been fun, but he was bored by men of the Lord Lanier ilk. Even his old friend Walter Brady was a stuffed shirt, and Terry considered himself well rid of such company. He loved the low-life, considered himself born for it, and—so long as the money came rolling in—wanted nothing better.

As for marriage, what was the point to it? Why tie yourself to a millstone if, like Terry, you could be in the bed of a Ziegfield girl one night and the arms of someone else's wife the next? Perhaps if he ever met a millionairess who was eager to marry him, he'd consider it, but no such person had come along.

Malloy often dropped into the saloon on Twenty-first Street late at night. Terry sensed that these visits were a means of checking up on his capability, and resented them, but he could hardly bite the hand that fed him, and he was unfailingly pleasant and courteous to his benefactor.

Mild rain was falling on the night, in late April, when Malloy stepped through the door and walked heavily to the bar. Terry thought he had changed in the last few months, and wondered if the old scoundrel might be ill. He was still jovial and sly, but there was a speculative, wounded look in the black eyes which had not been there before.

"Evening, Des," said Terry, taking a seat next to him. "How's McCabe looking?"

McCabe was a heavyweight boxer who showed distinct possibilities. Normally, this question would have interested Malloy, but tonight he spread his hands and shrugged, then ordered a whiskey. All around them, men were talking about horses, women, and money—and the casualty list from Verdun. Malloy sat in silence, contemplating his whiskey, and then turned to Terry abruptly.

"Do you ever think of yer cousin, Kieran?" he asked softly.

"Not often. He disappeared, you know. I haven't seen him for almost five years." The question surprised Terry.

Malloy downed his whiskey. "Spare him a thought," he said.

"Have another drink," said Terry. Privately, he imagined Malloy was already three sheets to the winds, although he didn't show it.

Malloy consulted his pocket watch. "I won't," he said. "It's just gone midnight."

Terry laughed. "What of it?" he said. "It's the shank of the evening. I never knew you to stop drinking at midnight, Malloy."

"It's the one day of the year I go dry, lad."

"What day is this, then?"

"Good Friday," said Malloy.

And then, astounding Terry, he clapped his hat back on his head and walked gloomily to the door, and out into the rain.

Dublin buzzed with ominous rumors all during Holy Week. Ordinary citizens were sure something was about to happen, but they didn't know what. British Army Intelligence was fully aware that a Rising was planned, but without arms, they reasoned, the rebels couldn't rise. By Easter Saturday, they had proof that all hopes of a rebellion had been smashed, and British soldiers and Irish police alike became complacent.

Sir Roger Casement, who had been landed on the Kerry coast by German submarine in the early hours of Good Friday morning, had been arrested later in the day. He was confined at Tralee Barracks, where he refused to admit his identity. On the morning of Holy Saturday the German ship *Aud,* bearing arms for the Irish rebels, exploded and went to the bottom of the sea. Casement and the *Aud* had failed to make contact, and Sir Roger, still refusing to give his name, was sent to Dublin Barracks and on to prison in London.

The Military Council sat in Liberty Hall on Easter Sunday morning and deliberated. Despite the loss of the German arms, the debate was not whether the Rising should take place, but when. Clarke wanted it to happen that evening, but he was over-ruled. It was decided to begin the next day, Easter Monday, at noon.

The strategy was a simple one. Marching on a routine maneuver as Irish Volunteers, the architects of the Rising would take over the General Post Office on Sackville Street. The post office would become the revolutionary headquarters of the Provisional Government. Other deployments would command outposts which would circle the heart of the city and form a barricade against the five British military barracks.

Although the hoped-for German reinforcements lay at the bottom of Tralee Bay, it was too late to turn back. The headquarters of the revolutionary army would be armed with the old German Mausers landed at Howthe, rifles of an even older make, shotguns, and pickaxes. With this unlikely arsenal, and a little gelignite, they hoped to bring the British Empire to its knees.

Kieran was under the command of Eamon de Valera. When word was sent to him that his battalion was to assemble at Great Brunswick Street at ten on Easter Monday, he felt a rush of joy so strong it made his legs tremble. He had waited so many years, and seen so many setbacks, it seemed nearly impossible to him that the time was at hand. He looked forward to the battle with fierce eagerness, and lay sleepless all the night before.

In the five months since he had left America, and Maureen, he had trained himself not to think of her. At the back of his mind was a lovely, reassuring picture: Maureen, safe in Newburgh, laughing with his Aunt Bridget near a warm fire. He was sure she would be happier with Bridget and Michael—surely Margaret's stern ways and fish-eye would freeze her—and thought of her there, with Patrick visiting, of course. How they would love her, his uncles and Bridget, and make much of her, and keep her safe! The child would be beginning to show by now; soon it would kick beneath her heart.

He could call this picture up whenever he needed to, but he would not go beyond the simple *tableau.* The longing for her would be too great, and he was a soldier now. Soldiers could not afford to pine. If they were secret soldiers, they could not even write letters. He lay, waiting for the morning, sure that he would be returning to Maureen within the month. When the child was born, all three of them would come to live in the new, free Ireland he and the others were struggling to create. He slept a little, just before dawn, and dreamed he was a child again, running at the bottom of the garden in Newburgh. With him was an older boy. They were great friends, but Kieran realized he didn't know the boy's name. He asked it. "Why, you know me," the boy said. "I'm Bobby. Bobby O'Donnell."

At ten the next morning, he presented himself at Great Brunswick Street. Of the five hundred men under de Valera's command, only a hundred and forty had received the message. They were to take their post at Boland's Mill. It commanded the route troops from England were most likely to take, and the fact that less than a third of de Valera's battalion had turned out on Easter Monday seemed ominous, indeed.

Shortly before noon, James Connolly stepped out of Liberty Hall, leading the Irish Volunteers. The men had made an attempt to appear like members of the military, but uniforms were in short supply and they made a motley crew. On Connolly's right marched Padraic Pearse; on his left, Joseph Plunkett. At Sackville Street they were joined by Tom Clarke and Mac-Diarmada. Bringing up the rear were two drays, packed full with Mausers, shotguns, rifles, pikes, and crude bombs fashioned of tin cans or pipes. The Irish citizenry watched with little curiosity. As far as they were concerned, it was simply another ordinary route march, staged by the Irish Volunteers.

Not until they drew opposite the General Post Office did anything of interest take place. Connolly gave the order: "Left turn—the G.P.O.—*Charge!*"

With a bewildering swiftness, the public was turned out of the post office and the marchers occupied it. Most of them went through the main door, a few ran through the Henry Street entrance, and a small group commanded the roof. While stunned onlookers gaped, a flag was run up the great pediment. To the north flew the green, white and orange flag of *Sinn Fein*, to the south a green flag emblazoned with a gold harp, and bearing the words: *Irish Republic*.

Ian Kavanaugh

Precisely three quarters of an hour from the time he had left Liberty Hall, Padraic Pearse came out onto the steps and read the Proclamation of the Republic. He spoke in the name of the Provisional Government.

"Irishmen and Irishwomen: In the name of God and of the dead generations from which she receives her old tradition of nationhood, Ireland, through us, summons her children to her flag and strikes for her freedom."

The bystanders were a small group. They listened to the long, high-flown passages of the stirring proclamation and muttered uneasily. What did it all mean? The document was signed with the names of seven men, which Pearse read out to them proudly. Then he went back inside the G.P.O., and most of those who had heard him shrugged, and went home. The Rising had begun.

Early that afternoon, a troop of British cavalrymen appeared at the north end of Sackville Street. They expected to find rebels rioting in the open and reckoned to ride over them. Gunshots rang out from the G.P.O., killing four of the soldiers and forcing the others to retreat. The British irritably admitted that the use of mounted cavalry would not work. By evening, the North Wall Quays, the Amiens Street Railway Station, and the Customs House were occupied by British forces. Eight hundred forty infantrymen from the 15th Irish Brigade were sent for.

The Post Office was left in peace, and the rebels waited. They could not know that, in the end, their original number of one thousand men would swell to sixteen hundred, nor could they know that their sixteen hundred would be pitted against an army of twelve thousand.

Kieran, at his post at Boland's Mill, waited for battle in silence.

By Tuesday, news of the Rising had filtered to America. People in Newburgh, as well as New York City, read accounts of the brave, misguided attempt to forge an Irish Republic.

"Shocking," Mrs. Parker said, when Peg read the headlines. "Them as doesn't die in the mischief is bound to be hanged."

"It's a bloody siege," Michael Flynn said to his brother-in-law. "It's medieval warfare, and in this modern age."

"They'll all be slaughtered," said Patrick.

In New York, Veronica whispered to her daughter, "As God is my witness, Bernadette, I'm with them."

Neither Terry nor Delia concerned themselves with events occurring three thousand miles away. Jim read of the Rising avidly, wondering what Liam would have said about it. He thought of it as fertile ground from which new songs might spring, and waited to catalogue them in his masterwork.

Patrick's comment, unfortunately, proved to be the most prophetic. A labor organizer named William O'Brien would later write that Connolly himself, at the beginning of the fateful march, had ordered him to mount his bicycle and go home. When O'Brien asked why, Connolly lowered his voice and whispered, calmly:

"We are going out to be slaughtered."

On Wednesday, April 26, 1916, Dublin began to
burn. A British incendiary shell, hurled into the printing offices of the *Irish Times,* started a conflagration
in the very heart of the city. Troops had moved to Upper Sackville Street, completing a circle around the
rebel headquarters. They fired on them from all sides.

Kieran O'Donnell, quartered at 25 Northumberland
Road, faced an entire battalion of British troops, which
moved up Northumberland straight into the fire at
Number 25. Inside the house were three men—Kieran
O'Donnell, Michael Malone, and James Grace.

They crouched at the barricaded windows, firing
steadily. Kieran, like a Celtic warrior, did fearful
damage to the enemy without feeling himself the in-
strument of their death. He took aim, with his old and
defective rifle, and shot an advancing British soldier
through the leg. The man fell and Kieran took aim
again and shot him in the head. He felt none of the
bracing, revolutionary tonic racing through his veins,
only a weary conviction that he must perform, mechanically, until he could perform no longer.

No matter how many times they re-loaded and fired,
the enemy kept coming. Reason told Kieran they were
hopelessly outnumbered, but reason had never played
a central role in his life. At three in the afternoon,
when they had been at the windows for over two
hours, he still hoped for the best.

At a little before five, he knew that it was useless.
He wished he could find paper and pen and write a
letter to Maureen, but there was no time; the moment
he stopped killing he would die. He knew that he

would never live to see the fine, free Ireland he had dreamed of, but it didn't matter. It would rise some time in the future, beyond his death, and his son—Maureen's son—would be alive to see it.

At five, the British blew the door in with bombs and machine gun reinforcements. Grace was knocked back against the wall so hard he was temporarily stunned. Kieran went to him, crouching low, and saw the look of despair in his friend's eyes. "I'm alright, lad," he said, "but we've had it now."

Outside, it was silent. The three waited for the inevitable charge.

When it came, Malone was killed immediately; his brains and fragments of his skull rained down on Kieran like a blessing. Grace miraculously managed to escape. Kieran, the lone, live member of the Northumberland Road resistance, rose from the rubble and fired a last shot into the assembled ranks of the advancing army.

As he fired, he shouted his father's name, and the soldiers—most of whom were too young to know that name—pumped two dozen bullets into his body. He was dead before he fell to the floor.

Kieran O'Donnell had lived to complete the dreadful rounds of his appointed destiny—to die for Ireland.

17

Pearse, MacDonagh, and Clarke were sentenced to death and executed on the third day of May. Nine more were court-martialed and shot during the next five days. To the pleas for leniency from such men as Bernard Shaw and John Dillon, the British government turned a deaf ear. On May 12th, Connolly and Mac-Diarmada went to their deaths. Connolly had been so badly injured in the fighting that he had to be carried to his place of execution tied to a chair.

The citizens of Dublin, who were at first outraged by the Rising, began to see the rebels as heroes. The brief rebellion, which had lasted but a week and had been counted a dismal failure, took on a new light as Dublin, and the world, watched England take her revenge.

The executions ceased, but sentences of penal servitude for life were given to hundreds of lesser members of the rebellion. Arrests were made in rural Ireland, which had not been part of the Rising, and the suffering continued.

Perhaps because he had been born in America, Eamon de Valera's death sentence had been commuted to penal servitude for life. From Dartmoor Prison, where he was sent, a letter was smuggled out. It was to be delivered to the closest relative of one of his fallen men, and although it took some time for the letter to reach its destination, its recipient was prepared.

Patrick read of the executions with sorrow and disgust. It was known that several Americans had been a part of the rebel army that Easter week, but so many had died anonymously it seemed he would never know if Kieran had been among them. The poet William Butler Yeats had written that a "terrible beauty" was born with the Rising, and Patrick was inclined to agree with him. Of all the O'Donnells, he was the only one to suspect that Kieran had been a part of it.

The letter did not reach him until mid-August, a week after Sir Roger Casement had been hanged in London for high treason.

"I have reason to believe," wrote de Valera, "that a man known to me as Patrick O'Rourke, who said he was the son of Robert O'Donnell, is your nephew. His true Christian name was Kieran."

The letter went on to say that Kieran had died in the recent "troubles," bravely defending his post against a battalion of British soldiers. In all respects, the letter resembled those written to bereaved families by commanding officers fighting in the Great War. It concluded with the usual condolences and assured Patrick that Kieran had been an exemplary soldier. It was signed *de Valera—written from Dartmoor Prison.*

Patrick read the letter twice. Then he folded it up and locked it away in the same safe-box which had once housed the ring bequeathed to Kieran. He sat for a long time, motionless. At length he rose and went to Front Street, where he contracted a job which would take three weeks. Then he went home to Ridge Street and wrote to his sister, his sons, and his nieces, and commanded them to come home on a date in early September. He confided what he knew, and what he planned, to his wife Margaret.

"If you persist in doing this," said Margaret coldly, "then I will never be buried there. I will not lie in earth where criminals are honored."

"It's as you like, Margaret. When the others arrive, you needn't be present. This is O'Donnell business."

They all arrived on the appointed day, even Terry, who was puzzled by the ambiguous wording of his father's letter and thought more money was coming his way. Robert Tyrone accompanied Veronica and Bernadette with a suspicious air. Since the item about his wife's arrest in the *Sun*, he had begun to distrust her again. His appearance in Newburgh was a concession. Delia and Jim arrived together. Delia ran to her father and hugged him, and Jim inquired politely after his mother's health. Margaret was confined to her bed with a headache.

Patrick stood in the middle of the drawing room and looked at what remained of his family.

"More than fifteen years ago," he began, "we were gathered together in this house to mourn my father. Since that time, we have lost my mother and my sister, Bridget. Their absence is felt by all of us. Mother, grandmother, father, grandfather, sister, aunt, and wife—each of us has lost three people dear to us.

"There has been another loss, the first in fifteen years of the younger generation, and that is why I have called you here."

He took the letter from de Valera and read it to them. When he had finished, there was a stunned silence.

Delia leaned into her father's sheltering arm, stricken and pale. "Forgive, and forget," she whispered.

Terry spoke suddenly, his brow furrowed as if trying to absorb a difficult lesson. "I met a man on Good Friday who told me to spare a thought for Kieran," he said.

In two automobiles, the party drove to the churchyard on the hill. There, in the lambent light of an Indian summer sun, they viewed a plain granite marker, erected on the O'Donnell plot. Cut into the stone were the words:

> ROBERT O'DONNELL 1858-1882
> KIERAN O'DONNELL 1883-1916
> *In Loving Memory*
> *Ba dhuthchas riamh d'ár geine cháidh*

"What does the Gaelic mean, da?" asked Delia.

"Well, dearie, it's from a soldier's song. It means 'children of a fighting race.'"

"That they surely were," said Veronica. She turned

to her daughter. "Don't cry, girl," she said gently. "If he had to die, be glad it was quick. Think of how Kieran would have hated to rot away in prison."

They ate their dinner together that night, silently and each wrapped in private thoughts. Only Patrick, Michael and Veronica were old enough to understand how inevitable Kieran's brief life and violent death had been. To the younger ones, it seemed an unnecessarily cruel loss. Delia felt betrayed and remembered Malloy's warning with sorrow. As for Terry—he admired his cousin's bravery but despised him, also, for a fool. Only a fool would give his life for a country not even his own.

Jim and Bernadette sat up long after the others had gone to bed. The warmth of the day had departed with the sun, and a chill wind blew down from the mountains.

"I wish I could have been in Dublin for the Rising," said Bernadette.

Jim laughed. "Ah, Bernie," he said. "You're one of them for sure."

"One of them?"

"Children of a fighting race. I'm not." He looked into the fire and sighed. "All the same," he said, "I may have to fight before long."

Italy had declared war on Germany a month earlier. Daily the war grew more threatening and vast. It stretched its arms out to drag all nations into the vortex, as if its appetite for blood was unappeasable. Many people now thought America would join the allies in the coming year.

Bernadette, part fighter and part pacifist, regarded her cousin with affection. "If you go, so will I," she said. "Perhaps I'll be a nurse, or an ambulance driver."

Jim confided that he wanted to leave the law. She was the first person to whom he had confided, and he waited uneasily to hear what she would say. Bernadette stood up and crossed the room. Gravely, she shook his hand. "Good for you," she said. "Anyone with an ounce of sense can see you were meant to be a musician and not a lawyer."

"It will be my contribution," Jim said, "to Ireland. It doesn't measure up to Kieran's, but it's my own."

At mention of Kieran, Bernadette grew sad again. She stood, holding her cousin's hand, her head cast down. "When I was a little girl, I thought I was in love with him," she whispered.

Jim squeezed her hand. "Look here," he said. "There's a song I'll teach you. It's a sad song, but proud too. It's perfect for remembering Kieran."

Bernadette sat beside him while he repeated the first stanza of the song. Then he taught her the melody.

"Got it?" he asked. She nodded.

And then, very quietly, so as not to disturb those sleeping above them, Jim and Bernadette joined their voices and sang, in memory of Kieran:

> *We drink the memory of the brave,*
> *The faithful and the few—*
> *Some lie far off beyond the wave,*

Some sleep in Ireland, too;
All, all are gone—but still—lives on
The fame of those who died,
All true men, like you, men,
Remember them with pride.